Praise for Rhyannon Byrd

"With a Byrd book, you know you will get plenty of sizzling sensuality, as well as molten emotion."

—*RT Book Reviews* on DEADLY IS THE KISS

"Byrd's Bloodrunner characters are the ultimate heroes."

—*RT Book Reviews* on DARK WOLF RISING

Praise for Lauren Hawkeye

"Readers who are looking for a sexy tale will be satisfied with this novella."

—*RT Book Reviews* on TAKE ME DOWN

RHYANNON BYRD

is an avid, longtime fan of romance and the author of more than twenty paranormal and erotic titles. She has been nominated for three *RT Book Reviews* Reviewers' Choice Awards, including best Shape-Shifter Romance, and her books have been translated into nine languages. After having spent years enjoying the glorious sunshine of the American South and Southwest, Rhyannon now lives in the beautiful, but often chilly, county of Warwickshire in England with her husband and family. For more information on Rhyannon's books and the latest news, you can visit her website at www.rhyannonbyrd.com or find her on Facebook at www.facebook.com/RhyannonByrd.

LAUREN HAWKEYE

is a writer, yoga newbie, knitting aficionado and animal lover who lives in the shadows of the great Rocky Mountains of Alberta, Canada. She's older than she looks—really—and younger than she feels—most of the time—and she loves to explore the journeys that take women through life in her stories. Hawkeye's stories include erotic historical, steamy paranormal and hot contemporary.

DARKEST DESIRE
OF THE VAMPIRE

RHYANNON BYRD
AND LAUREN HAWKEYE

HARLEQUIN® NOCTURNE™

Recycling programs
for this product may
not exist in your area.

ISBN-13: 978-0-373-88571-8

HARLEQUIN BOOKS

WICKED IN MOONLIGHT
Copyright © 2013 by Tabitha Bird

VAMPIRE ISLAND
Copyright © 2013 by Lauren Hawkeye

For questions and comments about the quality of this book,
please contact us at CustomerService@Harlequin.com.

® and ™ are trademarks of Harlequin Enterprises Limited or its
corporate affiliates. Trademarks indicated with ® are registered in the
United States Patent and Trademark Office, the Canadian Trade Marks
Office and in other countries.

Printed in U.S.A.

™ www.Harlequin.com

CONTENT

WICKED IN MOONLIGHT   7
Rhyannon Byrd

VAMPIRE ISLAND   161
Lauren Hawkeye

WICKED IN MOONLIGHT

RHYANNON BYRD

Dear Reader,

I'm so thrilled to have the chance to introduce you to the Santos brothers in my new Harlequin Nocturne novella, *Wicked in Moonlight*. These deliciously dark, dangerous vampires are as alpha as they come, and more than a little sinful. For too long, their lives have been about duty and responsibility, lacking the comfort and warmth of a woman's love. But that's about to change....

Nick Santos, the middle brother, is up first. And boy is this hard-edged, rugged vamp in for an eye-opener when he finds himself trapped in an underground bunker with a determined, intrepid human female named Lainey Maxwell. Lainey is unlike anyone Nick has ever encountered, and she soon becomes a temptation he simply can't resist. But nothing worth keeping ever comes easy. When their night of wild, wicked pleasure proves more than Nick can walk away from, he learns just how stubborn the little human can be. Lainey's willing to accept nothing less than the sexy vampire's heart....

I hope you come to love this wonderful couple as much as I do.

Rhy

To my readers...

Nick is one of my all-time favorites,

so I thought he should be for you. ;)

Love Rhy

Chapter 1

"I'm sorry, miss. But as you can see from the yellow police tape, this area has been restricted." The young, fresh-faced officer's voice rang with practiced conviction. "No one's allowed access."

Lainey Maxwell took a step closer to the cop, who was stubbornly standing his ground at the top of the wooden staircase that hugged the jagged cliff face, the deep blue of the roiling Pacific spreading out behind him. In another lifetime, she could have cleared out her savings account, bought a boat and simply sailed into that endless blue, leaving this nightmare behind. But she didn't want to run away from her problems. She just wanted to get down to that blasted beach.

"I swear I won't go snooping around." *Lie!* "All I want is to take some snapshots for my scrapbook." *Another lie!* "Pleeease," she begged, holding up the pink camera that hung around her neck as she gave him her brightest smile. But it was probably too strained to be believable. She never had been able to lie worth a damn, and this past week had pretty much zapped her dishonesty reserves to the point where there were only scraps lingering at the bottom of the bucket.

"Just one little picture," she pressed, wondering if she'd have better luck if she were one of those toothpick-sized girls instead of her too short, curvy self. "My father proposed to my mother on this beach a long time ago," she fibbed, "and it would really mean a lot to me if I could have a photo of it."

Shaking his head, the cop said, "I'm sorry. This is a crime scene. No photography is allowed."

She lowered her hands, letting the camera dangle around her neck again, resting against her colorful halter top. "Could you maybe just go down there with me?" she asked. It wouldn't be ideal to have him with her, but at this point she'd take what she could get.

"My boss would have my badge if I took you down there," he replied, though she could tell he was tempted. Surprise swept through her system in a rush. She should have been flattered, considering he was pretty cute, but she wasn't here for a date. She just wanted to search the caves on that damn beach. And because of the cliffs, this was the only way to get down there.

"Can you at least tell me what happened?"

Sandy hair fell over his brow as he shook his head again. "No, ma'am." Puffing up his chest a little, he added, "But there's nothing on that beach you need to worry your pretty little head about. We've got everything under control. You just enjoy your vacation."

Ha! Nothing to worry about, her ass. She felt like one of those poor beachgoers in the movie *Jaws,* listening to Mayor Vaughn tell them it was perfectly "safe" to go back in the water.

Yeah, right. And Godzilla was just a cuddly little lizard.

Despite the late afternoon California sunshine, the wind was brutal today, gusting over the cliffs with a vengeance. Lainey held her sun hat on her head with one hand, the hem of her top down with the other, and racked her brain for a way to get past Dudley Do-Right here. The police officer was trying to play it off like the local law in Moonlight Bay knew exactly what they were doing. But it was a crock. This beautiful little romantic getaway nestled on California's northern coast was about as far from "fine" as it could get. In the past four months, more than six people had gone missing while vacationing here, and another three had been found murdered, their bodies so mutilated it had been impossible for the coroner to determine the cause of death. A few sources had cried rogue shark. They claimed the victims had been swimming in the ocean and ended up a great white's snack before their remains washed up into the seaside caves with the tide. And the missing persons, they said, were simply eaten whole. But there were too many holes in that gruesome theory. She knew, because her brother had told her all about them.

Three weeks ago Lainey's big brother, Ryan Martin, one of Los Angeles's most respected crime journalists, had come here to blow the top off this story. But a few days after checking in to one of the local hotels, he'd gone out one night and never came back. No one had heard from him since.

Six days ago Lainey had shown up in town herself,

ready to get some answers about Ryan's disappearance because no one else seemed capable of providing any. Even the paper he worked for had decided not to send another reporter until the police had a lead on what had happened to Ryan. So she'd left her job managing a bookstore down in San Diego, caught a flight into the local airport and registered at one of the cliff-top inns under the pretense of being a vacationing tourist. Every instinct she possessed told her there was something fishy going on in this town, and until she knew what it was, she trusted no one. Which meant she hadn't told a single soul what she was really up to. Not her grandmother or her friends or anyone in the town. As far as they knew, she was here to do nothing more than enjoy herself. But she was getting damned tired of faking a smile when inside she was worried as hell about Ryan.

Since her arrival, Lainey had been on three different group hikes, two wine-tasting trips and a boat cruise around the bay. Without being obvious, she'd asked as many questions as she could about the reporter who had gone missing and the strange things that had been happening in town, but no one was willing to talk. This was a community that made its bread and butter from the tourist trade. The last thing they wanted to discuss with a client was a missing journalist and the chilling case he'd been investigating.

Determined to make one more try for access to the beach below this cliff, Lainey gave the officer what she hoped was a good sympathy-inspiring look. She knew that parts of the three murder victims had been found on this particular stretch of beach (the third one just two days ago)…and that, based on the information Ryan's editor had grudgingly given her, her brother had spent a lot time snooping around here. She'd avoided coming here for as long as she could because it quite frankly freaked her out to be in a place where some whack job had dumped pieces of his victims—but she was getting nowhere fast. Something told her that if she wanted to know what had happened to Ryan, she needed to get her backside down the staircase this cop was blocking and onto the beach, where she could take a look around the caves that cut into the cliff.

"I know I'm being a pain, but this is *really* important to me," she murmured to the officer before casting a quick glance over the surrounding area. She suddenly had the unnerving feeling that they were being watched, but there was no one else around. Shaking it off, she forced her attention back on the cop. "Could you please just let me take a quick little look around? My parents are both gone now and it would mean so much to me if I could see the place where my father proposed."

He swallowed, looking pained, color marking his cheekbones. "Miss, really. I'm so sorry, but I…I just can't."

She rubbed the back of her neck, her breaths starting to come a little faster, her pulse racing. The officer was looking at her kind of strangely, as if wondering what the hell her problem was, but she didn't know herself. Didn't have a freaking clue! Was she having a panic attack? Now? What was happening to— *Whoa!* She blinked like crazy, hearing herself make a soft little wheezing sound, like a gasp. *Oh…wow. Just holy-freaking-wow!*

Lainey actually *felt* the force of a physical presence, like a warm jolt of electricity coasting over the surface of her body, before she heard a deep, deliciously rugged voice behind her say, "You need any help here, Casey?"

Spinning around, she came face-to-face with a man whose short dark hair had been disheveled by the wind. He was incredibly tall, incredibly sexy and incredibly good-looking. As her best friend, Bailey, back in Alabama—where Lainey had spent her childhood—would sometimes say, the guy looked "good enough to lick like a Popsicle." But it was freaking weird, how he'd come up on them so fast. Had he been spying on her and the officer—Casey?—from the trees? There was a copse of pines off to their right, the winding dirt path that cut through the underbrush probably leading to one of the gorgeous, rustic cliff-top homes that dotted the coast. Had he been standing there listening to their conversation? Was that why she'd felt as if someone was watching her but hadn't been able to spot anyone when she'd looked around?

"Who are you?" she demanded, more sharply than she'd intended.

But her voice was overshadowed by his own as he said, "You should listen to Officer Munn, Miss Maxwell. You have no business down on that beach."

She glared, ready to tell the stranger to mind his own damn business, when the cop cut her off. "Mr. Santos," he gushed as he moved to Lainey's side, looking ready to ask the guy for an autograph. The young man's Adam's apple bobbed in his throat when he gave another hard swallow. "It's good to see you, sir."

A pair of dark sunglasses shielded the man's eyes as he turned toward the officer, his tone low but friendly. "Would you mind letting me speak to Miss Maxwell alone for a moment?"

"Of…of course not."

"Thanks, Casey. And tell your dad hi for me."

"Sure thing," the cop called out, waving as he backed away.

Huh, she thought, crossing her arms over her chest. *So this is the infamous Nick Santos.* Lainey had heard whispers about him all week long. The guy was like some kind of local legend. From what she'd gathered, he worked as a pricey private investigator. The kind she would have loved to hire but could never afford. If he'd looked at all friendly, she might have tried appealing to his sympathy and asking for his help in her search for answers about what had happened to Ryan. But there was nothing nice or soft-looking about this man. He was… She tried to think of how to describe him, but words failed her—and if that wasn't strange, she didn't know what was. According to Grandma Kate, since the moment she'd made her first sounds as an infant twenty-six years ago, Lainey had *never* been at a loss for words.

Determined to fight past her stunned reaction and pull her mental foot from her mouth, she decided the first thing that struck a person about Nick Santos was his height. The guy was freaking tall as hell. Probably six-four or six-five. The fact that he was jaw-droppingly gorgeous was the second. The kind of good-looking that probably had women turning their heads to look at him on the street. But he wasn't pretty. Just raw and hard and masculine. Every feature was cut in sharp, rugged detail. Blade of a nose, sensual slash of a grim mouth, high cheekbones and iron jaw. And then there were the muscles. The guy was lean but ripped. Like, seriously ripped. The sleeves of his black T-shirt were strained by the power of his biceps, his olive-toned skin stretched tight over long, lean lines of sinew and heavy veins that had been forced to the surface by all those mouthwatering muscles.

She hadn't seen how well the pair of worn-in jeans cupped his ass, but based on the front view, Lainey was pretty sure it would be a killer sight.

As soon as "Casey the Cop" had walked away, heading toward the small parking lot that stretched north of the trees, Santos turned his attention on her. Even with the dark aviator glasses, she could feel the force of his gaze as he looked her over, taking in the beach-bunny getup. She noticed a slight curl to his upper lip as he asked, "Why are you so desperate to visit this particular beach, Miss Maxwell?"

She felt ridiculous, like a kitten going up against the big bad wolf, and the feeling chafed. He was treating her like she was an irritating ball of fluff, and she wanted to tell the arrogant jerk where to stuff it but knew that wasn't going to help her cause. And she was irrationally hurt by his attitude. She was used to guys seeing the blond hair and colorful clothes and instantly judging her, thinking they knew every damn thing about her. Over the years, she'd gotten good at blowing off that particular kind of jerk-wad. But for some inexplicable reason, she felt a nearly uncontrollable fury that this man would act so shallow.

Nearly biting her words out through a tight smile, she said, "All I wanted was to take some photographs."

His sensual mouth twisted into a smirk. "Just another vacationer, huh?"

"What else would I be?" she muttered, knowing damn well he wasn't going to let her past him. Another thought occurred to her, and she narrowed her eyes. "And how do you know my name?"

She'd have given anything to be able to see the look in his eyes when he said, "Everyone in town knows your name. You've been asking some interesting questions for a tourist." He gestured with one of his large hands toward her camera. "And most of the tourists around here aren't looking to add morbid crime scene photos to their vacation pics."

Heat rushed into her face, the "Southern" in her accent getting thicker with her temper. "I wasn't aware that curiosity was a crime," she snapped.

He took a step closer, invading her personal space. A frown curved her lips as she craned her head back to hold his stare. "It might not be a crime," he said in a low rumble, "but it could land you in a serious amount of trouble."

Overwhelmed with frustration, Lainey tossed her hands in the air. "What's the big freaking deal? You're all acting like I want to go traipsing through a minefield. It's just a beach!"

The hard set of his mouth got even harder. "Even if it wasn't a crime scene, the stretch of beach down there is too treacherous for sightseeing. So pull your head out of your ass and forget it. You aren't setting foot on it or anywhere near those caves, and that's an order."

Oh…whoa. He was giving her *orders* now? "Exactly who do you think you are?" she demanded hoarsely, getting the strange feeling that they were having some kind of bizarre secondary conversation without any words. One that went along the lines of *Get the hell out of here, little girl, before you end up getting hurt by things you're too fluffy to handle,* while she shot back,

I'm not setting foot out of this town until I know what happened to my brother! I'm worried sick about him... and I'm freaking terrified he's already been killed!

Taking a deep breath, she added, "You have no right to tell me what I can and can't do."

"Actually," he replied in a low, brutally controlled voice, his accent impossible to place, "I have *every* right."

Wow. Talk about arrogant! "And how do you figure that?" she scoffed.

"Because I own it," he ground out.

Lainey blinked. "Own what?"

His voice got rougher. "The beach, Miss Maxwell." He took a few deep breaths, his handsome face twisting into a grimace as he added, "I also own the cliffs and the land you're currently standing on."

A sarcastic snort tickled her nose. He'd have to be a freaking multimillionaire for that to be true. "You're kidding, right?"

He responded with a slow shake of his head. There wasn't even a hint of a smile on his firm lips as he crossed his powerful arms over his chest, and Lainey found herself taking an unconscious step backward. He hadn't tried to hurt her, or even touch her, but there was something about the aggressive way he was staring down at her—*even though she couldn't see his damn eyes*—that told her to get away from him. Now. Before something really bad happened.

I'll just come back tonight, when no one's around, she whispered to herself, quickly turning her back on the incredibly strange Nick Santos and walking away. She could hear him mutter something rough under his breath, but she didn't look back, heading as swiftly as she could in the same direction Casey Munn had gone. Minutes later she'd reached her room at the inn, her pulse still hammering from the odd encounter. She didn't understand the weird current buzzing through her veins or the heated flush on her skin. Sheesh. The guy hadn't flirted with her or threatened her...and it's not like he'd said anything she hadn't already heard from the young cop, other than the bit about him owning everything. So why this bizarre reaction?

I don't know, but I don't have time for this. I need to just shake it off and focus.

Right. Stripping out of her clothes, Lainey took a quick shower, planning to make her way down to the inn's cozy restaurant for an early dinner. She always ate when she got nervous, which was why she could never drop a dress size. Well, that and the fact that she enjoyed food, like any other healthy human being. Why women wanted to starve themselves to look like skin stretched over bone had never been something she could wrap her head around, and she didn't even want to try. She'd take her forties pinup figure any day over the heroin-chic look.

But I bet that's how Nick Santos likes them. Skinny and simpering, terrified by the sight of an ice cream sundae.

"Oh, God. Listen to me," she muttered under her breath as she stepped from the shower. That kind of cattiness wasn't like her. And why on earth was she standing in front of the bathroom mirror, staring at her curvy figure while thinking about that arrogant asshead? Sure, he was gorgeous. But that didn't mean he was decent or kind or worth her mental energy. And, damn it, she didn't have any mental energy to spare!

She suddenly stilled…holding her breath…not liking the direction her thoughts were going. Was this some kind of new avoidance ploy on her part? Obsess about the cranky yet studly private investigator so that she didn't have to think about what she was going to do later that night? If so, she needed to get over it, and fast. Santos obviously had his suspicions about what she was doing, and for some reason, he didn't like it. With his influence in this town, he could make it so that no one was willing to lend her a helping hand—not that they'd been all that helpful to begin with.

Putting him out of her mind, Lainey dressed and headed down to the restaurant. After having a mouthwatering lobster bisque and fresh-baked bread for dinner, she took a walk along the path that hugged the cliff tops. She wrapped a light sweater around her shoulders to fight off the breeze still blowing in hard off the Pacific, enjoying the brilliant colors of the sunset. As she walked past the taped-off entrance to the stairs, she noted that there was an older policeman manning the site now. The corner of her mouth twitched as she wondered if that'd been Santos's doing. Had he thought Casey wasn't tough enough for the challenge if she decided to make another try for it?

Knowing it was best to bide her time, Lainey made her way past the officer in silence, her attention moving to the sprawling homes that rose out of the higher cliffs like rustic monuments to money and power. Which one belonged to Santos? And how in the world did someone who looked to be in his mid-thirties manage to afford one?

He must come from family money, which would explain the house. But why would someone so obviously

wealthy choose the gritty lifestyle of a P.I.? She'd spent
enough time in Ryan's world to know that the private
investigators glamorized in television shows were nothing more than Hollywood fiction. In order to earn such
a kick-ass reputation in his field, he had to be a serious
badass, which didn't exactly fit the "family money"
image. But who knew? Maybe he'd gotten lucky and
won the lottery but was too embarrassed to give up his
career and just enjoy the money.

The thought brought a bittersweet smile to her lips
because it reminded her of Ryan. He could have been
the richest man in the world, and he still would have
spent his days slugging through the seedy underbelly of
society, looking for a way to expose those who thought
they were above the law. She'd loved that about him as
much as she hated it and she had always been terrified
he'd go too far one day. Make a mistake that landed him
in a heap of trouble…or even cost him his life.

Taking a deep breath, she turned away from the ma-
jestic homes and stared out over the dark ocean, send-
ing a silent message to her brother. *Wherever you are,
Ry, I want you to know that I miss you and I won't stop
looking for you. I'll never stop looking.*

Working to psych herself up for what she knew she
had to do, Lainey blasted her favorite playlist on her
iPod as she made her way back to the inn. Once in her
room, she changed into black jeans, a black T-shirt,
black tennis shoes and a black knit cap to cover her
blond hair. Tucking her cell phone into a small black
backpack, she also packed a flashlight, extra batteries,
her camera and a utility knife. Then she pulled on a
black hoodie, propped her back against the headboard
and found one of the *Underworld* movies to watch on

TV while she waited. She wished she could be some kind of kick-ass heroine like Selene instead of a nervous, butterflies-in-her-stomach bookseller. But she wasn't going to let her nerves hold her back. Not when there was a chance Ryan might have left some kind of message for her down in those caves.

As the movie ended and a clock chimed midnight from somewhere in the inn, Lainey left her room and made her way down the back set of stairs. Hiking her small backpack on her shoulder, she headed toward the cliffs, surprised when she caught sight of another officer standing guard at the top of those damn stairs. She'd thought for sure they'd abandon the post once it hit midnight, but that didn't appear to be the case. Slinking back into the shadow of the cop's SUV, she nibbled on her thumbnail, trying to work out what to do. Did she dare try to create a distraction? Or did she simply bide her time, waiting for the opportunity to steal past the policeman?

She was still trying to decide when the cop's phone rang. He answered the call, then continued talking as he started making his way toward the SUV, saying something about the list being in the car. Hunched down by the front bumper on the passenger side, Lainey waited until the cop was rummaging around in the backseat before sprinting toward the stairs. With her heart hammering so loudly she was surprised the officer couldn't hear it, she rushed under the yellow police tape and started hurrying down the wooden staircase. It zigged and zagged its way down the rocky cliff, the weathered planks of wood slippery from the sea spray blowing in on the wind. She had to grip the handrail a few times to keep from stumbling but managed to make it to the bottom without being spotted by the cop.

"So far, so good," she murmured under her breath, thankful for the nearly full moon that illuminated her way without the use of her flashlight. But as she entered the first cave, she had to dig it out of her bag, needing the light to inspect the craggy walls. Though the sea often drifted into the caves at high tide, it hadn't quite reached that point tonight, leaving a moonlit strip of sand along the base of the cliffs.

She must have spent nearly a half hour in the first cave, the only sounds her breathing and the roar of the surf. As she moved into the second cave, she ran the beam of light from her flashlight over the walls in small sections, searching for…well, for *anything* that her brother might have left behind that the police could have missed. Their father had been a scholar of ancient symbols and had often used various cryptograms when playing games with her and Ryan when they'd been younger. The games had often entailed leaving secret messages for each other, and Ryan had even joked with her that if he ever found himself in a no-win situation while out on a case, he'd leave her a private message to let her know what had happened to him. It was a chilling thought, which was yet another reason why she'd put off coming down to the caves, afraid of what she might find.

When she found nothing etched into the cavern walls, Lainey moved her search to the sandy floor, but again she found nothing.

The moon seemed even brighter as Lainey stepped back out onto the beach, making her way to the third cave. The wind swept sand against her shins, the tiny granules slipping into her shoes, though she barely noticed. As she stood in the center of the dank, massive cave, her flashlight illuminating the sickening splotches of blood that still covered the sandy floor, she knew she'd found the place where the police had discovered the most recent remains. But she wasn't thinking about the killer. At the moment, the only thought running through her head was that she wanted to go back in time.

All she wanted was to lose a month. Four measly weeks in a lifetime of them. She just wanted to be back in a time when her brother was still in her life. When she knew he was healthy and alive, enjoying being a pain in the ass to his editors and the crooks he thrived on exposing.

Releasing a shuddering breath, Lainey shook off her melancholy and focused on her search. This cave was bigger than the first two, with the entrances to several tunnels on its back wall. She knew, from the research she'd done on the town, that a tangled network of tunnels connected many of the caves here. She wasn't venturing back into those eerie passageways unless she had to, hating the idea of being in such a dark, closed-in space.

A search of the floor with the beam of her flashlight revealed nothing more than those unsettling splotches of blood. Turning her attention to the walls, Lainey had just worked her way to the back wall when she finally found what she was looking for—a scrawled, intricate symbol etched several inches over her head. It looked like something he'd had to do in a hurry, but she had no idea what to make of it. The symbol was one from a set her father had created specifically for her and Ryan, and in her mind's eye she could visualize the translation:

M. O. N. S. T. E. R. S.

Monsters? What on earth did that mean? Ryan wasn't given to flights of fancy or practical jokes. And she knew there wasn't any way this message had been meant for anyone but her. With their father gone, there was no one else in the world who would have been able to understand the rudimentary symbol.

What had Ryan been trying to tell her? And what the hell was that sound out on the beach? Had she just heard...voices?

Shit!

She was no longer alone. She could hear someone coming—no, that was *more* than one person. At first, Lainey thought the cop must have caught sight of her sneaking under the tape and sent for backup. But something about the sounds told her this wasn't a group of cops. They were throwing out curse words like confetti, and her heart started pounding, blood rushing in her ears as she realized she was trapped. Reacting quickly, she reached into her pack for her phone and the knife she'd brought. Being a single woman living in a big city, she'd taken some self-defense courses a few years ago at one of the local community colleges. But her skills weren't going to be anything that could help her when confronted by an entire group of men. And those guttural, graveled voices were definitely male.

Struggling to control her shaking fingers, she ran into one of the tunnels, turned off her flashlight and tried to dial nine-one-one, but the call wouldn't go through. Cursing under her breath, she slipped the phone into her pocket as she crept farther into the tunnel, praying the men would gawk at the bloodstained cave, then quickly leave. But she was wrong. As if they knew exactly where she'd hidden, they headed right for her. She panicked, flicking on the flashlight and heading deeper into the network of tunnels as she did her best to outrun them. But they just kept coming until she found herself trapped in another cave that had only one way out.

And it was blocked.

Plastering her back against the rear wall of the cave, Lainey faced off against a group of what had to be at least a dozen men, the beam from her flashlight wavering over their faces as she tried to gauge the exact number. Then there was a cracking sound, and a strange green glow filled the center of the cave, emanating from the glow stick one of the men had just thrown on the ground.

"I've called the police!" she shouted, holding the knife in front of her. "If you don't want to end up in jail, you'll get the hell out of here!"

"You haven't called anyone," a man with greasy black hair sneered before taking a long swig from the whiskey bottle he held in his hand.

Her throat shook as she looked the group over again. There was a lot of leather and dark, stained denim. They smelled of oil and sweat and malice, their bodies tall and hard and packed with muscle. They were brawny and rough, with shaggy black hair and scruffy jaws. She could feel their leers against her skin like physical touches, and she wanted to scream like a banshee for help. But who was going to hear her? She was too deep within the caves now for her cries to reach the policeman standing watch atop the cliff.

"Is it just me," one of the men called out, "or does this little bitch smell familiar?"

The one to her far left narrowed his strange, bright-gold eyes. "You related to that reporter who was snooping around here?"

Fury spiked through her system so hard and fast she felt dizzy. "What do you know about my brother?"

Another male gave a low, gritty laugh. "Aw, that's so sweet. She's come here searching for her *big bwother*."

"I've probably got a bit of him still stuck in my back teeth!" another called out, making her flinch. Just what did the bastard mean by that? Before Lainey could ask, a few of the guys started taking off their leather jackets, their leering smiles making her skin crawl as she gripped the handle of her knife so tightly her fingers felt numb. Then the unthinkable happened.

Shaking her head, Lainey tried to clear her vision, but the nightmare before her still remained. They were all shedding their clothes now, something strange happening to their naked, aroused bodies, and fear unlike anything she'd ever known rolled through her system. Their muscles rippled beneath their sweat-covered skin, their bodies somehow getting even bigger, as if they were growing before her eyes. She racked her brain for a way out of this nightmarish situation, but she was trapped and she knew it.

"What the hell are you?" she croaked, unable to believe what she was seeing.

"Hey, Jace. What are we?"

"I think it might be more fun just to show her!" someone hollered, tossing several more glow sticks around the cave.

"Good idea! I'm starving!"

"Then let's do it!"

Monsters...monsters...monsters.

Oh, God. She got it now. As the men began to transform into the horrifying shape of towering, two-legged wolves, they tormented her with the story of Ryan's gruesome murder. The words were garbled as their mouths shifted into short snouts, their jaws filled with deadly fangs, but she understood enough to realize Ryan had suffered a long, horrifying death at their hands.

According to the...werewolves, he'd been targeted because he was getting too close to uncovering the truth about the pack's latest killing sprees in the little beach town—and now she was going to be their next victim.

Damn it! She was such a freaking idiot. Why in God's name hadn't she listened to Nick Santos when she'd had the chance?

And why was she thinking about the sexy P.I. when she should be focusing on her own horrifying torture and death?

Is that a trick question, Lainey? Why do you think?

Before she could answer her own question, one of the monsters lunged for her, and Lainey screamed as she tried to escape his hold. She didn't make it but a step or two when one of the other werewolves grabbed her, his gnarled, claw-tipped fingers yanking the knife from her hand. But she wasn't going down without a fight. Lifting her knee, she jammed it into his crotch, and he roared with fury as he backhanded her across the face. She crashed into the side of the cave, a piercing pain shooting through her head as she slumped to the ground.

Get up, Lainey. Don't let it end like this.

Gritting her teeth, she struggled up onto her hands

and knees, only dimly aware of the strange sounds now coming from the other side of the cave. There was a loud roaring in her ears, the ground literally shaking with violence as she lifted a hand, pushing her hair out of her face. But before she could get a clear look at what was happening, something slammed into her, flattening her against the ground. She screamed beneath the heavy, furry body, realizing she was pinned under a fully shifted werewolf. The thing had to be massive, its weight crushing her chest, making it impossible to breathe.

"Lainey!"

She could have sworn she heard someone shout her name, and a second later the crushing weight was lifted. Dragging in a much-needed breath of air, she started to move back onto her hands and knees when something picked her up as if she weighed little more than a feather. Then it shoved her against the wall before moving away. With her hair still hanging in her face, she felt her knees buckle, and a moment later she was lying on the sandy floor of the cave again, the bone-chilling sounds of what had to be a vicious fight echoing in her ears. But it sounded far away, as if she was drifting in and out of consciousness. Were the monsters fighting each other? For what? For *her*?

She tried to crawl away, keeping her head low, not wanting to watch the gruesome scene. Blood covered the sandy floor, dripping from the walls, and she knew she was in shock. When a body hit the side of the cave, then landed in front of her, she crawled around the fur-covered beast and kept going until something rank and hairy swept her off the ground, throwing her over its massive shoulder. Her stomach heaved, and then there was a terrible collision, like her abductor had been slammed by a Mack truck and she was suddenly falling again, feeling like she'd landed on some kind of life-threatening carnival ride. She landed with a thud, her breath knocked from her lungs as a hot spray of something wet and slick splashed over her. She felt something hard under her hip and reached down, coming back with one of the glow sticks clutched in her hand, the eerie green glow shining through the tangle of hair that covered her face. Before she could get her bearings, she was swept up into another powerful pair of arms, but the chest she was crushed against this time wasn't covered in fur. It was hard and hot, and as she lifted her hands, finally managing to shove her hair away from her eyes, she couldn't believe what she was seeing.

I must be dreaming, she thought, *because this can't be real.* A bloody, furious-looking Nick Santos couldn't possibly be holding her in his arms, running through one of the winding tunnels like a madman. But he didn't look like he had that afternoon. Bathed in the eerie green light, she could see that his sunglasses were gone, his dark eyes glowing with a blue, preternatural light, a sinister-looking set of fangs gleaming beneath the sculpted curve of his upper lip.

Wetting her own lips, she managed to mutter a single stammering word. "W-werewolf?"

He gave a curt shake of his head, not even bothering to look down at her as he kept running from the monsters she could hear chasing them, their harrowing howls echoing through the tunnels. She thought that nod was the only response Santos was going to give her until he worked his bruised jaw and growled, "I'm not a werewolf. I'm a…vampire."

"A v-vampire?"

He replied with a sharp nod, still running.

Lainey's response was little more than a hoarse croak. "Well, *shit*."

She didn't catch whatever he said next. She'd already passed out.

Chapter 2

Pacing from one side of the metal room to the other, Nick Santos kept a careful eye on the female he'd chained to the king-size bed wedged into the far corner and gritted his teeth.

Fuck! How the hell did I let this happen?

A mere hour ago, he'd been taking his nightly run on the beach, going hard and fast, hoping to work off some of the tension that had been riding him since that afternoon. It'd been hours since his little head-to-head with Lainey Maxwell, yet he hadn't been able to banish the human's face from his mind. Or her damn scent from his nose. When he'd argued with her that afternoon, she'd looked like a colorful, delectable little ice cream cone that he'd wanted to lick from head to toe, savoring all that creamy skin and those ripe curves with deliberate slowness.

Unfortunately, those were *not* the kind of thoughts

he normally had about human females, and he'd let it screw with his head. He should have known she'd try some stupid stunt like she had tonight, going into the caves by herself. And look where it'd gotten her.

Careless, infuriating, mouthwatering woman.

More times than he could count this past week, Nick had seen Lainey Maxwell prancing that sweet ass of hers all over town, acting clueless and cute. But it was a damn act. Not that she wasn't easy on the eyes. But he wasn't buying the ditzy blonde routine. She'd been carefully asking questions about Ryan Martin from the moment she hit town. Was she the journalist's girlfriend? And what the hell was she doing trying to track him down on her own? She should have left the investigating to the cops. They didn't have any more chance of solving Martin's disappearance than they did the others in the area, but damn it, at least she wouldn't be in the shit situation she was in now.

He should have been keeping a closer eye on her; instead, he got called away on a quick mission tonight, then arrived back in town just in time for his nightly run. He hadn't been running for more than ten minutes when he'd caught the scent of the wolves, wanting to go for their blood. For weeks now the bastards had been thumbing their noses at him by using his own goddamn caves for their kills whenever he'd left town on a hunt. But they'd screwed up tonight. He'd obviously made it back sooner than they'd thought he would, and he'd believed he finally had them.

But from their scent, Nick had known there were too many for him to take on single-handedly. Especially when he and his brothers had been given the directive to bring the wolves in for questioning rather than outright execution. The vampire council he and his brothers answered to wanted to know why the beasts had chosen Moonlight Bay for their new killing ground. They shared Nick's belief that the pack had learned his true identity, and the ones in power wanted to know how.

In his line of work, it was imperative that the preternatural killers he hunted never knew where he made his home.

Hating it, but fully aware that he needed to call his brothers for backup, Nick had reached into the pocket of his sweatpants for his phone only to realize he'd left it back at his house. Another frustrating sign that his fascination with Lainey Maxwell was screwing with his head because he never made mistakes like that. Cursing under his breath, he'd started to run back for it when he caught something light and sweet under the heavier, animal scent of the wolves. He'd known in an instant who that mouthwatering scent belonged to, and a cold terror had gripped his insides, as if the woman were something he badly needed to keep in this world.

At that point, he'd had a hell of a shitty choice to make. Reveal his true nature to the human female by going after her in an attempt to rescue her...or turn his back on the troublesome woman, leaving her to suffer the consequences of her recklessness on her own.

Of course, it was really no choice at all. Which meant he'd run into a lethal situation with no regard for his own safety, blatantly disregarding the orders he'd been given in regard to the pack.

He'd been lucky enough to get her to the bunker and seal the door behind them before the bastards caught up to him—but there was a time bomb ticking on her life, and now she was trapped inside with it.

And they were definitely trapped. The wolves' harrowing howls were echoing through the small air vents that led to various tunnels, their deadly claws making god-awful screeching noises as they tried to batter their way through the reinforced door.

You can keep on knocking, you bastards—but you won't get in.

Only problem was, he and the human couldn't get out either. And he could already feel himself starting to—

No, damn it. Don't even think about it!

When she gave a soft moan, slowly coming to, Nick braced himself for what was sure to be a screaming tantrum fueled by shock and terror. She shifted restlessly against the bed's gray, military-issue blankets, making her incredible scent even stronger.

From the middle of the room, he watched her eyelids tremble, then slowly open, her confused gaze whipping around the room before landing with a wide, fascinated look of shock on him.

"Don't panic," he scraped out, the thick sound of his voice catching him by surprise. Clearing his throat, he added, "I just saved your life, Miss Maxwell. Wouldn't make much sense for me to turn around and kill you, now would it?"

"I g-guess not," she stammered, cutting a dark look toward the shackles that looped her wrists, each manacle connected to a thick chain that was secured to a heavy metal hook high on the wall above the bed. The chains had been pulled tight enough that her arms had to rest above her head, and he tried like hell not to notice the provocative thrust of her breasts that was a result of the position. Tried…but didn't come anywhere close to succeeding.

"Are you okay?" he asked, still standing in the center of the room, not daring to move any closer. "Do you hurt anywhere?"

She brought her gaze back to his, her astonishment increasing, appearing surprised that he genuinely seemed worried about her condition. "I'm f-fine," she murmured, sounding a little rattled but not as terrified as he would have expected. Maybe she was still in too much shock to fully process what was happening. But at least she was no longer covered in blood.

After cutting off her blood-drenched hoodie—it'd thankfully been covered in wolf's blood and not her own—Nick had used a warm washcloth to wipe the spatters of crimson from her face and hands, though her hair had been more difficult to get clean. While he'd worked, it'd been hard as hell not to lose the cloth and touch that soft skin and silken hair with his bare hand. By the time he'd finished the task, his hand had been visibly shaking. He'd opted to leave her jeans and T-shirt in place, knowing better than to tempt himself by redressing her in something of his own, and they hadn't been splattered nearly as bad as the hoodie.

Determined to get his mind off the way she looked all trussed up on the bed and into safer territory, Nick crossed his arms over his chest and said, "Since you're all right, now might be a good time to go ahead and tell me who you really are."

Her eyes still had that shocked look in them, but her voice came out a little steadier. "Ryan's sister."

"Ryan? Are you talking about Ryan Martin?"

"Yes," she whispered, subtly tugging at the chains as if she didn't want him to notice. "Martin is his p-pen name. He started using one when he got death threats because of some articles he'd written. He didn't want to make it easy for some jackass to trace the members of his family."

Nick narrowed his gaze, wanting to throttle her for being so careless with her safety. "You came here looking for him after he went missing, didn't you? That's what you were doing in that fucking cave! Am I right?"

"There's no need for you to go all potty mouth on me, Mr. Santos." She sounded a little feistier, her own gaze now as sharp as his.

"I'll speak however I damn well please, lady. And call me Nick."

"My name isn't lady," she growled, her breasts quivering as she tried to wriggle herself into a sitting position against the pillows. "It's Lainey!"

"I know that!"

"Then use it!" she shouted.

"I don't believe this shit," he muttered, shoving both hands back through his hair before dropping them to his sides. Shooting her a frustrated glare, he ground out, "I've got you chained to a fucking bed, and you want to argue about your name?"

She gave him a withering look. "You could always unchain me if it makes you feel better!"

"Like hell."

"You told me not to panic—" another mouthwatering jiggle before she collapsed back on the bed, glaring up at the chains "—but restraining me like this hardly inspires confidence."

"The chains stay. And since they're for your protection, I wouldn't waste your breath arguing about it."

"Oh, come on," she scoffed, turning her head to glare

at him. "They're for my *protection?* Seriously? Do I look like a freaking idiot?"

No. She looked… *Shit.* Scratch that thought. No way in hell was he going *there.* The last thing in the world he needed to be thinking about was how incredible she looked stretched out over that bed, her tight clothes hugging every inch of her sweet little body.

When it became clear he wasn't going to answer her question, she said, "Will you at least tell me where we are?"

"In one of my caves."

She cast a suspicious look around the grim, gray room, and then stared up at the chains that hung from the walls by long, sturdy hooks that few creatures would have had the strength to break. "This doesn't look like a cave."

Feeling restless as hell, Nick crossed his arms again and explained. "I've built a bunker inside one of the larger caves that was buried deep in the cliffs. The walls, floor and ceiling are reinforced steel and titanium. So nothing's getting in, no matter how hard they try."

A shadow of fear moved through her light brown eyes. "Does that mean those things that were chasing us aren't…dead?"

His jaw hardened. "Not all of them, no."

"Oh." She swiped her tongue over her bottom lip, leaving it glossy and pink. "Are they, um, still after us then?"

As if in answer to her question, a bone-chilling howl sounded outside the thick, reinforced door.

"I guess that's a yes," she said a little unsteadily.

Forcing his attention away from that juicy lip, Nick

locked his gaze with hers. "The good news is that we're protected here," he told her. "The bad news is that we're essentially trapped. There's no cell phone coverage either, so calling someone is out of the question."

Of course it was. If they could call for help, Lainey assumed Santos would have already done it. From the tense looks he was giving her, it was obvious he wanted to be anywhere in the world but trapped in this bunker with her. Hardly flattering, but then, she hadn't expected any less from the man…er, *vampire.* He'd made it clear that afternoon that she wasn't his type.

She'd heard the term "vacation hell" before, but she was pretty sure it had never so appropriately applied to a situation as it did to this one. So many questions crowded her brain. How was it that nobody knew vampires and werewolves truly existed? And exactly what did being a vampire entail?

More than a little unnerved by the situation and everything she'd been through, she asked, "What do you use this place for?"

He cast her an uneasy look from the corner of his eye as he started pacing, and for the first time since she'd lifted her lashes in this bizarre room, Lainey noticed the bloodied gauze wrapped around his right biceps, just visible beneath the sleeve of his black, lightweight T-shirt. "Interrogations," he said in response to her question.

Oh…yikes. From his cold tone, she could tell it wasn't a topic she wanted to pursue at the moment. Maybe later, but right now she was trying to process everything else that was happening. She didn't need to start thinking about what kind of "interrogations" a vampire would hold in an underground bunker that had chains hanging from every wall.

"Can't we…you know. Just sneak out through a back door or something?"

Shaking his head, he ran one of those large hands through his dark hair. "There's no back door, Lainey. No escape route."

"You didn't think to put in an escape route when you built this place?"

His response was wry, as was the look he cut her from those impossibly sexy, dark blue eyes. "After this clusterfuck, you can be sure it's going on the top of my To Do list."

Lainey started to laugh, but the sound quickly dissolved into something wrenching and raw. From the moment she'd opened her eyes, she'd been focusing on the shock and fear coursing through her system. But the crushing truth she'd learned about her brother in that nightmarish cave was never far from the surface. Like a dam suddenly buckling under the pressure, her emotions rushed to the surface, her laughter becoming the choked sobs of someone who had lost something they loved that could never be replaced.

When she'd finally managed to calm down, Santos spoke in a low voice. "I'm sorry about your brother."

She sniffed, swiping her fingertips across her damp, puffy cheeks. "Thanks."

"You were close?" he asked, sounding a bit closer to the bed than he'd been before.

She nodded as she pressed her head into the pillow, staring up at the metal ceiling with burning eyes. "Always. He was never one of those pain-in-the-ass older siblings who detests the sight of their brothers or sisters. Our mother died when I was only two, and Ryan took me under his wing. I was lucky to have an incredible dad and grandmother, but it was Ryan who walked me to and from school. Who dealt with bullies, making sure no one ever messed with me. My dad lived with his head stuck in his books and computer programs, but Ryan was my rock." She turned her head on the pillow to look at him, her voice thick with pride. "I bet he gave those assholes a hell of a fight when they attacked him."

Standing with his hands in his pockets, no more than a few yards from the side of the bed, he said, "I'm sure he did."

"Did you try to warn him?" she asked in a rush, her mouth barely able to keep up with the words as they poured out of her.

"About what?" he asked, head cocked a bit to the side.

"The…werewolves," she said hoarsely, blinking away her tears. "About what he was going up against."

He lifted his hand and rubbed at the back of his neck, his expression grim. "I warned him off this case, several times, but he wouldn't listen."

"But did you tell him the truth?"

He rasped a quiet curse as he stared at the floor. "No, I didn't," he said after a moment, lifting his head and locking that dark blue gaze with hers. "Your brother was a reporter, Lainey. It would have been disastrous if I had revealed the truth about the wolf pack to him."

"But you had to know that they would target him!"

Frustration hardened the rugged angles of his face. "I thought my brothers and I would have them contained before that happened. But I give you my word that I did everything I could to convince Ryan to go home."

She thought about what he'd said, desperately wanting to believe him, though she didn't understand why. "Did you think you would have the wolves contained… or eliminated?" she finally asked, aching for her brother.

Holding her troubled gaze, he spoke in a low, gritty voice. "We didn't plan on letting them walk away. And we still don't. They'll be questioned extensively before they're put down."

"What is it exactly that you and your brothers do? I'm assuming the P.I. job is just a cover for the town, right?"

He nodded, scrubbing a hand against the dark stubble on his jaw, before saying, "We…hunt."

Lainey lifted her brows. "You hunt? That's all you're going to tell me?"

In that dry tone she'd already heard a few times, he said, "It's more than enough, trust me."

Wow, this guy was the king of cryptic responses. "Do you really live here? Not in this…bunker, but in Moonlight Bay?"

She noticed that he winced a little as he moved his hand to his arm, applying pressure to the bloody gauze on his biceps, a husky note in his voice as he told her that he did.

With a frown wedged between her brows, she asked, "Then isn't it a little strange that a werewolf pack would start terrorizing your home ground?"

"That's why they need to be questioned," he murmured, a scowl on his face as he gave a hard squeeze to his injured arm, then wiped his bloody palm on his dark sweats.

"You didn't try questioning anyone tonight." Her head might have been spinning during the fight, but she sure as hell would have remembered the sound of Nick's voice if he'd started talking to the bastards.

"No, I didn't exactly get around to questioning them." His tone was dry again as he flicked her a shuttered look from under his lashes. "I was too busy trying to save your little ass."

Which was the only reason why she wasn't currently having a complete and total breakdown. The guy had risked his life going into that cave to save her when he could have just as easily left her to suffer at the pack's hands. To Lainey's way of thinking, that meant she owed him more than she could ever repay, and *that* meant she had to keep her crap together until she was alone. Then she could fall apart and bawl like a raving lunatic. "Will you be in trouble for making the kills?"

"No," he answered, sounding…distracted. He was standing in profile to her now, looking in the other direction, at the heavily fortified door on the other side of the room. She had the uncomfortable feeling that something out there in the tunnels had snagged his attention. But she hadn't heard anything. Not even a howl.

"Santos?"

"Yeah?" he grunted, still staring at the door.

"Are you going to unchain me now?" she asked, tugging at the heavy manacles. If something was going to come through that monstrosity of a door, she wanted to be able to run. Not that there was anywhere to run to. A few interior doorways led out of the room, one a bit smaller than the other, but they were just going to lead to other rooms in the bunker, based on what Santos had said.

Pulling his focus away from the door, he walked to

the side of the bed and stared down at her. With a slow shake of his head, he said, "No. The chains stay."

"Come on, Santos. I'm human. You're…not. It's not like I could hurt you even if I tried."

He let that statement go and simply said, "I told you to call me Nick."

"Look. If you're not going to unchain me, can you at least loosen them enough that I can have a little more movement? I'd like to be able to sit up and put my hands in my lap."

He didn't look happy about the request. Or maybe, she realized, as he braced one knee beside her on the mattress and lifted his arms, reaching for the hook on the wall behind the bed, he just didn't *like* getting this close to her. He was careful not to touch her as he adjusted the chains, and it looked as if he was holding his breath. Humiliation burned like a flame under her skin. Did humans just smell crappy to him…or was she that rank after the fight with the wolves?

Feeling the need to fill the awkward silence, she asked, "How did you hurt your arm?"

He cast a disgusted look at the wound after he finished with the chains, moving back to his feet so quickly you would have thought she had some kind of contagious disease. "One of the bastards bit me."

Oh, wow. Freaking ouch. "Does it hurt?" The second she heard herself saying the words, she winced. What kind of stupid question was that? Of course it hurt. The guy was a vampire, not dead!

She expected him to deny any pain, but he surprised her by saying, "Throbs like a bitch."

"Can you take anything for it?"

"Painkillers don't work on my kind," he said, shaking his head.

"Speaking of your...kind—" She stopped for a moment as she finally managed to push herself up into a sitting position with her back against the wall, relieved to be able to lower her arms. "Exactly how old are you?"

He snorted, a crooked smile on those beautiful, sensual lips as he lifted his brows. "How old do I look?"

"I'd say...mid-thirties?" she murmured, trying not to think about her appearance. After everything she'd been through, she probably had some kind of funky Bride of Frankenstein look going on, while he managed to look extremely edible in nothing but a sweaty, blood-spattered pair of sweats and a T-shirt. If that wasn't unfair, she didn't know what was.

A low, gritty laugh shook his chest. "I'm nearly 240."

"Wow. You're, uh, holding together well," she offered lamely. But what the hell did you say to a man who had just told you he was older than the Constitution?

He gave another quiet snort, the flare of heat in his eyes as he stared down at her face making her breath catch. "Thanks. It's always good to hear that one's... holding together."

"And your brothers? How old are they?"

"Val is my older brother by ten years," he said, turning and walking over to the table and chairs that were pushed against one of the walls, his big, masculine body moving with a breathtaking predatory grace despite his height and powerful build. "Seb is the youngest at only 220."

"Only 220?" She quietly laughed, thinking this must have been close to how Alice felt after slipping down into that blasted hole. "Still in his prime, eh?"

He turned and looked at her as he grabbed the back of one of the wooden chairs one-handed, his dark gaze a sexy cross between perplexed and impressed. "You're taking this all very well, Lainey."

With a philosophical shrug, she said, "It's kinda hard to be disbelieving after what I saw tonight. And you *did* save my life. You could have just left me, but you didn't. Based on what I could hear, you must have come charging into that cave like some kind of avenging angel."

"I'm no damn angel," he snapped, any softening edges she might have glimpsed in his expression going razor sharp again. "You'd do well to remember that."

"Just tell me more about your family," she prompted, unfazed by his anger.

A scowl formed between his dark brows. "Why?"

Gathering her tangled hair and pulling it over her shoulder, she said, "Because it's helping me stay calm, and I'm too tired to freak out."

For the first time since she'd met him, Nick Santos looked a little lost. "I...don't know what you want to know."

"Well, after you bring that chair over here and sit down—that *is* what you were doing, right?—you can start by telling me about your parents."

He was quiet as he carried the chair across the room, setting it on the floor about five feet from the side of the bed. He turned it so that he was straddling the seat, his powerful arms crossed over the top rung at the back as he settled his curious, slightly uncertain gaze back on her face. In that deliciously low, rugged voice, he said, "My father is Spanish, but he settled in the colonies not long after meeting my mother. She was born and raised in Britain."

"Are they both vampires?" she asked, thinking he must have gotten his olive-toned skin and dark hair from his father, whereas those sinful baby blues probably came from his mother's side of the family.

"Yeah, they're both vamps, which means my brothers and I are born vampires and not made ones. There's not much difference between the two once a made vampire has reached full maturity."

"And how long does that take?"

With a shrug of those massive shoulders, he said, "Fifty years or so."

Oh, sure. Just a drop in the bucket for a guy who was going to live forever. Or would he? "Are you immortal?"

His chest shook with a breathless laugh. "Unless someone decides to kill me I am. More or less."

"I know you have a heartbeat because I can see the pulse at the base of your throat." A strong, dark, corded throat that looked good enough to nibble, even if she *wasn't* a vampire. "You, um, also look like you're breathing."

Brushing his bottom lip with his thumb, he said, "That's because I am. But unlike a human, going without oxygen won't kill me. It just gives me a hell of a headache."

"I can imagine," she murmured, thinking her own head wasn't feeling too great at the moment. But considering how lucky she was to have come out of the violent battle without anything more than a few bumps and bruises, she wasn't going to complain. "And what do your parents do?" she asked, determined to keep the conversation going. Of course, she was also curious as hell about his life and everything else that had to do with him.

"My mother is an artist," he explained, the look on his face making her feel as if she, quirky little ol' Lainey Maxwell, were some kind of mystifying puzzle he was still trying to figure out. "My father now holds a place of authority on the council that oversees our kind. Before that, he worked for many years as an Enforcer."

"An Enforcer?" It sounded like some kind of ancient military term to her.

His voice was rough and deep. "It's a vampire who hunts."

"Hunts what?" she asked, remembering him say that he and his brothers were hunters.

He held her stare with his piercing gaze, then looked down at his hands as he rubbed the thumb of one hand into the palm of the other. "Whatever we need to."

For a moment, Lainey was chilled by the coldness in his expression and in his tone, but then she realized what he was doing. Like so many other things in life, there was clearly a hell of a lot more to Nick Santos than met the eye. He might have been built like the perfect predator, long and lean and impossibly powerful, but the killing took its toll on him. When he went cold like this, she would have been willing to bet it was his means of coping with what he had to do, encasing his emotions in ice so that they couldn't interfere with his work.

Did anything, or anyone, ever crack through that ice deeply enough to actually touch him? Or did he use it as a shield to keep the rest of the world at a comfortable distance?

Uneasy with how important the answers to those questions were to her, she forced her attention back on the conversation. "Would werewolves be something that needs to be hunted?"

"Not all of them," he told her, bringing that compelling gaze back to hers. "Just the ones who feed on humans rather than other animals." He waited a moment, then added, "It's the role of an Enforcer to cull any preternatural creature that threatens the life of a human or a vampire."

"And you and your brothers? You've followed in your father's footsteps?"

When he nodded, she asked, "Are you any good at it?"

His jaw went hard and he gave her a sharp look as if she'd just insulted him by questioning his ability. Prickly vampire. "We've all reached the level of Prime."

"Is that high?"

"It's the highest," he said with obvious pride.

"And how does one become a Prime Enforcer?"

A grim smile twisted his lips. "With a hell of a lot of work," he supplied with a tired laugh.

"And a lot of smarts, too, I'd be willing to wager."

Shrugging, he said, "When you've been around as long as I have, you learn or you die."

"So you *can* be killed?"

He slowly arched one of those dark brows. "You planning to off me, little human?"

"No, of course not. I'm just curious…about your abilities. I mean, I met you this afternoon, in the sunlight. Isn't that meant to kill a vampire?"

His mouth twitched, as if he was trying not to smile. "In folklore, yes. But we're more resistant to the sun's rays the older we get. I can go out into the daylight for small intervals of time as long as I wear sunglasses. My eyes are more sensitive than my skin."

"What else?"

Without arrogance, he said, "I'm faster, stronger and harder to kill than a human."

"And you have fangs and claws," she pointed out, remembering the way he'd looked when he'd rescued her.

"That's right," he murmured, watching her closely, as if he was trying to figure out why she wasn't sobbing hysterically at this point. "But we call them talons."

"Can you—?"

"I think it's my turn to ask the questions," he cut in. "Let's start with what you do for a living."

"Great," she muttered, feeling her face go warm. "This'll be the part of our night that goes from fascinating to frightfully dull. Are you sure you want to go through with it? Wouldn't you rather just answer *my* questions? I mean, I've got, like, thousands of them."

"So do I," he returned with a quiet but firm force. "And something tells me you're anything but dull, Lainey."

She rolled her eyes. "That's sweet but far from the truth."

"Just answer the question," he ground out, probably irritated by the "sweet" comment.

"Fine!" she huffed, deciding just to get it over and done with. "I run a bookstore in San Diego. We also sell local arts and crafts and have a great little café, so we still get a lot of business even with the e-book boom."

Watching her carefully, he asked, "Are you married?"

"What? No!"

He lifted his brows. "Boyfriend? Girlfriend?"

"Uh, no. If there was, you can bet I'd have had them here with me, helping me search for Ryan." She paused for a moment, then added, "And I'm hetero, by the way.

Not that I would have a problem being a lesbian. One of my closest friends is gay and she's gorgeous. It's just not the way I...swing. If it was, I'd have begged her to marry me years ago."

His mouth twitched with one of those sexy, crooked smiles. "How old are you?"

"I turn twenty-seven next month."

Surprise shone in that deep, dark blue. "You look even younger."

"It's the hair," she said, ignoring the rattle of the chain as she lifted one of the long, curly locks.

"And what's with all the black?" he asked, his voice a little huskier than before as he ran his intense gaze over her dark clothing before lifting it back to her face.

She slowly arched a brow as she stretched out her legs, thinking that she just might kick him if he said something unkind. "What do you mean?"

"It doesn't really seem your kind of color scheme," he offered with a cocky smirk, as if she was too fluffy to pull it off. What an ass!

Lainey narrowed her eyes. "You have no idea what my color scheme is. For all you know, I wear black *all* the damn time. I might be the freaking Goth queen of black clothing."

He gave a masculine snort, looking too mouthwatering to be real. "Doubt it."

"Just because I wasn't wearing it earlier today doesn't mean anything. That outfit you saw me in could have just been a way to fit in around here."

"Whatever it was," he said in a low, husky rumble, "I thought it was cute as hell on you."

She blinked, those unexpected words taking the oomph right out of her pique. "Oh. You...uh, did?"

"Any man would have," he muttered, his gaze starting to glow a little as he rubbed his jaw. "Hell, you looked like a pink ice cream cone."

She gave a soft, startled laugh. "Well, if it makes you feel better, I didn't opt for *all* black tonight. My thong is pink."

As if drawn by a magnet, his gaze shot straight to her crotch. She shivered, feeling as if he was actually seeing her in nothing but the skimpy panties, and her entire body went hot.

What on earth was she doing? Was she actually... *flirting* with him?

Considering the look he was giving her, Lainey thought it might be a good time to finally ask, "What exactly is the plan? You know...for the two of us?"

He moved to his feet so quickly he was little more than a blur, turning his back to her as he carried the chair back over to the table. Apparently question time was over.

"Nick, seriously. Please just answer the question."

"I'm hoping my brothers will find us," he said, crossing his arms over his chest as he turned to face her. "If they return to town tomorrow and realize I'm missing and not answering my phone, they'll start searching the area. This should be one of the first places they look."

"And if they don't make it back to town tomorrow? What then?"

Everything about him, from his stance to his tone, said he didn't want to be having this conversation. "We'll talk about it tomorrow night."

"Tomorrow night? Why? What's happening tomorrow night?"

His voice became dangerously low. "Take my word for it, Lainey. You don't want to know."

Feeling a little sick inside, she said, "I do, actually."

"Christ," he grunted, shoving one of those big hands back through his hair, his blue eyes beginning to burn with a hot, glittering glow. "You just can't leave well enough alone, can you?"

"Just answer the damn question, Nick. What's the big deal about tomorrow night?"

Narrowing his gaze, he took two steps toward her, then checked himself, his voice erupting in a guttural snarl of words as he roared, "That's when we're going to have a serious fucking problem!"

Chapter 3

And they didn't already? From her viewpoint, Lainey would have sworn that things were about as serious as they could get. When he'd bellowed, the wolves had taken up with their bloodcurdling howls again, the eerie cries echoing through the tunnels, until it sounded as if hundreds of them were out there…just waiting to get in.

Before she could ask Nick to explain his unsettling announcement, he turned and left the room, disappearing through one of the interior doorways that led to God only knew where. It didn't make any sense, but she felt bereft without him there. She'd have been worried she was developing that weird syndrome where victims became emotionally attached to their captors, except that he wasn't really her captor. He was her…hell, she didn't know what to call him. But for some inexplicable reason, Lainey was positive he would let her go as soon as he thought it was safe. She didn't understand the whole chained-to-the-wall thing, but she didn't think he was doing it to be a dick. He truly believed there was a good reason for it. Who knew? Maybe the guy was worried she was emotionally distraught enough to try and take her own life or something.

As she braced herself against the hard wall, she racked her brain for a way to explain why he'd reacted like that before he'd stormed off, but exhaustion soon won out over her curiosity. Not surprisingly, her sleep was fitful. She dozed off and on but could see from the clock on the far wall that only a few hours had passed when Nick finally came back into the room. Well, almost. He stood in the same doorway he'd disappeared through earlier, arms crossed over his chest, shoulder propped against the doorjamb.

Though it was after three in the morning, he obviously hadn't had any more success at sleeping than she had. If he'd even been trying. His hair was wet and he was wearing clean clothes, making her aware of just how grimy she was. But it was a distant thought because the majority of her brainpower was busy processing how freaking hot he looked. Dressed in nothing but a well-worn pair of jeans that hung low on his hips, his muscular chest and broad shoulders left bare, he was the most mouthwatering sight Lainey had ever set eyes on. Not even the fresh, crimson-stained gauze he had wrapped around his right biceps could detract from his provocative sex appeal. Instead, it just added to the hard, rugged warrior look he had going on, as if he were some ancient Highlander who'd just come in from fighting for his clan.

The modern jeans obviously didn't fit with that whole scenario, but if she squinted her eyes, she could easily imagine his sexy bod wrapped up in nothing but a kilt. One that he slowly unwrapped with a devilish grin when he caught her staring at him, his deep voice thick with lust as he prowled toward her, telling her in explicit, erotic detail all the wild, wicked, breathtaking things he was going to do to her. *Mmm...*

When he cast her a funny look and lifted his brows, she realized she'd drifted off into fantasyland, her expression no doubt glazed with lust. Clearing her throat, she sat up a little straighter, knowing damn well that her cheeks were burning with color. If the guy had any idea what she'd been thinking, he'd probably laugh in her face. She struggled to think of something to say.

"Did you, um, take a shower?" she asked, liking the way the golden light coming from the single overhead bulb played over the dark, gleaming strands of his hair.

"Yeah."

Lucky duck. He obviously had some kind of water tank set up in this place, and she hoped she'd eventually be allowed to shower, too. Despite being trapped in what was essentially an oversize metal prison, the air was warm and humid, making her feel like she was in the tropics, and she desperately wanted to get clean.

But first, Lainey wanted an answer to the question that had been burning its way through her brain ever since he'd stormed out on her. "Are you going to need blood?" She took a quick breath, licked her bottom lip, then tried to hear her own voice over the roaring of her pulse. "Is that why you're worried about your brothers getting here in time? Will you need to...feed? By tomorrow night?"

The look on his gorgeous face was almost...bemused, as if he found her funny and strange and more than a little confusing all at the same time. "I have blood stored here, Lainey."

"Oh." She told herself this was a good thing because it meant he wouldn't need to *feed* on her. But she still felt strangely deflated. "That's, um, good then." Because she hadn't been thinking of offering him her neck. Nope. The idea hadn't even crossed her mind.

And, God, was she bad at lying. Even to herself.

"I also have food," he murmured, watching her so intently she felt like he was trying to crawl inside her head and look around. But he simply said, "I stocked up on fresh supplies just a few days ago. There's a small kitchen behind me that runs off a generator. Are you hungry?"

She bit her bottom lip and nodded, surprised to realize that she actually was. "I had dinner last night at the inn, but I feel like I haven't eaten in years."

A brief smile touched his mouth. "That's the adrenaline working through your system."

Before she could say anything in response, he disappeared again. She could hear water running, then the sound of things being set on a counter, and a few minutes later the mouthwatering scent of fresh-brewed coffee reached her nose, making her want to whoop with joy. She knew the reaction was a bit extreme, making her wonder if there really was some truth behind the label of "severe coffee addict" that was always being thrown her way.

When Nick came back into the room, he was carrying a tray with two steaming mugs of coffee, along with a plate of hot scones that had already been sliced open and smeared with cream and jam. As she took in the sight of such a deliciously dark, gorgeous, dangerous male doing something so domestic, Lainey couldn't help but smile.

Who would have ever thought that a vampire could turn out to be such a nice guy? Oh, he could be grumpy and taciturn, with some of the most mercurial mood swings she'd ever witnessed. But it was obvious that he wanted to take care of her.

With the tray balanced on one hand, he pulled one of the chairs from the table over next to the bed, set the tray on it and then pulled over another chair for himself, though she could tell he was careful to keep a certain amount of distance between them, as if he didn't want to unsettle her any more than she already was. Or maybe he just didn't want to be that close to her. Whatever the reason, she was charmed by the fact that he'd made her a snack. Of course, she'd been pretty charmed by the way he'd saved her life before he ever set foot in that kitchen. The culinary skills were just a delightful bonus.

Then again, if a guy couldn't figure out how to heat scones and make coffee after more than two hundred years of life, he didn't deserve to still be breathing. But Santos didn't just *make* coffee. He made damn incredible coffee, she realized, after he'd handed her one of the mugs and half a scone.

As she watched him pick up a half for himself and take a bite, she murmured, "So you actually do eat real food? I half expected you to just pretend so that I would feel more comfortable."

The husky sound of his laughter was so sexy it made her toes curl. "I eat," he said in that deep, rugged voice that seemed to contain a blend of too many accents to name. "Probably about as much as any human male around my size would, even though I also drink blood.

I need both sources of energy because of an accelerated metabolism."

"From who?" she whispered, liking the way he sat with his body angled forward, elbows braced on his parted knees. It was one of those purely masculine poses that did great things to his chest and thighs, not to mention his powerful arms and rock-hard abs.

Swallowing another bite, he asked, "You mean who do I feed from?"

"Yes. Or is that too personal a question? I don't want to offend you," she told him, taking a bite of her scone.

He shrugged those incredibly broad shoulders. "I'm not offended. And I don't feed on...victims." He gave her a wry grin when he spotted the look of relief on her face. He went on, saying, "There have always been those who are willing to provide their blood for my kind, and they're well compensated for it. Occasionally, we might feed from a willing source, but we usually just store our supplies in the fridge the same way humans store their milk. When we need it, we heat the blood up and drink it from a glass."

"Oh." She was silent for a moment, then asked, "Which do you prefer? From the source...or from a glass?"

His chest shook with another one of those rugged laughs. "That's like asking which tastes better, tofu or steak? The tofu can nourish you," he drawled, "but it's nowhere near as good."

"Ahh...I understand."

Jerking his chin toward the plate, he asked, "You want another one?"

She shook her head, marveling once again at the bizarreness of the situation. Nibbling on the last bite of her scone, she said, "You know, you're pretty dangerous, Santos."

"I told you to call me Nick," he responded in a low voice, watching her from beneath his dark lashes as he set his empty mug on the tray and leaned back in the chair, fingers laced behind his head. She could see the dark tufts of hair beneath his arms, his biceps freaking huge in that position, straining the gauze on his right arm, his forearms corded with muscle and sinew. She'd never seen a man look so sexy, his voice a deep, throaty rumble as he added, "And I meant it when I said that I wouldn't hurt you."

"Not that kind of dangerous. You're the keeping kind," she mused, wondering if he'd put something in the coffee to make her loopy. Or maybe she was still suffering from shock? Out of her head crazy? One egg short of a dozen? But the words didn't feel…insane. They felt…real. Truthful. Even painfully honest.

His expression was almost comical in its surprise. "I'm afraid to ask, but what in God's name are you going on about now?"

"You." She took a quick sip of her coffee, holding the mug now with both hands as she studied him through her lashes. "You're all smoldering and intense. Smart and sexy and too masculine to be real. But you're also not afraid to set foot in a kitchen, which means you're the kind of guy that makes a woman think you'd be worth keeping around once the afterglow has faded."

He shook his head slowly, looking kind of worried about what she would say next. "Afterglow?"

Shrugging her shoulder, she said, "Sex. Orgasms. It's great and all, but a guy's got to offer more than some fun times between the sheets, right?"

"I'm afraid I wouldn't know," he croaked, his expression arrested.

She laughed at his reaction. "You know what I mean."

He studied her for a moment, and then his dark brows suddenly snapped together in stunned confusion. "Are you…are you saying that you'd like to *keep* me?"

Lainey's eyes went huge. "God, no!" she blurted, feeling her face go bright red. "I was just pointing out the obvious. But I'd never try for a man who wasn't even in the same league as I am."

"Why's that?"

She didn't know what to make of the hard, tight edge to his voice that hadn't been there a moment ago. With a frown, she said, "Well, you're…you know. And I'm… well, you've got eyes, Nick."

Confusion was quickly giving way to what looked like formidable anger. "So how many leagues under you am I, exactly?"

"What?" she gasped, reaching out and just managing to set her mug on the edge of the tray. "No! I meant *you*, Nick. You're way above me. Not the other way around!"

He scowled. "That's ridiculous."

Rolling her eyes, Lainey said, "You don't need to flatter me. I'm not fishing for compliments—I'm just stating the obvious. You can see *exactly* the kind of woman I am."

He didn't say anything at first. Just leaned forward in the chair again, braced his elbows back on his knees and took his time looking her over. He started with her face, his own expression impossible to read as he studied her individual features, one by one, then moved down to the rest of her. He looked at the way her breasts strained against the tight T-shirt, her nipples hard despite the fact she wasn't cold. Then he looked lower, at the soft swell of her stomach…her hips, before following the curvy shape of her legs encased in the black denim. When he was done, he slowly brought that dark, blistering gaze back to her face. His voice little more than a whisper, he rasped, "Considering my X-ray vision, Lainey, I can actually see a hell of a lot more of you than you think."

Her heart jerked into her throat so fast it nearly choked her. *"What?"* she wheezed, chains clanging as she quickly crossed her arms over her chest and threw one leg over the other.

The corner of his mouth twitched, and she saw an unmistakable, devilish gleam in his eyes. "Calm down. You don't need to pass out on me again," he said, holding up his hands. "That was a joke."

"Geez, Nick! Give me a heart attack, why don't you?"

"Sorry," he murmured with a wry twist of his lips, looking even more surprised by his teasing than she was. "I couldn't resist."

"Try," she told him, her tone sharp and her eyes narrowed to piercing slits. "Or I'll make you sorry."

"And how would you do that?" he questioned, sounding more than a little curious as he leaned back and laced his fingers behind his head again, the position doing downright sinful things to the muscles in his arms and torso. Lainey took a moment to consider the question, more than a little distracted by those mouthwatering abs as she tried to think of something that would be really torturous for a vampire. Finally, she came up with one that brought a smirking smile to her lips. "I'd hold you down and tickle you until you were crying and begging for mercy."

He snorted. "You think you could?"

Shaking her wrists, she said, "We'll never know unless you take these chains off me. Will we?"

His head cocked a fraction to the side, his sky-blue stare deep and measuring. "You know, for a human captive at the mercy of a vampire who kills for a living, you're very...relaxed."

"Well, I don't think you want to kill me," she murmured, tucking a strand of hair behind her ear, "or you would have already done it."

"So now you're no longer afraid of me?" he asked, that inscrutable expression back on his face.

"Why should I be?"

His voice went eerily soft again. "There's a hell of a lot I could do to you without killing you, Lainey."

"True. But you wouldn't."

"Yeah?" His blue eyes were shadowed...dark. "And why's that?"

"I can just...tell."

"Christ, I don't believe what I'm hearing," he muttered, the moment of teasing over as he shoved to his feet. Suddenly she found herself staring up at almost six and a half feet of pissed-off vampire. "You can just *tell?*"

Her chin went up a notch. "That's right."

He gripped the chair they'd been using as a table, their mugs nearly tumbling from the tray as he shoved it out of his way, that raw, violent tension she'd glimpsed in him earlier riding his large body all over again. "The way I see it," he bit out, glaring down at her, "you should be screaming bloody murder right about now."

She would have explained if she could, but she barely understood her own mind at the moment. All she knew was that she felt safe with this man…or vampire…or whatever he wanted to call himself. Safer than she had in…a really long time.

Locking her gaze hard on his, Lainey looked him right in the eye and said, "I'm not afraid of you, Nick. So why would I scream?"

"Take off the goddamn blinders," he snarled, swiping one of those large hands through the air. "The world is shit, as evidenced by what happened to your brother. You shouldn't trust me. Hell, you shouldn't trust *any* man. The sooner you start to realize that, the better your chances of surviving."

"Yeah, well, you know what I think? I think you need a woman who can help you learn to lighten up a little."

He went completely still except for the hard rise and fall of his chest, those big hands fisted at his sides as he stared her down. "Is that right?" he finally asked, his voice doing that soft, raspy thing again that made her feel like the words were stroking her skin.

"Yes," she breathed out, trying not to shiver.

"You mean a woman like *you?*" He moved even closer to the side of the bed, the look in his eyes both dark and bright, as if the midnight sky had been spread out over a hot, molten glow. "Is that what I need, Lainey?"

Her temper spiked. As much as she wanted him to flirt with her, she knew damn well that wasn't where he was going with this. "Cut it out, Nick. Now I'm starting to think you just like being mean."

He came a little closer, his knees bumping the mattress. "Explain."

Tilting her head back farther so that she could hold his piercing gaze, she said, "You keep making references to the two of us...you know. So I'm wondering if you're actually trying to *make* me dislike you because I'm not afraid of you. Is it *that* important to you for me to keep my distance?"

His brows went so high they nearly reached his hair. "The idea of having sex with me is grounds for dislike?"

Gritting her teeth, she said, "Despite some of the comments you've made tonight...or this morning...or *whatever* it is, we both know you're just mocking me. I'm obviously not your...type."

"Not my type?" He made a sharp sound of frustration, absently rubbing his hand over his bandaged biceps. "You're being serious, aren't you? You really think you're not the type of woman I like to fuck?"

Her face went crimson. "I know I'm not."

"I don't screw around with human women," he grated, veins thickening beneath his dark skin as he squeezed his hand around the wound. "But it doesn't mean I wouldn't want to."

Her soft snort seemed to set his teeth on edge. "So it's my humanity that throws you off? *Right*."

He cursed under his breath as he turned away from the bed, starting that relentless pacing again. As if they could sense the tension in the room, the wolves started another incessant round of howling, accompanied by the nerve-racking scratch of their claws against the door.

Following him with her eyes, Lainey ignored the monsters and focused on the vampire in the room with her. "I'm not going to think you're a jerk for being honest," she told him, knowing damn well what he would say. Something along the lines of *You're a great gal,*

Lainey, but I just don't think of you that way. How many times had she heard that little spiel before? Lifting her chin, she tried not to sound upset as she added, "We both know you're not attracted to me, Nick."

"Is that so?" His voice was rough but soft. "You have no idea how tempted I am to prove you wrong."

She started to launch another argument but found the words drying up on her tongue when she caught the way he was looking at her. It was unlike anything she'd ever seen—a scorching look of savage, visceral hunger. She went breathless, her heart starting to pound with shocked excitement. "If...if that's true, then tell me."

He shuddered, the muscles beneath his dark skin bunching with tension as he clenched his hands. He looked like a caged animal prowling the confines of its cage, but she still wasn't afraid. Captivated, thankful, *hopeful*. Those were all far better words for what she was suddenly feeling.

Licking her bottom lip, she said, "Better yet, why don't you show me?"

There was something deliciously provocative about the way he angled his head as he cut her a sharp look of warning. But it was a little intimidating, too. Animalistic and raw, making it clear he was anything but human. Yet, she still wasn't frightened.

As if he read that in her eyes, he growled, "You're playing a dangerous game, Lainey."

"Oddly enough, Nick, this is the safest I've felt all night." Her voice was quiet but firm.

"Damn it, woman!" He turned toward her with a fierce scowl, eyes burning like blue chips of flame from beneath his dark brows. "You should be terrified!"

With a little shrug, she said, "If you want to scare

me, you're going to have to do a better job than you have so far."

"You have no idea what you're asking for," he snarled, moving so fast he was nothing more than a blur. Before she could process what was happening, she was upright, being pinned to the wall behind the bed by nearly six and a half feet of hard, muscled male. Sweat beaded on his brow, his breaths warm against her lips, eyes glowing and bright, the irises now a pure molten gold without a glimmer of blue. She could feel the hunter in him—that dark wildness that saw her as something more like food he could fuck than a woman he could make love to. Could see the battle he was fighting to keep that vicious predator in check. Keep it from breaking loose and doing something she knew they'd both regret.

He'd said he didn't screw around with humans, and she was beginning to see why.

As if he saw that flash of vulnerability in her eyes, he flinched, something shadowed and pained moving through that savage gaze. For a split second she thought he would pull away, but then his big hands were wrapping around her wrists, lifting them over her head and trapping them against the wall. He leaned harder into her, grinding his massive erection against her lower belly as he tilted his face down and stared into her eyes. Stroking his thumbs against the damp heat of her palms, he said, "When you're bound like this, I could do anything to you, Lainey. *Anything.* And there's nothing you could do to stop me."

"Chains or no chains, Nick, you could take what you want from me anytime you wanted it."

"And that frightens you," he whispered, the look in

those inhuman eyes daring her to disagree. But despite everything, she still wasn't afraid. Just because he *could* hurt her didn't mean that he would.

When she shook her head in response to his statement, he cursed something guttural in Spanish that sounded exceptionally dirty. In English he simply demanded, "Why, damn it? I know you're not stupid, so what the hell is your problem?"

"I don't know how to make you understand," she whispered, wishing she could break out of his hold and touch him. She wanted to rub her hands all over that hard, breathtaking body. "I'm not sure I even understand it myself. Did you…have you used some kind of vampire trick to mesmerize me or something?"

He gave a sharp snort. "We have enough advantages over humans without needing to be able to control your lust."

"Then I guess I just want you," she whispered, giving him a tremulous smile.

"Goddamn it!" His body shook as he pressed his forehead against hers, releasing his grip on her wrists. But he didn't take his hands off her. Instead, he ran them down her body—across her forearms and over her biceps, and when he reached her breasts, he made a thick, guttural sound in the back of his throat. "You feel so fucking good," he growled, rubbing her nipples through her shirt with his thumbs. She groaned in surrender, tilting her pelvis toward him, and his hands left her breasts in a flash, his breath hissing sharply through his teeth, as if she'd hurt him.

Before Lainey could ask him what was wrong, he slammed his hands against the wall on either side of her head, his breaths coming hard and fast and rough.

In the next instant, she heard an odd, high-pitched grating sound, a gasp of shock rushing past her lips when she looked from side to side and saw that he was scraping two vicious sets of talons down the metal surface of the wall. When she brought her startled gaze back to his face, she gasped again at the sight of the deadly fangs hanging beneath his upper lip. They were long… sharp…gleaming.

If ever there was a time to be out of her head with terror, Lainey knew it was now—but the haunted look on his beautiful face nearly broke her heart. In that single instant, she could see and understand so much, as if she were slipping right inside him, strolling through his mind, sneaking peeks at his secrets. Sensing, with some unknown skill, what he needed to ease the struggle and tension seething inside him.

He started to pull away, but she caught his face in her hands and leaned forward, pressing a tender kiss to the corner of his mouth. He drew in a ragged breath as she kissed the other side, his chest working like a bellows. "Shh," she whispered. "Just take a deep breath and trust me."

"I can't," he panted, jerking his head to the side. "Goddamn it! Breathing you in is the *last* thing I should be doing. You're too—"

He cut himself off with a low growl, and she wanted to stamp her foot with frustration. "I'm too what?"

"Forget it," he snapped, jerking away from her. "This isn't happening, Lainey."

"Nick, it's okay," she murmured, sinking to her haunches as she watched him step off the bed with pantherish skill. "Come back."

She could see how badly he wanted to, but he jerked

his head in a sharp, negative shake, refusing to look at her as he scrubbed his hands down his face. "Can't."

"You *can*. I trust you. Come back to me." She didn't understand *why* this was so important to her, but it was. It mattered in ways that meant a hell of a lot more than sex—though she had a feeling that any kind of sex with Nick Santos would be pretty damn meaningful. *"Please."*

"Christ, Lainey." Dropping his hands, he turned his head toward her, his expression tight with lust and things that were too primal for her to even understand. "I might be the vampire, but *you're* the dangerous one."

She shook her head, filled with confusion. "I doubt that. I mean, I'm practically a librarian!"

He gave a throaty laugh as he rubbed a hand over his eyes, the dark, husky sound making her tremble and melt. "I never would have guessed that a smart-ass little bookworm could tie me up in so many knots."

"I'll take that as a compliment, so thanks."

With those simple words, she had him clenching his jaw all over again. "You shouldn't be *thanking* me!" he roared. "You should be slapping my face and demanding I get you out of here. You should be cursing me to the depths of hell and telling me to keep my bloody hands off you!"

"But I happen to like your hands on me, Nick. And call me practical, but I'd rather be in here with you than out there with them any day of the week."

He glanced at the bite mark on his arm. "You might not think that come nightfall tonight."

"Why?"

Instead of answering, he grabbed the tray and started heading for one of the doorways. "You must still be exhausted," he said over his shoulder, his tone low and flat. "You should get some more sleep before we talk any more. Once the sun is up, the wolves will quiet down a bit, so the howling won't keep you awake."

"Nick, wait! I want to—"

But he'd already touched a switch on the wall that muted the light and disappeared through a doorway, leaving her alone.

Scooting down onto her side, Lainey huddled beneath one of the light blankets and tried not to dwell on how frustrating Nick Santos, badass vampire with a serious attitude problem, could be. Or all the things he wouldn't tell her. Prickly, irritating male!

But most of all, Lainey tried not to think about how badly she wanted him.

Chapter 4

Dripping in sweat, Nick attacked the set of weights he kept in the back room of the bunker, so furious he probably could have taken on the entire wolf pack on his own. But he wouldn't risk putting Lainey in harm's way. If his rage weren't enough to cut them down, she'd be the one to pay the price. Which meant he'd just have to find some other way to work through the most severe, excruciating case of sexual craving he'd ever experienced...for a woman he couldn't—*shouldn't*—touch.

He was a hairsbreadth away from ripping the clothes off her delectable little body and claiming her in ways so raw and hard and possessive most humans wouldn't even be able to comprehend them. He wanted her marked and filled with his seed. Wanted his tongue on her clit...then lower, plunging into her hot sex while he closed his lips over her opening and sucked in every juicy drop of her pleasure. Wanted to eat at the tender flesh between her thighs until she was coming so hard he could drink her in, drowning in her, while he drove himself into her beautiful, smart-ass little mouth.

And that was before he even got to the blood. To the idea of sinking his fangs into her tender throat and feeling her spill, warm and slick and sweet, across his tongue.

Though it had confused him at first, this morning Nick had more clarity. He now understood why he'd been so short-tempered with her. His pissy attitude was nothing more than a cover. A way to hide the fact that he wanted her so badly it was twisting him into knots. Hell, his natural hungers were violent enough—no telling where they could go with the wolf's blood flowing through his veins, creating havoc in his body.

Yet, the instant he heard the rustling of the bedding in the main room, his heart started to pound with anticipation. When a glance at the clock showed it was already nine, he figured she was probably awake. Making his way through the narrow passageway that connected to the bathroom, he took another quick, deliberately cold shower.

When he was done, Nick sent up a silent prayer that his brothers would hurry up and find their asses soon, not knowing how much longer he could keep it together, and headed into the kitchen to put on a fresh pot of coffee. A few minutes later, he'd doctored Lainey's with cream and sugar, keeping his black, and carried the two mugs into the main room, hoping they could start fresh for the day. He didn't want to spend what time he had left with her arguing. He just wanted to soak up as much of her as he could from as safe a distance as possible.

"I've got coffee," he said, his heart giving a strange

thump when he caught sight of her. She looked completely adorable sitting there on the bed with her back propped against the wall, her hair a wild tangle of golden waves that tumbled around her flushed face. If not for the chains manacling her delicate wrists, she'd have looked like a drowsy, brown-eyed nymph.

Then again, knowing what he did about nymphs, the chains might have been fairly appropriate.

With a half smile on those rosy lips, she eyed his bare chest, bit her lip as she did a quick visual sweep over the front of his jeans, then locked that heavy-lidded gaze on the steaming mugs of coffee. "Mmm. You're an angel."

She must have caught the word he muttered under his breath because she laughed and said, "Oops, sorry. I know how much you hate that. Would devil be better?"

"Did you sleep okay?" he asked, ignoring her question as he used his elbow to flick the light switch to a brighter setting, then walked over and handed her one of the mugs.

"Better than I thought I would. The howls woke me up a few times, but you were right about them quieting down."

"Most of them are probably asleep," he told her, taking a sip of his coffee. "In fact, four of them are actually sleeping against the door."

Her brows lifted. "How do you know?"

"For one thing, I can smell them through the air vents."

A strange look crossed her face. "Your sense of smell is *that* good?"

He took another drink from his mug, then said, "Think bloodhound but about a hundred times better."

"Whoa!"

"I'm a vampire, Lainey. Not a human. I might look like you, but I'm not." And the sooner she got that through her stubborn little head, the better off they'd both be.

"I know what you are, Nick. Trust me, the fangs were a dead giveaway. But that's not the problem," she murmured. "The problem is that I need a shower." He couldn't read her mind, but it was obvious from the look on her face that she was embarrassed.

"There's no need to worry," he said with a wry smile, sitting in one of the chairs he'd left by the bed. "You smell incredible, Miss Maxwell."

"Hardly," she scoffed.

He cocked his head to the side as he studied her. "But you can have a shower if you want one."

That brightened her right up. "Really? In private?"

Shit. Just the thought of watching her soap up that sexy little body made his dick twitch. But he knew better than to tempt himself. "Yeah," he practically croaked. "In private. You want one right now?"

"God, yes. I'd love that. Thank you."

Moving back to his feet, Nick took a small key from one of his front pockets. He was careful not to touch her as he took her mug, set it on the floor beside his own, then unlocked the shackles as she held her wrists out to him. As soon as she was released, she rubbed her wrists and scooted off the side of the bed, then moved to her feet, her body no doubt feeling stiff and achy from lying down for so long.

"I'm afraid the water won't be very hot," he told her, watching as she lifted a slender hand to rub at the knotted muscles in her neck.

"I don't care. It'll still feel great." Looking down at

her bloodstained clothes, she added, "But it sucks that I don't have anything clean to change into."

"Wait here." He headed through the doorway on the right and made his way back to the small bedroom he kept at the rear of the bunker. When he came back into the main room, he handed her a stack of clothing. "They'll be too big for you, but you can use these."

She gave him a blinding smile that damn near knocked him on his ass. "Thanks, Nick."

"Come on, then," he grunted.

She followed him through the doorway on the left, through the small kitchen, then into the narrow surveillance room that connected to the bathroom. He'd been hoping she wouldn't stop to study the wall of video screens that covered the right side of the room. But he should have known she was too curious to pass them by. The instant she spotted them, she walked over to the desk that hugged the wall, keeping the clothes he'd given her clutched in her arms as she leaned forward and studied the screen that revealed the wolves gathered just outside the door. She could see the shadowy shapes of others in the distance, a few glowing sets of eyes burning in the stygian darkness, while the others slept.

"Will they just stay there all day?" she asked. "All of them?"

"Yeah," he grunted, hands shoved deep in his front pockets as he moved to her side. He hadn't stood next to her since the previous afternoon, and he almost grinned, surprised by how petite she was beside him. But then he looked at the wolves, and the urge to smile fled as quickly as it'd come. "They won't risk lowering their numbers, knowing damn well that we'd try to escape if they did. They can't take the risk of you getting away."

There was a notch between her brows as she turned her head to look at him. "The risk?"

Nodding, he rubbed his fingers against his bristled jaw and explained. "You know the truth about them now, which means they can't risk you going to the authorities with that information. To keep that from happening, they'll block our only exit for however long it takes, probably thinking hunger will eventually drive us out. Idiots have no idea how much food I've stockpiled in this place," he finished with a derisive snort.

"But even if I *did* go to the authorities, they wouldn't ever believe me."

"That's true." He jerked his chin toward the screen that showed the sleeping wolves. "But you've also seen their human faces, which could definitely cause trouble for them if the police were able to identify who they are from your descriptions."

"Crap. I didn't even think about that." She took a shaky breath and closed her eyes for a moment, looking distraught. Nick frowned, completely at a loss for what to do—he'd never comforted anyone in his life. Clearly, it wasn't going to be one of his strong points. But he was saved from making an ass of himself when she lifted those long eyelashes and glared at the screen. "They're still in their wolf forms, but it's daytime. How is that even possible?"

"So long as they're in the dark, the older ones can control and retain the shape of their beasts. It's only the juveniles who are completely governed by the moon."

"They're massive, aren't they?"

"I've seen bigger," he offered dryly, thinking how horrified she'd have been by some of the werewolves he'd faced in the past. "It's their numbers that's the problem."

"How many do you think you killed last night?"

"I injured a lot of them but probably only killed one or two. Bastards are hard to destroy."

She'd just started to ask him another question when she finally noticed what was on the center screen. Nick winced, dreading her next question.

Without looking at him, she asked, "Were you…did you watch me while I was sleeping?"

Deciding the best way to deal with the situation was to not deal with it at all, Nick grabbed her shoulder, steering her away from the screens and toward the bathroom. "If you want that shower, get moving."

"But—"

"Move it, Lainey."

She muttered under her breath about bossy alpha males, knowing damn well he could hear her, and he had to bite back a low rumble of laughter. He didn't trust what he would do if he let himself loosen up around her.

The ferocity of his reaction to the little human was not only unexpected, it was unfamiliar as hell. Nick understood lust and had felt it often over the years, indulging whenever he wanted, though he'd never met a woman he wanted to tie himself down to. But he didn't know how to explain the way Lainey made him feel. It was almost as if something essential in his life that had always been missing had suddenly clicked into place— yet, the timing and circumstances couldn't have been worse.

"Nick?" she whispered, making him realize he'd just been standing there in the doorway to the bathroom, breathing hard as he stared at her mouth.

"Don't take too long," he muttered, forcing himself to step back and shove the metal door closed. He stood there for a moment, forehead pressed to the cool steel, and struggled to slow his breathing…his pulse, fighting for control. Finally, he forced himself to walk back into the main room, where he paced…and paced, his vampire hearing enabling him to follow her every movement even with the distance he'd put between them.

When she came back into the main room nearly fifteen minutes later, he'd already replaced the bedding with clean blankets and was now sitting at the table trying to clean the bloody wound on his arm just to keep himself busy. As she set her bundle of dirty clothes on the floor by the bed, then started making her way over to the table, Nick struggled to keep his attention focused on his task, but it wasn't easy. She looked incredible wearing his white button-down shirt with the sleeves rolled up, his brow misting with sweat when he realized she hadn't put her bra back on. And the shirt's hem was just long enough that it hid the stretchy boxer shorts he'd given her to wear. Her wet hair had been finger combed, curls already twining through the damp strands, her skin flushed and incredibly lovely. Her legs were shapely and smooth, her feet small, with coral-colored polish on her nails. It was amazing how much visual detail he could gather from the corner of his eye when he was really motivated.

"Before you put the chains back on me," she said, pulling her damp hair over one shoulder, "I want to talk to you about them."

Nick slid her a wary look. "All right."

"You can let me go now," she told him. "I mean, you can leave the chains off. I won't try to run. I swear."

Nick gave a derisive snort. "If you ran, you'd be dead."

"I know," she agreed, holding up her hands. "So what's the point of the chains?"

"You're better off not knowing," he muttered under his breath.

"Don't worry so much," she said with a smile. "I'll be golden, I swear."

He smirked as he ran his gaze over her hair. "You're definitely that, little human." He glanced at the shackles lying empty against the blankets, then back at Lainey, and he slowly shook his head. "I have a feeling I'm going to regret this, but fine, have it your way." He narrowed his eyes in warning. "But for your own sake, don't do anything to rile me."

He could see the questions in her big eyes and knew she wanted to ask what he meant, but he gave her a hard look that said *Leave it* and lowered his head, focusing his attention back on his arm.

"I'd like to feel like I'm earning my keep in here," she murmured, coming a little closer. "Why don't you let me help with your arm?" she offered, already pulling back one of the chairs and sitting down kitty-corner to him at the small table.

Lifting his head, he slid her a skeptical look. "And what exactly do you know about caring for wounds?"

"Absolutely nothing," she said brightly, giving him another one of those disarming smiles. "But it seems common sense can help me out, right? So just turn toward me a little and I'll be able to reach your arm."

Common sense? Jesus, the woman didn't have any. If she did, she'd know that getting within ten feet of him was a seriously bad idea, as was sitting her sweet little ass down right beside him. But his body had a mind of its own, and the next thing Nick knew, he was sitting sideways in his chair, staring down at her delicate profile as she leaned over his arm and gently dabbed with one of the antiseptic wipes he'd laid out.

"Why hasn't this already healed?" she asked, setting the bloody wipe aside and reaching for a fresh one. "In the vampire books I've read, the heroes always heal super fast from their injuries."

His response was dry. "Maybe because that's in books and this is the real world?"

She shot him a curious glance. "Are you saying that you don't have accelerated healing abilities?"

"No, that's not what I'm saying." Was it his imagination, or was his voice getting huskier? Clearing his throat, he added, "But it depends on the wound. A wolf bite is one of the few injuries that a vampire can't heal from quickly."

"Ahh," she murmured, as if that made perfect sense to her. She continued to carefully work her way across the raw bite marks and asked, "If you knew it was a werewolf pack that has been doing the killings here in Moonlight Bay, why not just hunt them down and destroy them?"

"You don't think I've been trying?" he muttered. "But the bastards are good at covering their tracks. Someone's taught them and taught them well."

Lifting her head, she gave him another questioning look. "Taught them what?"

"How to avoid detection by my species."

"Hmm. You mean like a rogue vamp?"

Nick lifted his brows. "A rogue vamp?"

"You know what I mean," she murmured, lowering her head again as she returned her attention to his arm. "A criminal vampire who knows how to keep from being found. As a vampire himself, or herself, he or she would know tricks to keep you from finding them, right?"

"Yes," he admitted, thinking she had to be the most unusual, fascinating human he'd ever known. "But we don't know why the wolves would have this information. My brothers have been up in Seattle talking to a few sources, seeking answers. So far, we haven't found any."

"If you knew they were using the caves for their kills, why not simply set up a stakeout?"

"We're not idiots, Lainey." His voice was getting a little tighter. "We tried that. But they knew."

"Hmm. Sounds to me like you have a mole in the system."

"Yeah," Nick muttered, rubbing his free hand over his face. Whoever it was, he just hoped the bastard wouldn't do anything to keep his brothers from reaching them in time.

"So how am I doing?" she asked with a grin, dabbing a fresh wipe on the wound. "Are my first aid skills up to scratch?"

"If you hadn't been so tempted by books, you could have been a nurse," he murmured, feeling a little uncomfortable giving the compliment. Or maybe it was just how good she made him feel that had his nerves jumping.

"A nurse?" She wrinkled her nose. "I like the idea of helping people, but that would have never worked out. I can't stand the sight of blood."

He didn't say anything for a moment, simply watching her clean the wound with sure, careful strokes. His blood had quickly soaked through the fresh cotton square and was now staining her fingers. "You're holding up pretty well with mine."

She smiled a little as she glanced at him through her lashes. "I guess that makes you special."

He kept staring at her slightly crooked smile until she finally asked, "What? Do I have food in my teeth?"

"No," he rasped, his voice rough with emotions he didn't dare think about or try to put a name to. "But you're very beautiful."

She blushed. "That's sweet of you to say."

God, she was insulting. "Please stop saying that. I'm a lot of things, but *sweet* isn't one of them. Neither is angelic or heroic or any of the other crap you keep throwing in my face."

"I'm entitled to my opinions, Nick. And I happen to think that you're sweet and more than a little scary at times—" her lips curled "—though the sexy helps smooth out those sharp edges. My best friend would go crazy over you. Bailey always does go head over heels for the bad boys."

"But not you?" *Of course not her. Get real. Why would she choose a killer over someone who can give her a family and a white picket fence?*

"I—" She broke off from whatever she'd been going to say, took a shaky breath and looked right at him. "Why did you almost kiss me?" she blurted.

"What are you talking about?"

She licked her lips, the look in her eyes hot and soft. "You left me when I tried to kiss you this morning. You know, when you had me against the wall. But before I took my shower, I could have sworn *you* were about to kiss *me*. Why?"

"Why does any man want to kiss a beautiful woman?" he muttered, rolling his shoulder with a fresh wave of agitation.

Her throat worked with a nervous swallow, but she managed to keep her voice steady as she said, "Then you *are* attracted to me? You really want to…"

"Fuck you?" he supplied when she didn't seem capable of saying the words.

"Yes," she said on a breathless sigh.

"I do," he ground out, knowing damn well she didn't understand what kind of danger she was courting with her questions.

She shook her head, her white teeth biting into the sexy swell of her bottom lip. "I find that so hard to believe, Nick."

With his thoughts going in so many different directions, he could only imagine what kind of look was on his face. "Why? You're… *Oh, hell, Lainey.* You're not a *virgin,* are you?" He couldn't have sounded more appalled if he'd tried.

A husky laugh slipped past her lips. "No. I've had a few relationships over the years," she told him, wrapping fresh gauze around his arm. "They never lasted very long, but a few of them were…sexual."

At that moment, it was a good thing for her ex-lovers that he was trapped in this bloody bunker. If free, Nick knew he'd have had a hell of a time keeping himself from doing something stupid. Like tracking her exes down and making it clear why they should *never* go near her again.

Not that I have any right to do it. But it would sure as hell make me feel better.

Needing a distraction from the dangerous direction of his thoughts, he asked, "What happened with the men?"

"They left me for other women."

He made a derisive sound under his breath. "Human males are such idiots."

She gave a careless shrug. "They were both going through bad times."

"So you helped them and then they betrayed you?"

Her expression was pinched as she leaned back in her chair and looked at him. "I guess you could say that."

Oh yeah, he would definitely enjoy getting his hands on the bastards if he could.

"Is that why you don't see yourself as beautiful?" he asked, thinking he understood her a little better now.

The color in her cheeks got brighter, the drawl in her speech a little more pronounced. "I didn't need their betrayals to see what I am," she said, crossing her arms over her chest. "Like I told you before, I have a mirror, Nick."

"Then surely you know that you're…"

"What? Chubby? Short? Quirky?"

"I was going to say beautiful again," he said in a low rumble.

She snorted. "You're such a smooth liar."

"I don't lie."

Eying him with an expression that was equal parts pleasure and skepticism, she asked, "Are you…trying to tell me that you're interested in me?"

"No!" he said so sharply that she flinched, making

him feel like seven different kinds of shit. "I'm sorry. I, uh, didn't mean it like that."

Wait a minute? Had he actually just *apologized*? And since when did a centuries-old vampire say things like "Uh"? Damn woman was making him dotty!

"Don't worry about it," she murmured, using her hair to conceal her expression as she pushed to her feet. But he didn't let her get away, holding out his uninjured arm to block her path.

"Lainey, I…" He exhaled a frustrated breath, trying to figure out how to explain. "Just trust me when I say that a woman like you is *not* for me."

"Ahh." He could feel the force of her stare against his face like a physical touch but kept his gaze focused on the rapid pulse at the base of her throat. "So you go for the tall, swizzle-stick look, then?"

With a wry grin, he shook his head, his hot gaze moving slowly over her curvy form, lingering on her breasts and thighs. "No. I actually prefer a woman to feel like a woman, not an ironing board."

She didn't say anything, but Nick could sense that she didn't believe him. Her confidence had taken more than one hit in the past, and he wondered what was *wrong* with the human males she'd known. How had they not lost themselves in lust for her? Been charmed by her quirky sense of humor? How had they not been awed by her bravery and loyalty?

Or maybe that had been the problem right there. Maybe they *had* been all of those things and just didn't have the balls to handle how she made them feel. In each century of his life, Nick had seen humans run from the things they wanted most, but he had never really thought of the flaw with anything more than confusion. But now…now he felt a raw, blistering fury at their petty reactions. Those men had run because they were too afraid of not being able to keep her happy and eventually losing her, whereas Nick was forced to hold himself back from what he most wanted because he was terrified of taking her fucking life.

And on that note, he knew it was time to put some more distance between them.

Lowering his arm, he started to move back to his feet, but she chose that moment to lean over, picking up one of the bloody wipes that had fallen on the floor, and Nick found himself staring down at a smooth, feminine shoulder. The neckline of his shirt had slipped to the side, revealing the creamy expanse of flesh, and his breath seized in his lungs.

Unable to resist, he lifted his hand…and ran two callused fingertips over that incredibly tender skin.

"So soft," he breathed out, sounding more like he was talking to himself than to her.

Lainey tried not to let the joy his words gave her show. She knew damn well it would just make the sexy vampire even more skittish than he already was where she was concerned.

He had a wary look in his dark eyes when he finally dropped his hand and lifted his smoldering gaze to hers as she straightened. But she couldn't stop herself from asking, "If you enjoy touching me, then why the whole 'a woman like you isn't for me' line?"

"It's not a line. It's the truth."

"Why then?"

His nostrils flared. "Because I'm a goddamn vampire."

"And I've read *Twilight*. I—"

"Just stop," he suddenly growled, holding up a hand. "And. Don't. Even. Go. There."

She blinked, then started to laugh. "Okay, I get it. I wasn't trying to say that you're some work of fiction. But if real vampires are anything like the ones in the romance novels, then it's possible for you to touch a human woman. Maybe not simple or uncomplicated... but it *is* possible." With a shrug, she added, "Just look at Sookie on *True Blood*."

"Jesus Christ!" he roared, surging to his feet so quickly that his chair fell over behind him. "This isn't a fucking TV show! Open your eyes, Lainey, and use your head. I'm a vampire who's been bitten by a bloody werewolf. Exactly how do you think this is going to play out? It's a goddamn full moon tonight!"

She took a moment to think about what he'd just said, and suddenly all those cryptic remarks about his brothers arriving in time started to make sense.

"That's what you meant last night, isn't it? You're worried about the full moon tonight, aren't you? About how it will affect you."

"I don't want to hurt you," he said in a low voice, sounding as if he was suffering the torments of the damned.

"And you think you will?"

"I don't know what to think," he forced out through his gritted teeth, backing away from her. He didn't stop until he came up against the wall behind him.

"Explain, please."

He looked to the left of her as he said, "When a werewolf bites, its blood enters the victim's system. Humans either change or die, but every vampire is affected differently when bitten by a wolf. They might take on all the physical attributes of the beast—or none of them. Some completely lose themselves to the wolf's feral hungers and end up having to be destroyed. Others are capable of mastering the more aggressive hungers of the beast and accept them as a part of his or her nature. But there's no way of knowing how a particular vampire will be affected until the first full moon after their bite."

"So why borrow trouble? Maybe we'll get lucky."

He cut her a sharp, furious look from the corner of his eye. "I'd rather not risk your life on a maybe."

"And what if I said that I trust you not to hurt me?"

"Then I'd say you're being an idiot," he muttered under his breath.

Rolling her eyes, she said, "Wow, Nick. Don't try to spare my feelings or anything."

"I don't have the privilege of worrying about your feelings, Lainey. I'm trying to keep you alive."

"Nick, I—"

"No! Just drop it or I'm putting you back in those damn chains."

She huffed with frustration. "Why did you even have me in them in the first place?" she demanded. "Because you thought it'd be easier to deal with me? I'm surprised you didn't put me in a gag and just leave me in here all alone, trying to pretend I don't even exist!"

"The gag's not a bad idea," he growled, looking like he could chew nails. "And I put you in those chains be-cause I was worried you would try to attack me."

Confusion filled her gaze, a little notch etched be-tween her brows. "You can't really think that I'd hurt you."

"It's not that. But I'm worried about how the wolf's

blood in my system will make me react if you try. I could be…violent and end up doing something that can't be taken back."

Her head tipped a bit to the side as she studied him. "And now you trust me not to attack you?"

"Either that," he muttered, "or I've lost my goddamn mind."

Chapter 5

The woman was trying to kill him. That was the only reason Nick could think of for this incessant flirting that was slowly driving him mad. He didn't believe for a second that she truly understood just how badly he craved her...or how aggressive he could be when it came to sex. An aggression he knew damn well was only going to be magnified by the werewolf blood churning through his system.

After she'd washed his blood from her hands at the kitchen sink, he made them a late breakfast of eggs, bacon and toast. Watching her eat was more arousing than any strip joint he'd ever visited in his long lifetime. She had a good appetite, and the way her full lips closed around her fork each time she took a bite made it damn hard for him to sit still. When she nibbled on a piece of bacon, then ran her tongue over her lower lip, leaving it shiny and wet, he finally exploded with a sharp, clipped, "Stop torturing me, Lainey."

Her eyes went wide. "I didn't know that I was. I'm just eating, Nick."

He stifled a groan as he closed his eyes. More to himself than to her, he said, "I *can't* fuck you."

"I know," she whispered. "But, um, if you *hadn't* been bitten, would you be trying to get me into bed with you while we're stuck in here?"

He opened his eyes again to glare at her. "No."

She scowled at his quick, gruff reply, then gave him another confused frown. "Why not, if you're attracted to me?"

Because even if a miracle happened and I didn't hurt you, we'd have an even bigger problem to deal with. Because I have a strong feeling I'd want to keep you, golden girl. But he didn't say any of that out loud. To Lainey he simply muttered, "Because it isn't done."

"You mean even if you weren't worried about the bite, you wouldn't sleep with me because I'm human?" She sounded thoroughly insulted. "Didn't we already establish that that wasn't a valid excuse?"

"And like I said before, this isn't a work of fiction. I'm a danger to you in ways you can't even imagine."

Pushing her empty plate to the side, she said, "Then explain it to me."

"For one, I have enemies," he said in a low voice, sprawling against the back of his chair. "Ones who would be ruthless about going after any woman I was involved with. The kind of enemies who don't have any qualms about hurting innocent people."

"So did my brother."

"Not like mine," he snapped.

She cast a pained look toward the door. "I wouldn't be so sure about that."

He cursed under his breath but didn't argue. After a minute or so of awkward silence, she went into motion, busying herself cleaning up the plates, and he helped by carrying their coffee mugs into the small kitchen. He felt like a total ass for pushing her away, but didn't see that he had any other choice. She was hurting and worried and seeking a way to take her mind off everything that was happening to her. He'd only make it worse by ignoring his conscience and taking what he badly wanted.

"Nick?" she finally murmured, keeping her back to him as she set the last plate in the drainer beside the sink.

"Yeah?" he grunted, knowing he had it bad when he got hot just watching a woman wash dishes. He was growing increasingly restless, his heart thundering, fangs heavy in his gums, his body burning with heat. But was he being driven by the sexual needs of the vampire…or the primitive hungers of the wolf? And how was he going to make it through this day without losing his goddamn mind?

She kept her back to him as she gave a little cough, then quietly said, "I know you said we can't have sex, but can we…can we at least have some fun together?"

Fuck. She was definitely trying to kill him. If she suggested anything other than a game of Parcheesi, he was going to need to dunk himself into a tub of ice water. "Doing what?" he asked, forcing the words out through his clenched teeth.

Taking a deep breath, she turned around to face him. "You said you were attracted to me."

"So?" he muttered aggressively, staring to the right of her. "That doesn't mean—"

"We don't have to have…intercourse. We could just do other things," she blurted, cutting him off, "to… each other."

He froze, but Lainey could feel the hunger and energy pulsing beneath his skin, like an electrical current flowing from him to her. He swallowed, then locked that hot, scorching gaze with hers. "Yeah?" His voice was low…*husky.* "Like what?"

She sucked in a quick breath for courage, determined not to cower like a wimp. But she could feel the heat burning in her face as she said, "We could…that is, you could let me, um…I could use my mouth on you."

He shuddered, and a low, guttural sound vibrated in the back of his throat, predatory and raw. "You want that?"

"Yes."

"Why?" Nick stalked toward her, unable to keep his distance, as if a powerful force was drawing them together. "Because you're hurting inside? Because you think we're going to die in here?"

Shaking her head, she said, "No. I could use those things as an excuse to do something reckless, but it wouldn't be the truth."

"And what's the truth, Lainey?"

She tilted her head back the way she did whenever he got close and she wanted to see his face. "The truth is that I've wanted you since the first second I saw you. And despite the crappy situation we're in, I want you more with each moment that goes by. If we make it out of this, I know you're going to walk away from me. When that happens, I don't want to regret not getting as much of you as I can while I've still got the chance."

He stared…in shock, unable to believe the things

she'd just said to him. He'd never known a woman who was so open and honest about her feelings. So courageous and full of life. And when she reached out and pressed her palm against his bare abs, that was it. Nick couldn't have kept himself back from her then if the fate of the world had hung in the balance.

Swearing every foul-mouthed curse he could think of inside his mind, his Spanish and English all garbled together, he grabbed the front of Lainey's shirt and ripped until buttons were pinging off the cabinets and sink. Then he yanked the ruined shirt off her shoulders, letting it slither to the floor, leaving her in nothing but the tight black boxers. She immediately raised her arms, trying to cover her naked breasts, her cheeks pink with embarrassment.

Breathing hard and rough, he said, "Lower your arms and let me look at you."

She licked her bottom lip as she looked him up and down, her precious face bright with color. "Can't we turn down the lights a little first?"

"No," he grunted. "I want to be able to see every inch of you. You're fucking gorgeous, Lainey."

"Hardly," she scoffed, just as her pretty brown gaze settled on the distinctive bulge of his hard-on, the buttons on his fly straining to the point he was surprised they hadn't burst open.

"You think I get this hard for just anyone?" he growled, flexing his hands at his sides, shaking from the effort of holding himself back.

"I…uh…"

"I *don't*." Unable to stop himself, Nick reached out and ran two fingers along one of her trembling forearms where it crossed her chest. Lifting his heavy-lidded gaze to hers, he said, "You started this, Lainey. You'd better be damn sure before we go any further because I'm not going to let you hide from me. I've been dying to get you naked and wet and under me from the moment you hit town."

"I'm not hiding," she whispered.

"Do you want me?"

"God, yes. I want you more than…" Something soft and vulnerable spilled through her gaze, and he could see her slender throat work as she swallowed. "Just trust me when I say that I want you a lot, Nick."

Curling his fingers around each of her wrists, he pulled them away from her shoulders, uncrossing her arms. "Then get your nipples wet for me," he told her, letting her wrists go.

"Wh-with what?"

Nick lifted his gaze from her gorgeous breasts and gave her a slow, sin-tipped smile. "What do you think?"

She took another nervous swallow, panting, but couldn't seem to find her voice. It was such a fascinating contradiction, the way she could be so bold and determined one minute, then turn shy and uncertain the next. He found it an incredible turn-on, which wasn't helping the situation. Lowering his gaze again, Nick stared at the bounty before him and ran his tongue over his upper lip. His voice little more than a guttural rasp, he said, "Your breasts are beautiful, Lainey. But I want to be able to eat your taste off them." Looking her right in the eye, he said, "Make them slick for me."

"Like this?" she whispered, slipping her hand into the front of the boxer shorts.

"Yeah." His nostrils flared as he watched her touch

herself, his jaw clenched so tight he could feel a muscle pulsing beneath his skin. "You know what to do."

Her lashes lowered, concealing the look in her eyes, as she pulled her hand from beneath the waistband, her slender fingers glistening. Being as tall as he was, Nick caught a glimpse of pale gold ringlets before the elastic band snapped back into place, a low growl rumbling in his throat as he watched her touch those trembling fingertips to a tight, berry-pink nipple.

"And the other one," he ground out, leaning forward and caging her in with his body as he braced his hands on the counter behind her.

Curling her fingers, she painted the other nipple until it was shiny and wet, and his mouth started watering. She was panting harder now, her lush breasts quivering with each shallow breath, the sight and scent of her juices on those pink little nipples making him burn with violent, visceral hunger.

"More," he growled. "I want them wetter, Lainey."

A mischievous glint sparked in her eyes, and she grinned. "You like being bossy when it comes to sex, don't you?"

Nick smirked. "I'm a vampire, Miss Maxwell. I like being bossy in *all* things." He stepped closer and snagged her wrist, lifting her hand up to his mouth. "But I'm getting a unique kind of pleasure out of being bossy with you." With a curl of his lips, he whispered, "Guess that means you bring out the worst in me."

"Or the b-best," she stammered breathlessly, when he sucked those glistening fingers into his mouth and cleaned them with his tongue. Her taste blasted against his senses with more force than he'd expected, making him groan, a surge of foreign thoughts and emotions flooding through his mind. They should have freaked the hell out of him, but he was too lost in her to care, his body throbbing with the need to claim her as something that would belong to him…and *only* to him…forever. How she could taste even better than she smelled he didn't know. But she did.

"You look so freaking sexy doing that," she whispered, her brown eyes wide and bright, glittering with passion.

"You taste incredible," he growled when he finally pulled her fingers free, his voice thick with lust. "Now tell me to touch you."

He didn't have to instruct her twice, her voice a soft, husky plea. "Yes. Please, Nick. Touch me. Right now."

His hands shoved into the back of the shorts, over her lush ass, and he gripped the soft globes in a tight, possessive hold. Jerking her onto her toes, he took one of those slick, pink-tipped breasts in his mouth and nearly died. Her nipple was small and sweet on his tongue, the sounds she made as he sucked on her damn near turning him inside out. He moved his mouth to her other breast, hungry for the feel of her…the intimate taste. His fingers slipped between her legs, touching tender female flesh that was swollen and wet, and he wanted so badly to thrust his fingers inside that tiny opening, feeling her from the inside. Wanted it more than anything in the world. But he…couldn't.

Oh, shit. Christ… He couldn't do this!

With each thundering beat of his heart, Nick could feel the aggression surging inside him, powerful and addictive, fed by his craving for this fragile human. His fangs were only seconds away from dropping, his fingertips burning for the release of his talons, his pulse raging as scenes from a nightmare played through his brain. Ones that showed him completely losing control with her.

"Nick! What's wrong?" she gasped as he stumbled back, then turned and staggered into the main room, his ragged breaths coming hard and fast. He could feel her come up behind him as his frantic gaze darted around the room, searching for an answer. For a way out of this.

"Nick! Answer me, damn it!"

"I'm losing control." When his narrow gaze skimmed over the bed and the manacles lying there, he growled, "You need to use the chains on me."

"What?"

"You heard me," he barked, heading for the bed as he reached into his pocket for the key that would lock them. "Do it," he snapped, careful not to look at her as he lay down and clamped the manacles around his thick wrists. There was just enough room inside the adjustable shackles for them to fit, but he needed her to lock them.

Edging closer to the bed, she shook her head as she wrapped her trembling arms across the front of her body. "No, Nick. I won't do this to you. I *trust* you."

"Fuck trust!" he roared, glaring up at her. "Lock the damn manacles and then tighten the goddamn chains!"

Tears tracked down her cheeks as she shook her head again, taking a step back, refusing to help him save her. Stubborn, infuriating, beautiful woman. She was going to be the fucking death of him!

Or the other way around—which was exactly what he was trying to avoid.

"If you won't do it, then I will," he snarled, cursing viciously as he used his knees to hold each manacle in place while he locked them with the key. When he had both wrists imprisoned in the steel, he reached up, struggling to tighten the chains until his arms were stretched over his head. Then he tossed the key across the room, watching it bounce across the cold metal floor until it finally came to a stop beneath the table.

Closing his eyes, Nick breathed a ragged sound of relief.

"Will they hold you?" she asked shakily, the direction of her voice telling him that she was now standing at the foot of the bed.

He hoped to God they would.

Then he felt the mattress dip near his feet. When he opened his eyes and saw her crawling onto the end of the bed, Nick bellowed with fury. "Lainey?"

"Shh," she whispered, the determined glint in her luminous eyes making him shudder with terror. "It's okay, Nick. I have a plan."

"What the hell are you doing?" he demanded, shaking so hard it nearly tumbled her from the bed.

Crawling over his legs, she said, "Last night, when you got...on edge, you calmed down when I touched you."

"For maybe a split second. That doesn't mean a damn thing. So stay the hell back!"

"No," she argued, "because I honestly think I can help. You just need a little TLC, Nick. You just need to be...soothed."

"Damn it, Lainey!" Completely ignoring his protests, she straddled his waist and leaned down, placing a soft kiss against his chest, right over the furious pounding of his heart. He was breathing so hard and deep he was practically panting, and that was *before* she dragged her pink tongue across one of his nipples. Nick's back arched as if he'd been struck by a violent jolt of electricity, a rough shout on his lips as he strained against the bonds. And his urgency didn't have a damn thing to do with the bite on his arm.

Christ, maybe she was right. Maybe she *had* gentled the beast, mesmerizing it, because in that moment all he could feel was a pure, overwhelming, mind-shattering sexual need for connection that he'd never experienced before. But he was drowning in it now, and if he didn't get to have at least this *one* moment with her—this one stolen moment—he thought it might literally kill him.

He didn't need to connect with just anyone. He needed *her*. Lainey.

Nick was still struggling to understand what was happening to him, *inside him,* when she scooted higher, putting her beautiful face right above his, her soft hands cupping his jaw as she smiled and said, "Prepare yourself, Nick. I'm going to kiss you now, and it's going to be our first kiss, so try not to curse at me when it happens, okay?"

He wanted to tell her this was a bad idea—that she should stay away from his mouth in case he couldn't hold back his fangs—but there wasn't time. He was already groaning in hunger and need and ecstasy as her hands moved through his hair and she leaned closer, the tender brush of her soft lips against his making him tremble. He opened his mouth, flicking his tongue against her lips, and she responded by rubbing her clever little tongue against his. He made some kind of raw, animal sound in the back of his throat, thankful as hell that it didn't scare her away as he tilted his head, going in for a deeper angle. She moaned, clutching his hair tighter, her gorgeous breasts pressed hard against his chest, and they were off, their lips and tongues moving together with wild, desperate need, as if they were addicted to the taste of the other's mouth. And, damn it, he was.

When she finally had to break away for air, Nick lifted his head and drew in a deep breath at the base of her throat, where her pulse was fluttering like mad. "Christ, Lainey. You smell so incredible."

"You really think so?" she asked, eyes wide, an adorable look of pleasure on her face as she sat up, straddling his stomach.

"Mmm," he moaned, wishing like hell that she was completely naked and he could feel her against his skin. "Are you wet for me?"

She blinked down at him, the color in her face getting brighter. "What?"

"Between your legs?" he growled, straining against the bonds until his veins were pressed against his skin by his hard, corded muscles. "Are you wet for me?"

"Y-yes."

His nostrils flared. "Then show me."

"Show you?" she whispered, looking shy…but intrigued.

Breathing in rough, uneven bursts, he said, "If this is going where I hope to God it is, and you're going to touch my cock, then I want you naked. Get rid of the shorts, Lainey. Let me see you."

She pulled that plush lower lip between her teeth, then blurted, "I'm not skinny, Nick."

"Thank God," he said with a heartfelt groan. "Because I *love* your body. I love your tits and your hips and those round thighs. And I'd be willing to bet my life on the fact that I'll love that tender flesh between them even more. So lose the fucking clothes, Lainey. Now!"

A blush covered almost every inch of her skin, but she moved to his side and slipped the shorts over her hips. When she moved to straddle him again, his gaze locked in sharp and tight on the pale ringlets glistening at the top of her mound, his mouth already watering as her warm, lush scent drifted to his nose.

Voice thick and graveled with lust, he said, "Now use your fingers to open yourself up. I want to see how pink and wet you are. How swollen your clit is."

She shivered, her heady scent getting richer, ripe and sweet and delicious. And because he already knew she tasted even better, he had no doubt he could happily live with his face buried in that sweet little sex and never get his fill of it.

His body shuddered as he drew in a deep, rumbling breath. "Do it, Lainey."

"I will, but I think…I think you should lose some of your clothes first," she breathed out, trembling with excitement. "Fair is fair, Nick. If you get to look at me, then I want to be able to look at you." She scooted down his legs, her smoky gaze locked on the ridge of his hard, thick cock. "You have no idea how badly I'm dying to taste you."

As Nick's breath hissed through his teeth, his stomach went so rigid that Lainey could see each hard, delineated muscle. Her sexy-ass vampire was perfectly ripped, and damn, but the guy was impressively hung. She would have been a little worried about the fit if she wasn't so freaking excited.

"You should know right now that if you put your

mouth on me," he warned in a raw, guttural voice, "then I'm coming in it."

"Mmm. Sounds good to me," she murmured, licking the tight skin just above the waistband of his jeans. He cursed something gritty and harsh, and she smiled, drunk on the pleasure of knowing he wanted her. *Badly.* It was the headiest feeling she'd ever experienced, momentarily cushioning the pain of Ryan's loss that was buried inside her heart. Yes, the pain was still there, but these stolen moments with Nick were proving that she didn't have to let it destroy her. That she could still love and laugh and enjoy something good when it found her. And right now, she was going to enjoy the hell out of Nick Santos.

Breathless with anticipation, Lainey knelt beside him and started working the buttons on his fly. A low, continual growl rumbled up from his throat as the backs of her fingers brushed against the rigid length of his cock. Only a thin pair of boxers separated her flesh from his, his heat stunning, the warm, mouthwatering scent of his body only ramping up her need to a feverish pitch. She was so desperate for touch and sight and taste that she was shaking as she told him to lift his hips, wrenching the jeans and boxers down his legs. His erection was even bigger than she'd guessed, and she knew it wasn't going to be easy to take, but she didn't give a damn.

"Lainey!" he shouted, making her jump. She blinked, surprised to realize she'd just been kneeling there, staring down at him in a daze. Nothing she'd ever seen had come anywhere close to this kind of hard, masculine perfection.

"Sorry I spaced out there," she whispered, tossing his clothes on the floor. "You just took my breath away."

He swore, writhing a little, then parting his knees for her when she asked him to. Deep, guttural curses continued to rip up from his chest as she knelt between his muscular thighs and took his cock in her hands, squeezing and stroking the heavy, vein-ridged shaft. And when she leaned down, licking her tongue across the broad, slick crown, tasting him, he shouted so loudly it echoed off the walls.

When the wolves started to howl out in the tunnel, they both ignored them.

"God, Nick. You taste so good," she moaned, loving the rough sounds he made as she took him between her lips and started to lick and suck as if she was starved for him. She fisted her hand around the swollen inches at the base that wouldn't fit in her mouth, rubbing her tongue against the veins pulsing beneath his velvety skin, his flavor salty and warm and completely addictive. This was something she'd only done in the past because she knew it'd been expected. She'd never craved it—never *needed* it—but that was exactly how she felt with Nick. She couldn't get enough of him and told him so the next time she stopped to draw in a ragged breath.

"You're killing me," he gasped, shoving deeper into her mouth. His body was burning hotter, the tremoring of his muscles beneath his dark, sweat-slick skin making the bed shake. She gripped his hips to steady herself, sucking him a little harder…faster. In the next instant, there was a terrible groaning sound, followed by a sharp snap, and then his strong hands were suddenly curving around her head, holding her to him as he arched and blasted into her mouth, a ragged shout on his lips as he came hard and long, the wrenching pulses going on…and on…and on.

Oh, wow. Just holy freaking wow!

Lainey lifted her head when he was finally spent, pressing a tender kiss to the glistening head, surprised that he was still so hard and thick. She wanted to ask him if that was normal for a vampire. But before she could catch her breath, she found herself lying on her back, more than two hundred and fifty hard-muscled pounds of aggressive vampire holding her down.

"Payback," he rasped with a low growl, the look on his rugged face as he slowly lifted his head and looked up at her from between her legs the hottest damn thing she'd ever seen. And when he lowered his head, burying his face against her hot, swollen sex as he spread her with his thumbs, it was even better than she'd imagined.

His mouth was insatiable, doing things to her that Lainey had only read about in books—and a few she'd never even heard of. He went at her with lips and tongue and teeth, feasting on her as if the provocatively intimate, wildly explicit act gave him even more pleasure than it gave her, which didn't seem possible. But he seemed starved for the taste and the feel of her, eating at her with a carnal desperation that had raw cries climbing up her throat. And when he replaced his thrusting tongue with two long, thick fingers, hungrily latched on to her clit, and the pulsing waves of pleasure slammed into her with the force of a nuclear detonation, she screamed so loud she wouldn't have been surprised if people could hear her out on the beach.

He pulled back a little the instant she started to come, watching her sex as she convulsed. He gave another one of those low, rumbling growls, then put his mouth back on her, ravaging her pulsing flesh with a kiss that was savage in its violence. He knew just where and how to touch her to prolong the spasms, making the climax go on and on, until she was limp with exhaustion, every cell throbbing and sensitized.

His mouth was shiny and wet when he finally looked up at her with eyes that were pure, molten gold, the smile on his lips so wicked it nearly sent her into another mind-shattering orgasm. He'd started to crawl over her, muscles shifting beneath his tight skin like a sleek jungle predator, his rock-hard cock looking even bigger than it had before, when he suddenly froze, that sexy, glowing gaze cutting toward the broken chain connected to the manacle on his right wrist.

"Oh, shit," he gasped, as if only just realizing what he'd done. The shackles were still on his wrists, but he'd snapped the chains and was now free to do whatever he wanted.

Reaching up to cup his hot face in her hands, she said, "Don't worry, Nick. It'll be okay."

He slowly brought his gaze back to hers, the look in those hooded eyes making her breath catch.

"I mean it," she told him, trailing one of her hands down to his chest and pressing it to the heavy beat of his heart. "I'm not afraid of you."

He exhaled a jagged breath as he bent his arms, lowering himself until his rugged, beautiful face was right above hers....

Then, in a voice that was far more animal than man, he growled, "You *should* be."

Chapter 6

Before Lainey could ask him why, a deafening screech of sound came from the kitchen area of the bunker.

"Son of a bitch," he snarled, climbing off her so quickly she'd barely seen him move.

As another horrific sound came from the kitchen, he yanked his jeans on and ran over to the table, then bent down and retrieved the key he'd tossed there. A handful of seconds later, he had the manacles, with their broken chains, unlocked. He left them lying in a heap of metal on the table as he headed toward the large cabinet that sat against the opposite wall from the bed, his fingers quickly keying a combination into the numeric lock. When the door gave a little pop, he wrenched it open, heading back to her with a heavy handgun that he put in her shaking hands. "Don't hesitate to use this if you need to," he instructed her in a low, cold voice, the sexy lover she'd known only a moment ago replaced by this hard, focused warrior. "It won't kill them, but if you aim for the head, it'll put them out of commission for a while."

If the wolves were to somehow breach the bunker, they both knew she wouldn't be able to shoot them all, but neither of them said it. And she didn't have time to worry about that possible scenario anyway. She was too freaking terrified about *his* neck to worry about her own.

"What are you going to do?" she asked in a choked voice. "What's happening?"

"There's an air vent in the kitchen ceiling. I didn't think they'd find it, but it sounds like one of those bastards is trying to crawl through it."

"Oh, my God," she gasped, setting the gun down so she could wrap one of the thin blankets around her naked body as she sat on the edge of the bed.

"If I can kill him," Nick said, heading back over to the cabinet, "I should be able to set off a small explosion that will seal the vent."

"But if there's a vent, why can't we use it to escape?" she asked, watching him slip a different gun into the back of his jeans, then grab what looked like a heavy black toolbox out of the cabinet.

"We can't escape through it, Lainey, because it leads right back into the tunnel they're blocking."

"Oh. But if you set off an explosion to block the vent, won't it cut off our air?"

He cut a quick glance at the clock on the wall. "We'll be okay. There are other, smaller vents that will provide us with enough oxygen."

He didn't say they wouldn't be staying in the bunker much longer anyway. But she knew that's what he was thinking. Before she could ask him just what he planned if his brothers didn't arrive in time, he came over, leaned down to put a hard, much-too-brief kiss on her lips, then left the room in another one of those dizzying bursts of speed. The door to the kitchen slammed shut behind him.

No! Lainey immediately ran to the door, but Nick had locked it from the other side! "You jackass!" she screamed, unable to believe he would just go like that. She'd planned on being right there with him, not letting him out of her sight. Damn it, she hadn't even gotten the chance to tell him goodbye! What if he didn't come back? What if he died in there with that freaking monster and she never saw him again?

Sobs rose in her throat, wrenching and raw, as she banged her fists on the door. Then she suddenly remembered the other entrance, but when she reached the second doorway to the kitchen she screeched with fury to find it had also been locked.

"Damn you, Nick," she croaked, her eyes blinded by tears as she made her way back into the main room, the blanket that was still wrapped around her body dragging on the floor behind her. Though the sounds were muted, she could tell some kind of fight was taking place in the vent. Then she heard the loud *thwump* of a gun being fired, followed by a guttural, bone-chilling roar of pain.

Oh, God...Oh, God. Please don't let that be Nick. Please...please...please...

If she'd had any doubt that what she felt for him was real, and not just an intense, overwhelming case of lust, the devastating depth of her fear for his safety suddenly made things perfectly clear.

Nick Santos didn't just mean something to her—he meant *everything*.

A second later, a quick explosion went off, violent enough to make her worry for the integrity of the bunker. But the walls and ceiling held their shape, refusing to buckle. She started to pace, frantic with worry and fear, until the door to the kitchen finally opened and he stepped back into the room. As remnants of smoke billowed behind him, he just stood there with his hands fisted at his sides, his massive body glistening with blood and sweat. As his dark gaze locked on hers with a violent, visceral look of hunger, Lainey couldn't help but tremble in reaction.

She swiped at the tears on her cheeks and somehow managed to say, "I was so freaking scared for you, Nick. Don't ever lock me away from you again! If you're going to be in danger, then I can damn well be in danger with you."

She thought he would say something sarcastic, like tell her she was crazy or delusional, but he didn't. He didn't say anything at all. Instead, he kept his mouth shut…and used his battle-hardened body to convey what he was feeling.

One instant he was standing there, staring at her with that blistering gaze from across the room—and in the next, a hard, primitive growl climbed from his throat and he was on her, tearing the blanket away as he took her down to the bed. Ripping his jeans open with one hand, he wrapped a strong, powerful arm around her hips to lock her in place—and then his body was shoving itself inside hers, going hard and thick and impossibly deep. She screamed from the shock and the sharp burn of pain that was already fading, drowned out by the unbelievable surge of pleasure she felt at having him inside her…a part of her.

Gasping for breath, she managed to moan, "God, Nick. You're, um…*really* deep."

Clenching his jaw, it took every ounce of strength that Nick possessed to hold himself perfectly still. "You want me to stop?" he scraped out, shuddering from the way her hot, cushiony sex was rippling around him. He'd only just gotten inside her and the woman was already on the cusp of orgasm.

"No. Don't you dare stop!" she cried, digging her nails into his rigid biceps.

"You want all of me then?" He buried his face in the tender curve of her shoulder, undone by the way she felt beneath him…around him. "You want me to fuck you with every inch, Lainey? You want them all?"

"God, yes!"

"If I do, I won't go easy on you," he groaned, feeling it was only fair to warn her. She was so hot and tight and perfect, he knew there was no bloody way he was going to have any control once he got going.

"After all this buildup, I sure as hell hope not." With no idea of the danger she was courting, she nipped his earlobe with her teeth. Crazy, beautiful, fascinating woman.

"Then spread your legs for me." His voice was raw. "As wide as they'll go, knees out at your sides."

As soon as she'd done it, Nick braced himself on his straightened arms, grunted a sharp curse as he pulled back his hips, then pushed forward in a heavy lunge, working against her tight resistance until he was nearly all the way in. Watching her flushed face, he pulled back again, loving the way all those plush muscles in her sex clutched at him, trying to hold him inside. Then he told her to brace her hands against his chest, dug his knees into the mattress and drove himself back in with bruising force, the power of the thrust taking him all the way to the root.

For a moment his heart nearly stopped when she arched beneath him with a sharp, hoarse cry on her lips, terrified that he'd hurt her. But she settled back to the bed with a provocative moan, lifted her long lashes to reveal eyes that were smoky with need and curled her lips in the most beautiful, pleasure-rich smile he'd ever seen.

"Again," she purred, now digging her nails into his pecs, and a thick, husky laugh rumbled up from his chest while a sense of happiness spread through him that was so potent and unfamiliar, he almost didn't recognize what it was. It made his brain soft…and his dick even harder, which didn't seem possible.

"Ah, God, Lainey." Sweat dripped from his face, splattering on her beautiful breasts as he ground himself against her, every brutal inch of his shaft packed up tight inside her. "You'd better hold on now," he growled just as his control shattered. And, God, did it shatter. The bed bashed against the wall again and again as he rode her snug body with thick, hammering thrusts until the first orgasm slammed into her so hard that she screamed, her slick sheath pulsing around him with such a tight, greedy clasp it damn near stopped his heart. He pressed in hard and deep, then just held there, gritting his teeth, wanting to feel every single ripple.

"Nick," she gasped, writhing beneath him as she grasped his waist, "drink from me. Take my vein."

"I...can't," he growled, his voice so guttural he wasn't even sure she could understand him.

"Please," she whispered, turning her head to the side. "I can take it. I swear I can. I just need to feel that connection with you."

He needed it, too. Badly. But Nick figured it was a miracle they'd managed to get this far without him hurting her. As desperately as he wanted her blood, he wasn't willing to risk destroying what they had for it. Not when he might take it too far...or she might decide that having a set of fangs buried in her throat was a hell of a lot more intense than she'd expected. Whether his brothers showed or not, he still had *this* day with her, and he wasn't willing to lose it if she freaked out and told him to get lost.

"I might be human, but I'm not so easily broken," she murmured, as if she knew his thoughts...and his fears. "You know that, right?"

"I know," he grunted. But he was still unwilling to take the chance. As badly as he wanted a bite of that pale, delicate throat, he wanted to keep losing himself in her *more*. And he needed to move again...starting *now*.

With his pulse roaring in his ears, Nick let himself go, his hips pistoning between her sprawled thighs as he fisted his hands in the bedding and took her with the single-minded focus of a man making a claim on a woman's body. It was more than sex. More than raw, aggressive fucking. It was a goddamn act of possession, and when he came the eruption was so intense it bowed his back, a guttural shout echoing through the room as he shoved himself inside her, nudging deeper with each thrust until she was gripping every part of him. Body, heart, soul.

"Feel good?" she whispered when he finally stilled, running her smooth palms down the slick length of his back as he settled over her, bracing his weight on his forearms at the last moment so he didn't crush her.

"Feels bloody incredible," he growled, shifting his arms higher so that he could spear his fingers into the wild tangle of her hair, gripping handfuls of the soft, silky locks. With his body pinning hers to the bed, Nick had her under his complete control, and he loved it. Couldn't get enough of it. Leaning down, he took her mouth with barely restrained violence, kissing her so hard and deep that neither of them could breathe. When they finally had to drag in gulping breaths of air, he buried his face against the side of her neck, licking the soft, tender flesh there. "Did I hurt you?" he rasped, tasting the tears he'd seen slipping across her cheeks as he kissed his way up over her jaw.

"No," she moaned, hugging him to her as if she never wanted to let him go. "I loved it, Nick. Every second of it."

He rolled his hips, enjoying the wetness, his chest filled with potent male satisfaction at the fact that she was drenched in him. And as that thought immediately led to another, he froze. "Hell," he rumbled. "I never even thought to ask you if you're on the pill."

"It's okay," she murmured, slipping her fingers through the damp locks of his hair. "I am."

He nodded, knowing he should be relieved. Considering what he was going to ask of her if his brothers didn't get there in time, he had no right putting a child inside her. But damn if he didn't feel a fresh surge of lust at the thought of her round and heavy with his babe.

Huh. Guess you could take the guy out of the 1700s,

but you could never take the 1700s out of the guy. He might hold his own in the modern world, but there were some old-fashioned sentiments that he found damn hard to leave behind. Though his job made it nearly impossible, he thrived on the idea of a wife and family. Of having that kind of closeness with another person. That incredible sense of belonging.

And this is a waste of my time now that the clock's counting down.

Biting back a bitter curse, Nick wrapped his arms around Lainey and held her close as he rolled to his back, reversing their positions.

As she settled against his chest, she rested her chin on her stacked hands and stared directly into his eyes. "Why didn't you take my vein?"

He tried to control his reaction to the provocative words but knew from the catch in her breath that she'd felt him get harder. "Please tell me," she murmured. "I just want to understand you.".

"I didn't do it because it's too dangerous," he told her, loving the little gasp she gave as he used his grip on her hips to hold her still as he pushed in a little deeper, already hopelessly addicted to the way she felt around him. "If I lost it," he added, "I could drain you."

Exasperation quirked the soft curve of her lips. "You wouldn't. You'd stop before you risked hurting me. And I think that however that bite ends up affecting you, you're still stronger than it is. I don't believe for a second that it could ever control you."

"I wish that were true," he grated, his thumb rubbing against her soft skin as he cupped her cheek in his hand. "But I can't stop what's coming, Lainey."

"But you can be prepared for it," she argued, bracing

her hands against his chest as she pushed herself up into a sitting position, his cock giving a hard pulse inside her as she straddled his hips. "Did you ever think that my blood might give you more control when you need it tonight? That everything that's happening between us might be for a reason?" she asked in a soft, firm voice that rang with challenge and conviction. "That you might actually *need* me, Nick?"

Need her? Of course he needed her! But just because the beautiful, beguiling, brave little human was willing to give him *everything* didn't mean it was right for him to take it. His heart and his mind knew that. But his body... The rising heat in his gums told him his body had a mind of its own.

When Nick's fangs shot out, longer and sharper than they'd ever been, she pulled her hair over her shoulder and smiled at him. "Will you drink from me now, Nick?" she whispered, the clenching of her slick sex around his thick cock telling him exactly how excited she was. But he had to keep his fucking head!

"No," he groaned, shaking his head...and wishing he could shake some kind of sense into *her.* "Don't ever ask me that again. You have no idea what you're doing, Lainey."

"It'll be okay," she said breathlessly, the rolling movement of her hips nearly making his eyes roll back in his head. Holding still like he was, he could feel every little ripple inside her...the seductive rhythm of her pulse making him want to howl, and God only knew that couldn't be a good sign. "I trust you," she told him. "I know you won't hurt me. I don't know why you even think you could."

"Damn it," he growled, his fingers biting into her

hips so hard he knew they'd leave bruises. "For once in your life just shut up!"

But he was simply wasting his breath. He should have known she wouldn't listen to reason, especially when her eyes got that hot, determined look in them. Before Nick realized what she was doing, she'd reached down and dug the pad of her thumb into one of his fangs. He was still shuddering from the scorching drop of blood she'd left in his mouth when she lifted her thumb to her pale throat, smearing a seductive line of crimson down the side. "Do it, Nick. I dare you."

"You reckless little bitch," he growled, already surging up as he fisted his hands in her long hair and jerked her toward him. She screamed when they came together, his fangs thrusting deep into her tender flesh with a sharp, searing pop. He growled with violent, mind-shattering pleasure as her blood pumped out over his tongue, hotter…sweeter…and more intoxicating than anything he'd ever known. He'd thought for sure that, if they ever got to this point, she'd panic and start trying to pull him off. But she didn't.

Instead, she curved her fingers around his head and held him tighter to her, her husky voice thick with emotion as she groaned, "More, Nick. Oh, God, *more.*"

And so he took more, greedy…driven…ravenous for every drop, until he knew he was nearing a point he wouldn't be able to come back from. Somehow finding the strength to stop, he tore his mouth away, struggling for breath as he sealed the wounds. Then he lifted his head and stared down into her flushed face, knowing damn well he had to look like a monster to her. Glowing eyes, bloody mouth, his fangs still dripping beneath the crimson curve of his upper lip.

Still angry with Lainey for pushing him, Nick gave her a dangerous look that said *Scared now, little girl?*

But, really, when was he going to learn?

"No," she drawled with a sly, cat-ate-the-canary smile. "I'm afraid you'll have to keep trying."

With a stunned, gritty laugh rumbling deep in his chest, Nick held her bright, challenging gaze as he slowly dropped back down to the bed and spread his bent knees farther apart. He rubbed his hands over her lush hips and squeezed, loving how soft and feminine she was, then started to move, thrusting up into all that hot, slippery wetness as she reached behind her and braced herself on his thighs.

Fascinated by the sight of the pale curls on her mound meshing with his black ones whenever he slammed up against her, Nick ran the pad of his thumb through her soft hair. "You're so damn sexy, golden girl."

There was a smile in her voice as she said, "I'm glad you think so."

"I *know* so." Tilting his head back on the pillows, Nick closed his eyes and simply savored the sensation of driving up into her lush, sumptuous heat again... and again, utterly lost in her. Watching her through his lashes, he said, "I could stay inside you forever, Lainey, and still not get enough."

"Then do it," she whispered, bracing her hands on his chest as she leaned forward, staring down into his face. Her eyes filled with hot, vibrant desire as he continued thrusting inside her. "Stay inside me forever, Nick. I'd be more than happy to keep you here."

He groaned her name, fisting one hand in her hair and pulling her down to his mouth. As he sank his tongue into that warm, sweet haven, he tried to put into the ravaging kiss all the powerful, confusing feelings he couldn't put into words. And she was right there with him, relaying emotions with her lips and tongue and the salty taste of her tears, making him want to rage against the unfairness of what was coming.

"I'm going to come in you so damn hard," he growled against her lips, needing to imprint himself on her so deeply she'd never be able to forget him. "You ready?"

"Yes!" she hissed. "Do it now. I want to feel it. Want your heat deep inside me."

He cursed, completely undone. With both hands firmly gripping her hips, he moved with inhuman speed, pumping up inside her as he came in a heavy stream of violent pulses. The end of the world probably wouldn't have left him so shattered, their heat-glazed bodies twitching with aftershocks of sensation.

Barely able to move, Nick took her with him as he rolled to his side, loving the way she hitched her leg over his hip to keep them together. He anchored his hands on her ass for the same purpose—and, well, just because he loved gripping it. The woman had an ass to die for, along with all the other mouthwatering parts of her.

As he licked his lower lip, where he could still taste her blood, her eyes turned smoky. "Did you like doing that?" she asked, her soft fingertips tracing the shell of his ear.

"You know I did," he rasped. "If you were mine, I'd be at your vein and buried deep in this hot little body so often you'd probably never even make it out of bed."

"Mmm. Sounds nice."

With a grin tugging at the corner of his mouth, he asked, "Did you know your accent is strongest just after you've come?"

She gave one of those soft, throaty laughs that made him think of sex, though that could pretty much be applied to everything about her. "Are you serious?"

"Mmm," he murmured, squeezing her beautiful ass. When she'd laughed, he'd been able to feel it around his shaft, and he wanted to feel it again. "Especially when you're screaming my name like a banshee."

She gave another throaty chuckle as she lifted her hand higher, brushing his dark hair back from his face. "Does it bother you?"

"Your accent?" he asked, lifting his brows.

When she nodded, he told her, "Of course not. I think it's beautiful."

"When I first moved out to California to be close to Ryan," she said with a quiet laugh that was softer this time, "he'd introduce me as Daisy Duke to everyone." Her eyes glistened with tears. "He could be such a smart-ass, but I'm…I'm going to miss the hell out of him," she finished with a broken sob. And as the dam broke and her tears came in a hot, blinding rush, Nick tightened his arms and held her hard against his chest, determined to see her through the storm.

She must have dozed for a bit because the first thing Lainey realized as she opened her eyes was that the wolves were clawing at the door in a frenzy now, no doubt able to hear or smell what they'd been doing inside the bunker. But she'd been so wrapped up in her wicked-as-sin vampire, she hadn't even noticed. Make that a sinful, *saintly* vampire, considering the way he'd held her through her tears. She'd known men who practically ran at the first sign of crying, but Nick had just held her tighter, his lips moving against the top of her head as he murmured comforting words that she'd felt more than heard.

Now, she felt him lift his head for a moment, and when she realized he was looking at the clock again, she scooted back enough to see his face. "What happens when your brothers get here?"

"Then you're safe," he said, locking his dark blue gaze with hers.

"But what happens…with us?"

His jaw hardened as he rolled to his back, staring up at the ceiling. "There can be no *us,* Lainey. You know that."

She braced herself on an elbow beside him. "Is it just sex then?" she whispered, trying not to let him see how deeply his words had devastated her. "Because it…it felt like more to me."

There was a long, pain-filled pause before he finally gave her an answer. "It *is* more. But that doesn't give me the right to destroy your life."

"Destroy it how?"

He turned his head to look at her, his deep voice rough with frustration. "Christ, haven't you been listening to a single word I've said? I'm a killer, constantly surrounded by death. Courting it. Hunting it. I've taken more lives over the years than you can even imagine."

"You're not telling me anything that I don't already know. But that's your job, Nick. It doesn't define you."

"It doesn't matter how you look at it. I'm not a good man, Lainey."

With a frown, she snapped, "That's such bullshit. There's a difference between killing something for pleasure and killing it because it needs to be put down."

He watched her with a hooded gaze, the barest hint

of a smile on his hard, sensual mouth. "You're assuming I don't enjoy it."

"I'm sure you enjoy the hunt," she offered quietly, sensing just how closely he was studying her reaction. "The challenge of tracking down your target. But that's different from enjoying the kill, Nick. It doesn't make you a monster."

For a moment, she thought he was going to make some mocking comment about how blind or naive she was. But when he finally spoke, his low voice held an odd note of wonder in it, as if he didn't quite know what to make of her. "There are many who would disagree with you, Miss Maxwell."

"Then they're idiots," she said, lifting her brows. "And anyway, you don't really care what they think, do you?"

Moving in a blur of speed, he rolled her beneath him, his lips brushing against her ear as he said, "Just leave it, Lainey. Please. I don't want to spend the time I have left with you arguing."

Tears burned her eyes at the painful reminder that their time together was limited, but she willingly opened her legs to him, letting him press against her. His long, thick erection nestled against her tender, swollen folds, and he groaned so deep she could feel it.

"I love how unbelievably warm you are," he rasped against the sensitive side of her throat. "Can't get enough of it."

"Aren't female vampires warm?"

"Not like this. Not like you." He lifted his head, a strange look in his deep blue eyes that made her heart hurt. Roughly, he said, "Unless they embrace true emotion, they remain cold. Both physically and emotionally."

"Sounds lonely," she murmured.

"It's just the way we are, Lainey. Very few of us end up like my parents."

"Are they happy together?"

A crooked smile lifted the corner of his mouth. "Ridiculously happy. It's enough to make you sick if you don't love them."

"That's sweet."

"Not as sweet as you," he groaned, kissing his way down her chest until he'd reached the sensitive tips of her breasts. Then he kissed his way even lower. He was ruthless in the pursuit of her orgasms, making her come again and again until she was utterly boneless with pleasure.

They made love five more times as the day progressed into late afternoon…and late afternoon slowly turned into evening. Each time, he took her in increasingly revealing positions, pushing her until she'd given him every part of her. Until she was devoid of shyness and insecurities and worries about her figure.

As the hour grew later, she knew he was keeping a close eye on the clock but wasn't sure what he was waiting for. Some kind of sign? Or a specific time?

Eventually, they pulled themselves from the sex-wrecked bed and took a long, enjoyable shower that consisted of lots of laughter and sensual moans of satisfaction, then put a meal together in the kitchen. With each minute that passed, Lainey could feel Nick's tension increasing and wished there was something she could do to reassure him.

The howls of the werewolves were growing steadily

louder, the screech of their claws against the door coming more and more frequently. The monsters were growing restless with the rise of the moon, and she should have been terrified. But it was impossible to feel anything but pleasure when she was in Nick's arms, their bodies so close she could feel the pounding of his heart against hers.

"They're angrier now, aren't they?" she asked, lying beside him on the bed. "Hungrier?"

"It's the moon," he said in a dark rasp.

She braced herself on an elbow. "Can you feel it? The moon's pull?"

Instead of answering, he tangled his hand in her hair and yanked her down to him, plunging his tongue into her mouth with a hungry, sexy thrust. He kissed her hard and raw and deep, as if it was the last time he was going to taste her mouth and he needed to get his fill. Tears sprang to her eyes at the feel of his desperation, and she kissed him back just as greedily, determined to show him that she accepted all of him. Even the parts she didn't completely understand.

With one of those deep, rumbling growls on his lips, he rolled her to her back, his wicked mouth lowering to her breasts once again. He sucked on her nipples until they were throbbing and achingly tight, then sucked on them more, each pulling suction of his lips and wicked rasp of his tongue ripping a pleasure-cry from her throat that only made the wolves howl louder. But she didn't care. All that mattered was the man—the *vampire*—suddenly sinking his fangs into her throat as he thrust back into her body. She could feel the relentless desperation in his touch as he used his strong hands to grip her hip and the back of her neck, holding her steady for his brutal, pounding rhythm. He ground himself against her with each perfect, devastating stroke, as if trying to imprint the memory of his lovemaking on her body…in her mind. He didn't stop until she'd shattered in a blinding, screaming orgasm that she was shocked to realize had made her claw her nails down his back.

"Nick, I'm so sorry," she gasped the moment she could find her voice, horrified to have hurt him.

Pulling his fangs from her throat, he licked the wounds closed and lifted his head, a lazy, sexy smile on his lips that made her breath catch. "Don't be sorry," he told her, his voice warm and husky with pleasure as he rubbed his lips against hers. "I loved it. Can't wait for you to do it again."

"I…I didn't hurt you?" she asked, stealing his question for once.

He gave a low, deliciously gritty laugh. "I'm a vampire, sweetheart. We sometimes like a little pain with our pleasure."

Her eyes went wide with surprise. "Oh…I, uh…"

"Don't you like it when I'm so deep inside you that it hurts a little?" he asked with a rough, wicked purr. He hadn't come with her, and he gripped her ass with those big hands, holding her in place as he rammed against her, shoving so deep there was a sweet, sharp pain, and her sex spasmed with a shocking jolt of sensation.

"I see what you mean," she gasped, but the quiet words were drowned out by his deep, guttural groan, and she could feel the rippling of powerful muscle beneath his skin as he lost control, driving them to a place where the pleasure was so intense she nearly passed out.

When the sweat had finally cooled on their skin, he carefully pulled out of her and moved into a sitting position at the side of the bed. "You okay?" he rasped, scrubbing his hands down his face, then shoving them back through his hair. Staring at the door, he said, "I didn't hurt you, did I?"

He'd asked her that question so many times today, but her answer was always the same. "No, Nick. I'm fine," she whispered, reaching out to touch the strong, beautiful length of his back. But when he flinched from her touch, a low, animal sound vibrating in his throat, she drew her hand back, knowing something was wrong. "Nick?"

Without a word he pushed himself to his feet. He grabbed his jeans off the floor and her eyes watered as she watched him hike the well-worn denim over his hips, the fly still undone as he padded toward the tall cabinet against the wall and keyed in the combination. A second later the door popped open, and Nick reached inside, his broad shoulders making it impossible for Lainey to see what he was doing. But a chill started to creep its way down her spine. In that moment, she was a thousand times more terrified by what Nick was doing than she was by the monsters trying to break their way into the bunker.

When he finally pulled something out of the cabinet, then turned around to face her, she knew she'd been right to be afraid.

He was holding what looked like a wooden stake in his fist, gripping it so tightly his veins were popping up beneath his dark skin. She scrambled to her feet and quickly pulled on the T-shirt he'd given her to wear earlier, never taking her eyes off the stake.

"What the hell is that?" she asked, even though she knew damn well what it was.

Instead of answering the question, he walked toward her, saying, "Lainey, I need you to do something for me."

Tears burst into her eyes, her voice little more than an emotional croak as she whispered, "What?"

He grabbed her wrist and tried to press the stake into her hand. But she refused to hold it.

"N-Nick?" she stammered, staring up into his beautiful face with blurry eyes that were wide with shock.

He exhaled a ragged breath, his own eyes burning with a cold, dark fire. "I hate to do this to you, sweetheart. But I need you to kill me."

Chapter 7

Shaking her head in stunned horror, Lainey couldn't believe what he'd said. "You *what?*" she gasped. "What are you talking about?"

His jaw was like iron. "You heard me."

"God, Nick. You must be out of your mind! Don't you think you're overreacting a bit? Because I think you *definitely* are!"

"You're a human, Lainey. What the hell do you know about it?" he sneered.

"I know I'm not doing this."

"You *will.*" His low voice shook with his rage. "You'll do it because it's our only choice."

She was trembling so hard she could barely speak. "N-no freaking way! If you're too worried to stay in here with m-me, then let's go out there and fight them together. I can use the gun and you can rip those bastards to shreds."

"We can't," he argued. "You'd be in too much danger, and I refuse to let that happen."

"Then we'll just keep waiting. It'll be okay, Nick. We made it through hours of sex and you taking my blood without any incidents, and we'll make it through this. You won't hurt me. I know you won't."

"Lainey, we're out of bloody time. Since we entered this bunker I've used every second that I wasn't obsessing about you to try to figure out another way. But there isn't one. I can't even do it myself because vampires *can't* commit suicide. It's part of our survival mechanism."

"Well, I'm not doing it either!"

He stepped closer, ignoring her struggles as he jammed the stake against her palm again, and this time he closed his fingers around hers as he lifted the tip to his chest. With a muscle pulsing in the side of his jaw, he said, "I knew I would refuse to gamble with your life when you were little more than a beautiful, infuriating stranger. You can bet your ass that after what happened between us in that bed today, I still refuse to gamble with it. This is the *only* choice. You are going to drive this damn stake through my heart, Lainey Maxwell, or I'll never forgive you."

She stared up into his furious eyes, barely able to see him through her tears. "No," she sobbed. "I won't!"

"You fucking will!" he roared, the savage force of his anger making her tremble so hard that her teeth chattered. "I can feel the moon pulling on me. It's getting stronger every goddamn second. So stop screwing around and do what needs to be done!"

"You don't get to do this!" she screamed, completely

losing it as she struggled to free her hand from his grip. "You don't get to leave me! To just give up on me!"

"I'm not giving up on you," he growled, his breathing loud and uneven. "Damn it, Lainey, I'm trying to save you."

She blinked her tears away. "By leaving me all alone?"

"You won't be alone," he scraped out, his dark eyes burning with emotion. "Not for long. When I'm dead, my family will be able to…sense it. The connection should be strong enough to lead them to my body. They'll find you, Lainey."

"And kill me," she said flatly.

He leaned down, pressing his warm lips to her forehead as he cradled the back of her head in his free hand. "No, sweetheart. When they see you they'll know that I…" His voice broke, and he cleared his throat. "Just trust me when I say that they would never hurt you."

She would have asked why he was so sure of that, but it didn't matter. No way in hell was she doing anything to harm him. Lifting her watery gaze to his, she said, "I'm sorry, Nick. I know you think this is the right thing to do. I know you're going to be angry with me. But I won't do it. I'd rather you kill me than be the one who takes your life."

With a chilling roar of frustration, he shoved her away from him, the stake dropping from her hand to clatter against the floor. Turning his back on her, he stalked across the room and started pounding his fists into the barricaded door until blood was flying from his knuckles, smearing across the steel gray metal.

Running to him, Lainey draped herself across his back, begging him to stop hurting himself. He continued as if he didn't even hear her, until he suddenly shoved away from the door, moving so quickly she nearly stumbled back on her bottom, only just managing to stay on her feet. She watched as his head shot back and he sniffed at the air. Then he lurched forward and put his ear to the door, listening.

"What's going on?" she whispered, terrified that more wolves had come for them.

Without answering her, he shoved away from the door again and headed toward the bed, buttoning his jeans along the way. Picking the handgun up from where she'd left it sitting on one of the chairs at the bedside, he made his way toward her and shoved the weapon into her hands. "Shoot anything that comes near you," he growled, his voice sounding even deeper than it had before, his eyes glowing with a strange golden light. "I mean it, Lainey. Even if it's me, you fucking shoot."

"What's g-going on?" she stammered, more terrified for his safety than she was for her own.

Running his tongue over the edge of his teeth, he said, "My brothers are here."

As if on cue, she heard the vicious sounds of battle coming from beyond the door.

Releasing his deadly talons from the tips of his fingers, he said, "I have to help them."

"No! Just…wait with me, Nick. Please! I don't want you going out there."

Ignoring her plea, he ordered her to stay in the room and headed back over to the door. It took him only a moment to wrench the bars off, unfasten the locks and pull it open. She made one move to go toward him, but he turned his head to snarl at her, and she could see the animal in his glowing eyes. He was already changing, and she heeded the warning in that visceral gaze, stepping away until the backs of her knees hit the bed. She went down with a thud, sitting on the edge of the mattress, tears streaming down her face as she watched him disappear around the edge of the door. Then he yanked the door shut behind him, no doubt expecting her to lock it again, but she couldn't move. All she could do was sit there and listen to the excruciating sounds of the battle, and it was the most horrifying thing she'd ever heard, seeming to go on forever...

And then there was a blessed, peaceful, terrifying silence.

Forcing herself into action, Lainey set the gun on the bed and wiped the tears from her face as she crept toward the door, using every ounce of strength she possessed to pull it open, praying she'd find Nick standing on the other side.

Please don't let him be dead. Please, please, please let him be alive.

As soon as she had the door opened enough that she could squeeze through the gap, she slipped into the shadowy tunnel, the only light coming from the room behind her. But it was enough to illuminate the tall, olive-skinned male who was standing about five feet away, his shoulders propped against the opposite side of the tunnel, his hands pressed against a bleeding wound in his side. When he turned his head to look at her, she gasped at the resemblance to Nick she could see in the man's face. He just looked a little younger, his dark hair long enough to touch his jaw.

This must be one of the brothers, she thought, while the male shouted, "Nick! She's out!"

She saw a flash of movement at the corner of her eye

followed by a strange gust of wind. Her skin tingled as she turned her head and realized there was suddenly someone standing right next to her. Tilting her head back, she gazed up at the hard, savage, blood-spattered face staring down at her and knew she should be terrified. In his "new" form, Nick was even taller than he'd been before, and broader, his talons replaced by long, gleaming claws that dripped with blood and could have easily sliced her in two. But though her heart was racing, she refused to react to him with fear; instead, she reached out and ran her fingertips over the new bluish-black tint of his skin. It was undeniably sexy, reminding her of the hero in the *Underworld* movie she'd been watching in her room at the inn. His eyes burned that same molten gold that she'd seen before and his long, sinister fangs gleamed white in the pale glow of light.

He was so powerful and huge, he probably could have killed her with nothing more than a flick of his wrist, but she wasn't afraid. There was enough of *her* Nick in this savage beauty for her to feel nothing but relief and need. And more love than she ever could have possibly imagined.

"You made it," she whispered, cupping his dark cheek in her hand. His now shoulder-length black hair brushed her wrist as he affectionately turned his head into her touch, nuzzling her palm.

"Nick!" another male shouted from behind him. "More wolves are coming!"

He snarled deep in his chest as he leaned down and took a rough, hungry sniff of her scent at the side of her throat, the primitive act striking her as intensely intimate. Then he pulled back and stepped away from her, his golden stare holding her own as he spoke to the tall, blood-covered male who was now standing beside him. The vampire had long, shaggy blond hair that reached his massive shoulders and a short blond beard. But his eyes were the same piercing shade of blue as Nick's, and she knew this was brother number two.

"Get her the hell out of here, Val," Nick commanded the male in a low, graveled voice, "and guard her with your life. I'll meet the three of you back up at the house when I'm done." Then he turned and disappeared in a blur of speed.

Within seconds, they heard more bone-chilling howls, and Lainey knew he was fighting the wolves on his own. Determined to help him, she'd just turned and started back for the room, where she'd left the gun, when a pair of strong hands gripped her waist. As if she weighed little more than a feather, they lifted her off the ground, her breath whooshing out of her chest as she landed over a hard, broad shoulder. "No!" she screamed, beating on Val's back, furious that he would take her away. She didn't want to leave when Nick was in so much danger. Couldn't stand the thought of not being there to help him if he got injured. Of never being able to tell him that he'd changed her life. That she'd fallen utterly and completely in love with him. And that if he died, she didn't know how she was going to go on without him.

But no matter how she screamed and thrashed, his brother didn't care. He just carried her out into the moonlit darkness of the night, leaving her heart in jeopardy behind them.

It was almost daybreak by the time Nick had dispatched the last werewolf, buried the bodies in one of the deepest, most difficult to reach caves and made his way back to his cliff-top home.

He entered the house through the French doors that opened into his master suite, snagging a clean pair of jeans and a T-shirt. An hour ago he'd started to return to his normal appearance, but the fabric of the clean clothes still chafed against his skin. His senses continued to be heightened beyond even his vampire abilities. He couldn't imagine how incredible it was going to feel when he had Lainey's soft, sumptuous body spread out beneath him, all velvety and lush. Damn it, he couldn't wait to feel her, period, needing to hold her in his arms so badly he was shaking.

Despite the fact that he'd managed to control himself in his strange, new hybrid vampire/wolf state, Nick knew the best thing he could do for her was to stay away—but it wasn't possible. It no doubt made him a selfish bastard, but he'd finally admitted to himself that he needed her too much to lose her. He'd just have to figure out a way to protect her from his enemies, whatever it took.

But when he opened his bedroom door and stepped out onto the open upstairs landing, Nick couldn't detect her scent, and he knew she wasn't in the house.

"Where the hell is she?" he bellowed, his heart banging against his ribs as he waited for his brothers to show their faces. Seb came from one of the guest rooms down the hallway on his left, while a stone-faced Val started up the wide stairs that hugged the wall on his right.

"She left," Seb told him, propping his bare shoulder against the wall. He'd been clawed open by a werewolf during the fight, and he kept one hand pressed to the white bandage that wrapped around his middle.

Nick glared at his younger brother, daring him to say those words to him again. Quietly, he asked, "What did the two of you say to her?"

"We didn't say anything," Val muttered, reaching the top of the stairs, his eyes hooded as he pushed his hands deep in the front pockets of his cargo pants. His tone was flat. "She simply refused to stay. Said this was all too much for her and demanded we let her go."

"Bullshit!" Nick snarled, his chest heaving. "That woman has more courage in her little pinkie than you could ever even begin to imagine! She's not like the women you've known. She's…damn it, even if she didn't want me, she would have had the guts to stay and say it to my face. So what the fuck did you do to make her run?"

Seb cut a worried look toward Val, then cleared his throat. "We didn't say anything that wasn't true, Nick. We were just worried as hell about you."

"And just what is your fucking idea of the truth?" he growled.

It was Val who answered him. "We could tell by the way you looked at her," he said, his hard tone thick with bitterness. "You were willing to tie your life to a human. To give up your immortality for her. I don't know what the hell you were thinking, Nick. But we're not just going to stand by and let that happen."

He was across the room in a burst of speed that was probably too fast for even a vampire to see. Wrapping his hand tightly around Val's throat, he pinned him to the wall and roared, "That wasn't your choice to make, you meddling son of a bitch! When will you ever learn?"

"It wasn't like that, man! We did it because we love you," Seb shouted at his back, trying to pull him off

Val. But Nick wasn't budging. From the cold look in Val's dark eyes, he knew exactly what his big brother had been thinking. And, God help him, Nick refused to head down that same dead-end road.

"If you cared anything about me at all," he grated around his rough breaths, releasing his hold on Val as he took a step back, "then you would have done as I asked and protected the woman who I pray to God is going to be my wife."

He didn't wait around to hear whatever Val had to say for himself. He simply turned and started making his way down the stairs, knowing he could grab everything he needed from his office.

"Where the hell are you going?" Seb demanded from midway down the stairs when Nick came out of his office ten minutes later, fully dressed. He held a leather duffel bag in one hand and his car keys in the other as he headed for the front door. "You need rest," Seb told him. "Don't be a jackass, Nick. You've got to be running on fumes."

Refusing to believe that Lainey had given up on him, he growled, "I'll rest when I've gotten her back." But with his hand on the doorknob, he stopped as a horrible thought occurred to him. Struggling not to panic, he cut a deadly look toward Val, who had appeared in the doorway to the kitchen with his hand clasped around a cold beer. "Did you cloud her mind?" Nick demanded, his voice raw. "Did you make her forget me?"

Val's jaw hardened, but Seb's gritty laughter drew Nick's attention back to him. "Val told her he could cloud her," he said. "He claimed it would make it easier for her to move on."

Nick's hand tightened on the doorknob with so much force that it dented. "And?"

Though he still looked worried as hell about him, Seb's blue eyes glittered with humor and admiration. "And she threatened to send his balls into his throat if he tried," he admitted in a wry drawl. "It was pretty impressive. For such a little thing, she's damned fearless."

That's exactly what Nick was counting on as he slammed the door behind him, determined to find Lainey as quickly as possible.

But it ended up taking a hell of a lot longer than he'd expected. By the time Nick finally tracked Lainey down, almost a week had passed since they'd escaped from the bunker. As he stared up at the softly glowing bedroom window in the rustic farmhouse situated in eastern Alabama, the air was warm and thick, redolent with the scent of apple trees and a summer garden. He'd never been to Alabama before, but he loved what he'd seen of it so far.

He loved the sight of the woman silhouetted in that upstairs bedroom window even more.

Because her grandmother's third husband's name—she'd apparently had eight of them—had been used on all the public records for the farm, Nick had had a hell of a time tracking it down. He'd gone to Lainey's condo in San Diego first, but there'd been no sign of her there. He'd even checked in at the bookstore where she worked, but no one had heard from her since she'd left town for her trip up to Moonlight Bay. He'd checked Ryan's house in L.A. next, but she hadn't been there either.

Long, frustrating, eviscerating days of searching had followed. Even now he was terrified that she'd changed her mind about wanting him.

Unwilling to wait a second longer to see her, Nick reached for the rungs of the ivy trellis that snaked up the side of the house, hoping the thing was strong enough to hold him. The fall wouldn't kill him, but sprawled on his ass in her grandmother's flower garden was hardly the impression he was hoping to make tonight.

If he weren't so desperate to see her, he would have just knocked on the front door. But he didn't think he could do the whole "meet her grandmother" thing until he and Lainey had had the chance to talk things over. God only knew there was *a lot* he needed to say.

"Nick!" Lainey gasped the moment he started through the open window. Her fair skin was flushed with color as she stared at him from across the room, her breathing rapid. Then she crumpled to the floor like a rag doll.

"Son of a bitch," Nick grunted, rushing over to scoop her off the hardwood floor. She was completely boneless in his arms, out for the count in her cute white cotton nightgown. He found a wry smile twitching at the corner of his mouth.

This wasn't the first time he'd held Lainey Maxwell's unconscious body in his arms—but when she woke up, Nick was determined to do whatever it took to keep her there.

Lainey was lost in that painful moment of dreaming when you know you're about to wake up but don't want to. In this dream world, Nick had finally come for her, and she wasn't ready to open her eyes, abandoning the fantasy to face reality.

She'd often heard people say that you could run, but you could never hide. She'd heard the words used in reference to things like fate and justice and karma. But she'd never thought about how true they were. Had never realized they could apply to something as huge and overwhelming as pain...and love.

It seemed like madness, pure and simple. The crazy-assed idea that she could have fallen in love with a man—a vampire—she'd known for little longer than a snap. But it was true. And now that she no longer had him—that almost the entire breadth of America separated them—she felt more pain than she'd believed was physically possible.

It was a different kind of pain from the grief she felt over the loss of her brother. More desperate—because she knew Nick was still out there, living his life without her. She was dark inside. Cold. Alone, even when she wasn't. She hadn't known emotion could hurt like this. Like a physical thing inside that pulsed and contracted and sliced until you wanted to cut it out with a knife.

Still refusing to open her eyes, she pulled in a deep breath and almost cried out when Nick's warm, mouth-watering scent filled her head. Could it possibly be real? Could he really be there with her?

Cracking her eyes open, she took a quick peek and nearly choked as her heart shot into her throat when she realized she was lying across his lap, cradled in his arms. "Nick?"

"Did you pass out because you're afraid of me?" he rasped, his dark, intense gaze shadowed with concern.

She couldn't help but laugh as she shook her head. "Of course I'm not afraid of you, you dolt. I'm just so freaking happy to see you! I've missed you like crazy."

"Then we can talk after," he said in a low voice, already working open the buttons that ran down the front of her nightgown. "Right now I just need to get inside you. I need to fuck you, Lainey. Badly."

"No, wait!" As she sat up, she saw that he was sitting on the little chair in front of her dressing table. He was still working on the tiny row of buttons that ran down her bodice, and she grabbed his thick wrist as he reached the last one, waiting for him to look at her. When he finally lifted that hungry, smoldering gaze from her breasts to her face, she asked, "You're not… you're not here to cloud my mind, are you?"

"No." With a tender look in his beautiful blue eyes, he lifted his hand and gently tucked a wayward curl behind her ear. "I wouldn't do that to you, sweetheart."

"But Val said—"

"I know." His lips twitched with a smile. "Seb told me you threatened to send Val's balls into his throat if he tried."

Sounding more than a little fierce, she said, "I would have, too. I didn't want anyone messing with my memories of you."

"Why?" His tone was rough, his gaze deep and measuring.

She swallowed, fighting back the tears. "Because they were the best memories of my life."

His arm tightened around her back. "Mine, too, Lainey."

Fighting hard to hold back her tears, she searched his gorgeous face, trying to read his expression. Recalling the painful reason she'd left, she said, "I can't even begin to describe how incredible it is to see you, but why…why are you here, Nick?"

"We'll get to that," he grated, the words rough with impatience. "But right now I'm about to have you on the nearest horizontal surface I can find. If you want it to be the bed, then you'd better get your ass on it. *Now.*"

"But we—"

With an arresting expression that was somehow as affectionate as it was aggressive, he growled, "Shut up, Lainey. All I want to hear from you is 'Harder, Nick.'" His voice dropped to a husky, provocative whisper. "'Deeper, Nick.'"

Oh...*wow.* All he had to do was look at her, and her body started melting for him, going liquid and hot and needy.

"And feel free to scream," he added with an impossibly sexy smirk, reaching under the hem of her gown and ripping her flimsy lace panties off her. "I love it when you do that."

A second later, he had two big fingers shoved deep inside her, stretching her tight sheath, and she gasped, "My God!"

His mouth curled with a wicked smile. "That's acceptable, too."

She was snorting with laughter as he rose to his feet, carrying her in his arms, and tossed her into the middle of the mattress, then quickly lost his shirt and jeans. But as he started to come down over her, wearing nothing but his tight black boxers, she pressed her hands to his chest, gazing up at him through a glistening sheen of tears. "Please, Nick," she whispered. "I need to know what's happening."

With a heartfelt groan, he rolled to his back beside her and shoved both hands back through his hair. "Okay," he said, and she could tell that he was trying to dredge up enough patience to do this because it was clear from the impressive bulge in his shorts what he'd *prefer* to be doing. "Where do you want to start?"

Moving onto her side, Lainey propped herself on an elbow, unable to get over the fact that he was lying there beside her. "What happened that night?" she asked. "After you had your brothers take me away?"

With his gaze focused on the ceiling, he said, "I hunted down every last one of those sadistic bastards. They're all dead."

Her brows lifted. "You didn't keep any for questioning?" she asked, knowing how important it was that he find out who had been helping the wolves.

"No, I didn't question them." He turned his head toward her, locking her in that deep, dark blue. "They knew who you were, Lainey. I couldn't risk one of them getting away and coming after you."

"Won't you be in trouble with your...bosses?"

Nick snorted. "They can try. But the ones I work for know better than to piss me off."

She made a small sound of relief. "Good."

Reaching out, he caught one of her curls, twining it around his finger as he asked, "Are you going to tell me what happened with my brothers?"

"Val said I was the last thing you needed," she whispered, unable to hide her worry in the husky words. Not to mention her pain. "He said that if I stayed, you would turn your back on them and give up eternity for me. That you would...suffer because of me."

"Val is full of bullshit," he snarled, his dark eyes flashing with anger. "You never should have listened to him."

"Are you saying you wouldn't die if we were together?" she asked, almost too afraid to hope. Yeah, they would still have some serious…issues. For one, she'd age…and he wouldn't. But in that moment, she didn't care. The only thing that mattered was having as much time with him as she could, and she was greedy as hell for it.

He got that closed look on his face that was impossible to read and let go of her hair before he sat up at the edge of the bed. With his back to her, he said, "You know vampires can't commit suicide, Lainey."

Frustrated by that half-assed answer, she sat up in the middle of the bed and said, "That's not what I'm talking about and you know it, Nick. Val said that vampires who pledge their lives to a single human will often choose to feed from only that one person, and by doing so, they begin to age and grow old so that they can die with their…loved one."

Moving to his feet, he started to pace across the hardwood floor. The way his powerful muscles shifted and flexed beneath his tight skin was the most magnificent thing she'd ever seen. "So you just left?" he ground out, cutting her a sharp look from the corner of his eye. "Without even talking to me about it?"

Using her fingertips to wipe away the tears spilling over her cheeks, she said, "I'm not…I'm not saying that you *love* me, but I knew if I stayed with you, there was a chance you would give up everything." A watery smile curled her lips. "You wouldn't have wanted to hurt me by breaking my heart. You're too much of a gentleman."

Shoving a hand back through his hair again, he gave a rough, masculine snort as he shook his head. "Christ, Lainey. You're the only person in the entire world who would ever accuse me of being noble."

"But you *are*. And that's why I won't let you do it.

There's got to be another way because I refuse to let you die for me, Nick."

He stopped at the side of the bed. "I choose to think of it as living for you," he murmured roughly, grabbing her ankles and pulling her toward him so that he was standing between her legs as she sat on the side of the mattress. He stared down at her with so much heat she felt burned. "I wouldn't want to live on without you, Lainey. I *couldn't*. And I know I should have told you how I felt before, but I'm saying it now." Dropping to his knees, he shoved his fingers into her hair, his blue eyes glittering with emotion as he said, "I fell completely in love with you in that bunker, Lainey Maxwell. And as sorry as I am that you lost your brother, I'm grateful as hell that you were brought into my life."

"I love you, too," she whispered breathlessly, unable to hold back a flood of tears. "So much, Nick."

With a heartfelt groan, he said, "Thank God." But then he rubbed the callused pad of his thumb across her damp cheek, and a frown wove its way between his dark brows as he said, "I want so badly to make you happy, but you know that life with me isn't going to be easy."

Touching her fingertips to the scar on his biceps where the werewolf had bitten him that first night, she asked, "How are you doing with…everything?"

"I'll be better now that I'm with you. I haven't been fit to be around since you left," he admitted sheepishly. "But I'm handling the bite okay."

"You're not in any pain?" she asked with obvious concern.

He shook his head. "It was frightening at first, changing like that, but the second night I had more control and even more the night after that. But I'll never be…normal for you, Lainey."

"Normal is boring," she told him with a soft smile, running her fingers through his dark hair. "I'd hate normal."

A wry grin twisted his lips. "I'm glad you feel that way. Because I'm sure I'll be a handful whenever it's a full moon, I probably won't even let you out of bed." He pushed her hair back from her face, his expression positively sinful. "But knowing you, it won't be anything you can't handle."

"You got that right," she agreed with a teasing purr. "I'm expecting you to be a handful *every* night in the sack, so the full-moon sex will just be a bonus."

A shock of heat flared in his blue eyes, one of those deliciously husky laughs rumbling up from his chest as he said, "Bite or no bite, I'll always be an animal with you, Lainey. You just…affect me."

"And I'm glad as hell about that." With a serious note creeping into her voice, she added, "So long as I'm the *only* woman who gets to see that side of you. We never really talked about—"

"We never talked about it," he grated, cutting her off, "because I thought you understood. I don't share. No other man *ever* gets his hand on you."

Pressing her palms against his warm, solid chest, she said, "I don't want any other man, Nick. But I feel the exact same way about you."

"I sure as hell hope so because you're the only woman I want." His voice was getting rougher, and she could feel the pounding of his heart. "The only woman I'll *ever* want or touch or kiss or make love to," he told her, his big hands suddenly landing on her hips as he jerked her closer.

"No flirting either," she warned him, so full of happiness she thought she might burst.

He got that haughty, insulted look that always made her smile. "Do I look like a bloody flirt, Lainey?"

"You flirt with me like crazy," she pointed out.

Eyes smoldering, he gripped her ass and gave a sexy growl. "That's because you're *mine,* woman. I can do whatever the hell I want with you."

"You got that right." She cupped the side of his beautiful face in her hand, her smile falling as she asked, "But what are we going to do about the future? Isn't there any way you can…keep me with you?"

"I love you, Lainey. That means I'm damn well going to marry you and keep you *with me* for the rest of our lives."

Though she was beyond excited about that "marry you" part, she knew they needed to talk this out. "But my life isn't like yours. I don't want you to die because of me, Nick. I couldn't stand that."

"And I can't stand the thought of hurting you," he muttered, his voice so low it was almost soundless. "Please don't ask me to do that, Lainey."

She studied his raw expression and suddenly realized what he meant. "Nick, is there a way that you could… change me? So that I could be like you?"

His face was tight with tension. "I don't want to talk about it now."

Almost too afraid to hope, she said, "Whatever it is, I love you, Nick. That means I'm willing to do whatever it takes to share my life with you. The more time we have, the better."

The look in his eyes was dark and wild and his breathing was getting jagged. "I love you, too," he groaned. "So much it scares the hell out of me. So much that the thought of you giving up your world for mine makes me want to—"

"Shh…" she whispered, pressing her mouth against his for a soft, quick kiss, knowing that anything more was only going to end one way, and as much as she craved making love with him, there were still things that needed to be said. Because she wasn't giving up on this. "It's going to be okay, Nick. Just trust me."

He drew back his head and parted his lips, and she knew he was going to argue. But then he got a funny look on his face, and said, "There's someone coming up the stairs."

Her eyes went wide with panic. "Oh, my God!" she gasped, pushing him away and clambering to her feet. "That's my grandmother! She doesn't believe in knocking and there's no lock on that door. Get your clothes on! She's about to bust right in here."

His brows drew together with a comical scowl. "She just walks into your room without knocking?"

Rolling her eyes, Lainey said, "I love her to death, but the woman has no concept of personal space."

It must have looked like some kind of screwball comedy as they both tried to get back in their clothes before the door was opened. When Nick caught his foot in the leg of his jeans and fell over, his sexy bod sprawled across the floor, Lainey collapsed against her dresser, laughing so hard she was crying. He'd only just managed to get back on his feet, yanking the jeans over his lean hips, when they ran out of time. Wiping the tears from her cheeks, Lainey looked over and saw her grandmother's weathered face poking into the room from around the edge of the door.

"There something you want to tell me, young lady?" Grandma Kate asked, her brown eyes bright with curiosity as she gazed at Nick, who had quickly moved to Lainey's side.

Taking Nick's hand, Lainey spoke in a breathless, excited rush. "Gram, this is Nick Santos and he's…. Well, I love him! He's the most incredible, wonderful man. And we're, um…well, you see…"

Squeezing her hand, Nick got right to the point. "I'm going to marry your granddaughter, ma'am. As soon as possible."

For a moment, there was nothing but a stunned, heavy silence. Then, with a knowing look at Nick…and a conspiratorial wink, her grandmother said, "I gotta say that I'm pretty excited about this wedding. It'll be the first one I've ever been to that takes place at night!"

Lainey shot a stunned look at Nick, whose dark brows were raised with surprise, and then they both started to laugh.

She didn't know how or why, but it was obvious that Grandma Kate had known about the existence of vampires all along.

Epilogue

Three months later...

The breeze that blew in off the Pacific this time of day was always his wife's favorite. Lainey often would crawl out of bed at sunset and enjoy her first cup of coffee on the balcony that extended off the master suite, and as he climbed the stairs with her mug in hand, that's exactly where Nick knew he would find her. She had only been a vampire for a few months now, and she still wasn't strong enough to go out in the daytime. But he knew she didn't mind.

As for Nick, he'd never dared to hope he could know happiness like this. Lainey had brought a light and warmth to his life that he'd never imagined could be his, and he was utterly devoted to her. His brothers teased him ruthlessly about being whipped, but he couldn't have cared less. He knew that deep down the jackasses were just jealous that he'd found the perfect woman. When they finally found theirs, he'd be able to get his own back at them, and he was going to enjoy every ruthless moment of it. With his wife's help, he had no doubt his retaliation would be satisfying and sweet.

For the first few weeks he and Lainey had been together there'd been countless arguments about their future. Still unwilling to put her through the excruciating process of becoming a vampire, he'd argued for her to remain human and for the two of them to grow old together. But in the end, it was his own greed that had been his downfall. Every time Lainey had talked about having an eternity to spend with him, his resistance had cracked a little more because he wanted as many forevers with her as he could get. The little imp had refused to marry him until he'd finally done what she called "accepting the inevitable," and on a blustery autumn night, with his family gathered around for support, Nick had drained her of her life's blood…and then filled her with his own.

They'd been married in a breathtaking ceremony at his parents' vineyard in Spain two weeks later in front of their closest friends and family. And after a decadent honeymoon in Mauritius, where they made love on the beach every night beneath the ethereal glow of the moon, they'd moved into the new seaside, cliff-top home they'd found in Malibu. Still suspicious of how the werewolf pack had learned about his home in Moonlight Bay, Nick hadn't been comfortable keeping Lainey in the house there. The estate had since been sold, the beach set up as a nature reserve in Ryan's name, and their new home was listed in one of their new aliases, making it difficult to trace back to them.

Though Nick had gone into their marriage intending to quit his work as an Enforcer, it hadn't worked out that way. Lainey had repeatedly argued that he couldn't quit something that was so much a part of him just because of her…and then the headstrong woman had gone and employed his family's help. Left with no other choice, Nick had grudgingly given in and resumed working with his brothers. And since Lainey had quit her job in San Diego, she'd decided to put her research skills to good use and help them with their investigations. Seb and Val now claimed that they didn't know how they'd ever managed without her.

The only rough spot had been when the first full moon came. Overcome by lust and love, he knew he'd been too aggressive with her, not to mention insatiable, keeping her in bed except for those brief moments when she'd needed to eat or visit the bathroom. But she'd never complained, promising him that she'd loved every minute of it, and he felt thankful as hell that he had such an incredible woman.

The morning after the night Nick had finally tracked Lainey down in Alabama, she'd had a long talk with her grandmother and learned much about her family that she'd never known before. According to Kate, her son's research into ancient texts had convinced him that there was a hidden world living among humanity in secret. A world that consisted of creatures and species most humans relegated to the realms of fiction and literature. It was a bittersweet moment for Lainey because she knew that Ryan might have been more careful if he'd known the true extent of the danger when he'd gone to investigate in Moonlight Bay. Her grandmother told her that her father had wanted to tell her and Ryan the

truth someday, but then he'd passed away, and she just
hadn't had the heart to do it herself. She'd been worried
about how they would react to the news and now blamed
herself for not coming forward sooner, but Lainey had
refused to let her feel guilty. As much as she grieved
for her brother, the last thing she wanted was for Kate
to spend the last years of her life burdened by grief.

They were expecting a visit from Kate closer to the
holidays, but today it was his parents who were coming to visit. Though Nick had known they would be
accepting of the woman he lost his heart to, he'd never
realized how completely they would come to love her.
But then this was Lainey he was talking about, so he
should have.

With his wife's coffee in hand, Nick had almost made
it to the top of the long, winding staircase when he
heard a knock at the front door. Turning to head back
down, he called out over his shoulder to let her know
his parents were there and made his way to the Spanish-
tiled foyer. Setting her mug down on a table beside a
vase filled with vibrant flowers, Nick pulled the heavy
wooden door open just as Lainey came rushing down
the stairs with an excited smile on her face. Her colorful, floral halter top and sexy low-rise jeans made him
grin despite his concern that she wasn't up for this visit.
She hadn't quite been herself the past week, tiring easily and losing her appetite.

Though he hadn't said anything to her yet, Nick was
worried that he'd been taking too much blood from her.
But as his parents stepped inside, his mother took one
look at Lainey as she reached the bottom of the stairs,
her happy exclamation laying his concerns regarding

feeding to rest…and giving him an entirely new mountain of worries to conquer.

"Oh, you precious, beautiful girl!" his mother said in a delighted rush, hurrying toward a startled-looking Lainey. "I knew it the moment I set eyes on you. You're making me a grandmother!"

His gorgeous wife, in typical Lainey fashion, shot him a stunned, breathtaking look of joy—then immediately passed out. Nick caught her in his arms before she hit the floor, and with a low, excited rumble of laughter, he told his parents they would join them later, then carried her up to their bedroom. When her lashes fluttered open a minute later, Nick was cuddled next to her on their bed, his face close to hers, his heart so full he thought it might burst. Now that he knew, he didn't know how he'd missed the obviousness of it, except that he'd never really been around many pregnant female vampires.

"Are you okay?" she whispered, locking her bright gaze with his. "I know you didn't marry me expecting to start a family so soon."

"I couldn't be happier about the baby, Lainey. And just so you know, I married you because I love you. Because I've pledged my heart and body and soul to you. And because I need you by me every day, and every night, until I take my final breath."

"I hope that day never comes because I want to be with you forever."

"You really think there's anything in this world, or beyond, that could keep me from you?"

With a smile, she said, "No."

His voice got lower. "You know your man well, little vampire."

"I love him even more."

"Tell him again," he murmured, lifting the hem of her top so that he could lean down and trail a line of tender kisses across her belly. "Because he never gets tired of hearing it."

Running her fingers through his hair, she said, "I love you, Nick. Now. Tomorrow. Forever."

Moving over her, he said, "I'll hold you to that, Lainey. Because you're *mine*."

"I've never wanted to be anything else," she whispered, and with the sweet, blistering touch of her mouth against his, he knew it was true.

* * * * *

VAMPIRE ISLAND

LAUREN HAWKEYE

Dear Reader,

The scenery surrounding a vampire tale is often like the creatures themselves—dark and full of shadows and mystery. When casting around for a premise for this story, I considered London, Paris, Ireland... where might an encounter with a vampire occur?

I decided that I wanted to do something a little bit different. Vampires are beautiful and deadly.... I thought that a tropical setting could be, too. Danger could lurk amongst the vices offered in paradise... and so the idea for *Vampire Island* was born.

I do hope you'll enjoy your visit to the island. If you'd like to tell me about it, I love hearing from readers! Find me on the web at www.laurenhawkeye.com.

Happy reading,

Lauren

For Ann Leslie,
whose nurturing nature is much appreciated.

Chapter 1

Isla Miller was not ready for the blast of humidity that descended on her like a wet blanket the moment she left the cabin of the boat.

Gasping a little for breath, she shifted uncomfortably as perspiration broke out over her skin, causing her sundress to cling and her pale red waves of hair to wilt. It was a radical change from the thin, dry mountain air of Colorado, and she wasn't entirely sure she liked it.

Maybe she should have stayed home.

Trying to keep her tread steady as the boat swayed beneath her feet, Isla looked hopefully to the captain for help disembarking. The man who dressed like a pirate had, however, thrown her bags over the edge of the vessel, onto the wide wooden dock, and scrambled back to the far side of the craft, where he looked to be preparing for departure already.

"Off with ya, missy!" His words were barely intelligible over the sudden roar of the motor. "Yer stayin' or yer comin' back, but best decide right quick!"

Isla blinked, not impressed with the service. That said, it had been far more difficult than she had thought to find transport from the small Tahitian airport out to Ile de Nuit. She had wandered nervously in the airport, searching for a sign with her name, held by the person who was supposed to collect her and take her to the resort. Finally an announcement over the static-filled PA system had connected her with Gaspar, who told her that he was her personal concierge for the week and that he was so very sorry—he had thought that their shuttle boat would be repaired by this time, but it was not. If she waited an hour and had a meal—on them, of course—they would come to get her.

If she waited an hour, she'd lose her nerve entirely and book a flight back home. She cringed when she thought of the fit her mother would have when she found out that Isla—predictable Isla—had hopped on a plane and taken off for parts unknown without her approval.

Isla decided that she would rather stay and wait it out than return home early and face that. She hadn't had many options for transport to the island, and the persistent old man who had followed her around the airport had finally worn her down.

Now she was feeling another change of heart. She wavered, not sure if she should actually disembark, or if she should go back to the airport and catch some transport back home, where she could curl up with a skinny cappuccino and a Matthew McConaughey movie. She could forget all about this trip, which had been foisted on her by her friend Jessie Spencer, and which she would never have agreed to if the details on the island hadn't sucked her right in.

"Ye look like a good girl, lassie. Come on back to shore." The words of the would-be pirate were what finally nudged Isla into action.

She wondered if all of the locals were as superstitious as this old man. Although the trip had originally been booked for Jessie, work had interfered, so her friend had given her the trip as a gift. Well, truthfully, Jessie had begged Isla to go in her stead. Isla knew how excited her friend had been, and though she wasn't overly interested in a resort of any kind, she hadn't been able to let down her best friend.

When she had, she'd warned her about the lore that surrounded the island. Locals thought that the island was full of vampires and werewolves and all kinds of things that went bump in the night—and during the day, apparently, or else the supposed vampires weren't very smart for settling on a tropical, sunshine-filled island.

She wasn't overly worried. Jessie was obsessed with the paranormal, which was why her friend had decided on a trip to this specific resort. For her own part, Isla didn't believe in spooky creatures, so the island's reputation didn't matter much to her.

Isla figured that this was a publicity stunt. She had grown up in a household with a mother who insisted that the paranormal didn't exist and that humans were ridiculous for perpetuating the legends. Isla hadn't even been permitted to watch *Sabrina, the Teenage Witch* or *Buffy the Vampire Slayer.*

As she looked around at the beautiful turquoise water, clear sky and white sand, she wondered why the resort would need any kind of publicity stunt.

It was beautiful. Though she had initially questioned Jessie about her resort selection—her lawyer friend was far more likely to enjoy a quirky gothic tone to her holiday than Isla was—now she was beginning to see why her friend had been so set on visiting the island.

It was beautiful. It was peaceful.

And better yet, it was miles away from her overbearing mother and her two perfect sisters.

The disreputable old man gunned the motor of the boat, urging her along. Frowning a bit—her version of a scowl—Isla shouted to him to wait a moment, then clambered over the edge of the boat. When she landed on the dock, she was red-faced and rumpled—not the sort of dignified impression that she'd hoped to present.

But then, she never came across as dignified, a fact that her family never let her forget.

Behind her, the motor of the small boat roared. She waved an American bill in her hand to leave him a tip, but the operator of the boat had already shoved the throttle back and was chugging quickly away from the dock.

Isla thought that she saw the old man cross himself dramatically as he piloted the boat away. She closed her eyes, then opened them again.

No. Surely not. Isla rolled her eyes. If vampires were roaming the island, then they were certainly hiding their existence well. There were no bodies, no missing persons reports…no evidence of anything other than a beautiful, lush resort that stood on an island with a wealth of local lore.

She'd checked. Not that she didn't trust Jessie to have chosen a safe vacation spot—but she knew her friend had a fascination with the supernatural. A few missing persons reports might just draw Jessie in, rather than repelling her. Thanks to the superstitions of Mr. Pirate, Isla was not feeling very positive about the start of her trip.

"Mademoiselle Miller?" Agitated, she turned as the voice with the lovely, cultured accent spoke her name. When she saw the speaker, her jaw dropped in disbelief.

"Um. Well. Hello." The man who had spoken was possibly the most perfectly beautiful person that she'd ever seen in real life—the type who looked as if he'd been airbrushed. Blond, with intense violet eyes, he had pale, perfect skin that gleamed in the bright sunlight.

Something about that seemed off to her, but she was far too off balance from the journey to think what it was. Still, even though he wasn't her type, he was very easy on the eyes. Pursing her lips with a hint of amusement, she began to see yet another reason that her man-hungry friend had chosen this place.

"Welcome to the Ile de Nuit, Mademoiselle Miller. I apologize that we were not able to arrange for better transportation to our resort." The beautiful man extended his hand for Isla's own. His palm was chilly against hers, as were his lips when he lifted her hand to his mouth for a small, discreet kiss.

"Well. It's all right, I guess." She was charmed by the gesture. If Jessie were here, she would have a date with the man already. Isla was far more reserved, however, and already knew that this man, handsome as he was, wasn't for her.

She wanted that visceral tug deep in her gut, that primal recognition of a soul mate.

And that was why she was always single. She wanted the real thing, not some tropical island fling.

"I am Gaspar." The man straightened back up and smiled flirtatiously at her, and Isla felt a bit of her agitation from the long day of travel melt. If the man had truly been flirting with her, she would have been intimidated, but she recognized the type of man that Gaspar was—he loved women, all women, and that included her.

She could handle that.

"We spoke on the phone earlier. I will be your personal concierge while you are here."

"My concierge?" Discreetly—or so she hoped—Isla brushed her hand over her forehead, wiping at the sweat accumulating there.

It was so *hot* here.

"Oui." Gaspar handed Isla a device that looked like a high-tech beeper. "If you need anything, anytime that you are in the resort, simply press this button. I will hear it, and provide you with whatever you want."

Shading her eyes, Isla looked past the man to the gates of the self-proclaimed haven and the massive, bone-white buildings behind them. She could see a huge pool that sparkled turquoise in the sun, the water glinting through the bars of the fence.

"I can't imagine what I could need. It looks fabulous." Yes, it looked fabulous indeed—luxurious, rich and relaxing.

"Still. Anything that you need, anything at all." Picking up Isla's massive suitcase and carry-on tote without even a grunt, Gaspar gestured with his head for Isla to precede him to the shiny black golf cart that sat at the end of the dock. "If you require a hamburger at two in the morning, you should press that button. If you wish for a dinner companion, press the button. If you need someone to apply sunscreen to your back, you contact me."

From two steps behind Gaspar, Isla started. To apply sunscreen to her back? Then Gaspar turned and winked at her, openly flirtatious, and she couldn't help but laugh.

"I think I'll manage, but thank you." Men who looked like him just weren't interested in women who looked like her. Petite and with curves that she often thought were a bit overly ripe, Isla wasn't the kind of woman who men typically checked out.

"After you, mademoiselle." Gingerly, Isla climbed onto the golf cart, and as she did, her heart started to pound. She didn't like new things and tried her best to avoid strange situations. Now, because she hadn't had the heart to turn her friend down and because deep down she knew that her life needed a kick in the pants, she was about to enter some fancy French resort on some tiny Tahitian island...and she was alone.

Alone. Nerves began to churn in her gut. Gaspar shifted in his seat, his nostrils flaring as if Isla's anxiety somehow had a scent.

She could do this. She could do this. She just needed to distract herself.

"Are you all right?" Gaspar cast a sidelong glance of concern in Isla's direction, and she gave herself a mental kick. No matter how fragile the hold on her self-esteem had been lately, she was a grown woman. She was taking an adult vacation. It wasn't that big of a deal.

Except that to her it was indeed a big deal, one that was loud and clear in her mind. Jessie knew it, too, and if Isla didn't know how much her friend had very much wanted to come here herself, she might have thought that Jessie had chosen this unique resort specifically to push Isla completely out of her comfort zone.

"I'm fine. Sorry. I'm just…a little overwhelmed from the day."

"We'll fix you up soon enough." Gaspar cast her a flirtatious smile. Isla felt as though she should be responding in some way, but she felt nothing.

Well…she did feel something, just not toward her cute concierge. She felt relief. Saying a silent but fervent thank-you to Jessie, she breathed the humid air in deeply. No matter how stressful the day had been, she was here now, on a tiny island in Tahiti, with a personal assistant who wanted to spoil her.

How bad could this possibly be?

He smelled her before he saw her.

The blood fizzing through the human's veins smelled, of all things, like fresh, juicy mango, overlaid with a hint of Tahitian vanilla. It made his mouth water, and no wonder.

He'd always been partial to dessert.

Sloane Goldhawk didn't trust anything, anyone, until they showed him why he should. The woman stepping neatly off the small boat that had ferried her to the island looked as sweet as she smelled, with her long strawberry hair pulled back in a simple braid, the color setting off the smooth-as-cream skin of her shoulders, which were bared to the sun by her white sundress.

She sure didn't look like the kind of woman to volunteer blood services to a colony of vampires. Hell, she didn't look like she'd ever even heard of the creatures in her life.

But then, he was certain that she had. Humans had

three trains of thought about Ile de Nuit—or Vampire Island. Some were superstitious locals who regarded the place as the devil's playground and wouldn't set a foot on the island for all the money in the world. Most were vampire groupies, that rare subset of humanity who not only believed in the reality of vampires, but who accepted what was right before their eyes and craved the thrill of being near nature's deadliest predator.

Most, however, were people who had heard the legends about the island and scoffed, certain that the stories were nothing but that—fiction made up to draw visitors to the island.

The exact opposite was true in the latter's case, however. Unless a human was a fanger—a proven vampire groupie, one who wanted to live on the island in exchange for providing blood—and had been invited personally by Lucian, then reservations at the resort had a mysterious habit of being full at the time of booking.

Lucian St. Baptiste, leader of the clan that lived on the island, had created the perfect little ecosystem. Humans who got a sexual thrill from being hunted, being fed on, were happy, and they were protected by rules against overfeeding. In turn, this gave the vampires a ready, fresh food source at all times, so long as they followed the rules of the clan.

Existence was peaceful in the hedonistic paradise of the island, far removed from the problems of the world.

That was why Sloane was there—for that peace. The mysterious owner of the island, who Sloane had yet to meet, had been searching for a mechanic for the resort. Though Sloane would have thought the man would want someone who would join his clan, strengthen it, he had offered Sloane the job, having heard that Sloane had been looking for some time away from his corporation. It wasn't at all odd for one vampire to reach out to another in that manner—the vampire community was small compared to that of humans.

In the six months he had been there, he had tried to keep mostly to himself, enjoying the beauty of the sun and the sea, using them to try to heal.

Though he didn't judge them for their sexual proclivities, Sloane still couldn't bring himself to feed off one of the fangers. Didn't those people understand that, clan rules or not, their lives were very much in danger whenever they were around a vampire at all, let alone in a sexual situation with one?

Though there were no official reports, neighboring islands whispered about the disappearances. No matter how invisible a person might be, someone always noticed when a person vanished as if they had never existed.

For vampires, sex and feeding were very much linked. Having sexual contact with one was like waving a red banner in front of a bull. And with her intoxicating scent, the fresh, innocent woman he was watching would attract more attention than most.

Tearing his eyes away from the sweet morsel of a human, Sloane found Pierre, the island's general maintenance worker, standing inches behind him, fangs out and lust in his eyes. The aggressive stance forced Sloane's own fangs to descend, and he hissed, long and deep.

Pierre blinked, some of his bloodlust clearing. He raked a hand through his long, scraggly hair and with visible difficulty retracted his fangs.

"Sorry, man." He took several deliberate steps back,

rocking a bit on the deck of the boat that Sloane was re-
pairing—the boat that would have picked the human up
at the airport had it been functional. The young vampire was still clumsy, unsure of his skin, not unlike a
newborn baby.

Sloane supposed that he should be nicer to the kid.
He had no more seniority on Vampire Island than Pierre
did—didn't consider himself a member of the clan that
inhabited it and had no interest in joining. But he was
a dangerous vampire all the same, a creature who had
been in the military before his death and after.

Still, no matter how young the newborn was, Sloane
did not like being snuck up on, and to emphasize his
point, he snarled for longer than was strictly necessary.

Pierre issued a noise not unlike the whine of a puppy.
"Dude. I said I was sorry. I just…I mean, look at her.
She's so sweet. I didn't mean to disrespect you. I just
couldn't help myself."

Sloane stared down the younger vamp, then nodded once, seriously. He was itching to turn back to the
woman. He could still smell her, and though he was old
enough to know better, he understood completely why
Pierre had lost momentary control.

Since arriving on the island six months earlier, he
had hunted animals to get his blood. Before that he
would drink either animal blood from the butcher's, or
human blood that had been donated to a blood bank, but
he hadn't fed from a human vein in a very long time.
In his mind, doing so made him no better than an animal himself, and he wasn't sure that he could control
himself if he did.

The smell of this beautiful woman, however, was
tempting him like nothing he had ever known. No mat-

ter that she likely wasn't as innocent as she appeared, that very same quality tugged at him, likely, he knew, because he had so long ago lost any shred of his own.

"Doesn't look like a fanger, eh?" Pulling his fangs back into his gum line, Sloane resisted the urge to grab Pierre by the scruff of his neck and throw him off the small boat and into the water for the comment.

If he wanted to stay on Vampire Island, and for the time being he did, he couldn't. Though he hadn't pledged allegiance to the clan, he still had to abide by its rules. The vampire version of "my roof, my rules."

Though he was now acquainted with the rumors about Lucian St. Baptiste's illness, the vampire still cast a dark shadow. Sloane knew his reputation well. Outsiders did not lay hands on any of his children, vampire or human, without facing dire consequences. The vampire kept a tight rein on the rules because if he did not, his entire delicate ecosystem could crumble in an instant.

Not that that scared Sloane, at least not overmuch. It was more that he didn't wish to rock the boat, not while current circumstances suited him so well. Though he did find it odd that he hadn't yet met his employer, he figured the man was ill, eccentric or both, and it was no business of his.

"Go away, Pierre." Looking down at the boat that he was standing on, Sloane chose words instead of fists. He didn't want to argue with the young pup of a vampire—he wanted to retreat, away from the enticing smell of the woman, away from the disturbing memories that she evoked. He wanted to go sequester himself on the houseboat on which he currently lived with the tequila that he kept in the freezer for the occasions when he needed oblivion.

He couldn't, nor could he toss Pierre into the water the way that he wanted to. He was old enough himself, had learned enough control, to do so. "And stay away from that human if you know what's good for you. Any who are that pretty are for Lucian, and you know it."

"I was just looking, man." Surly like a teenager, Pierre began to skulk off the boat, his white skin looking even paler in the mid-afternoon sun. "Besides, Marcus wanted to know if this boat will be ready soon."

"It'll be done by the time you get back there to tell him." Tightening one last screw, Sloane straightened and, stretching to his full height of six foot five, pulled his water bottle from the small cooler beside him. It was opaque plastic, the better to hide the contents—nicely chilled pig's blood—from the humans on the island, although many knew exactly what was in it.

Most would have even offered to provide it.

"Fine." Sloane sighed as Pierre finally—finally— left, breaking into a full run at vampire speed the moment his feet touched the sand, off to report back to Marcus, his master.

Sloane watched as the woman and Gaspar, who in his opinion was far too friendly with all of the females on the island, drove away to the complex. Her scent lingered in the air around him, teasing his senses and making him hungry.

Making him hungry in more ways than one. The thirst that burned in his throat despite his drink made him full of irritation with himself.

He'd been off his game lately, true enough—that was why he was hiding away in the middle of the South Pacific to begin with. Once upon a time, he had had no qualms about biting—and having sex with—beautiful human women. Then he had met Ana and had wanted to keep her with him forever. He'd turned her.

The result had shown him that he would likely never touch another human woman again.

Still, of late he had been feeling lonely. His best friend, a human male, had passed away only months earlier, and Sloane had been reminded of why humans in general were bad news. He needed to stay away from them entirely.

Drooling—and lusting—after tiny little redheaded warm blood was not a good start.

"Has she arrived?" Lucian St. Baptiste pursed his lips in agitation at the overly eager female voice on the other end of the phone line. Humans were, to him, no more than a source for food and sex, and to have his occasional dinner call his personal line irritated him to no end.

"You got her on the plane?"

"I did. It wasn't easy to convince her to go." He could hear the frown in Jessie Spencer's voice. Really, it had been too perfect to discover that his descendant's friend had a serious fascination for the occult. The vampire he had sent to gather information on Isla had only had to do some gentle convincing for Jessie to agree to a consensual bite.

After that she had been hooked, an addict desperate for her next fix. She would have done anything for an invitation to come live on Vampire Island—and that included setting up the woman who had once been her best friend.

"This number was given to you for use if, and only if, you had difficulties getting Isla on her way to the island." Lucian layered his voice with steel. "I do not understand why you are calling. I am not pleased."

There was a momentary silence, followed by panic so rich that he could almost smell it. "I'm sorry, sir. Truly. I…I just wanted to make sure that everything else was still in place. You know…about me moving to the island."

Lucian hissed out a breath.

He needed the blood of his descendant, and this woman had delivered Isla to the island. In return, he had promised her residence.

"I gave you my word, and it will be honored." Having lost interest in the conversation, he turned his attention to the text that had just come through on his cell phone. It was from Gaspar, the man he had assigned to be the woman's shadow for the time it took to woo her to his side.

He would take blood by force, if need be, but it was so much sweeter when the human came willingly. And he had been waiting a very long time for this blood.

Subject has arrived.

This was all that Gaspar wrote, but Lucian's lips curled into a smile. He cut off the stammering woman on the other end of the phone.

"Details will be sent soon. Do not call here again." Standing as he hung up the private line, Lucian paced to the window of his office, staring out at the sunshine that he no longer enjoyed. The legend of vampires burning in the sun was nonsense, of course, but he found that it worsened his headaches.

Yes, he couldn't wait to taste Miss Isla Miller's blood. It couldn't come soon enough.

Chapter 2

Isla had grown up in a wealthy suburban neighborhood in a large house with a manicured lawn. Even still, the small bungalow to which she had been assigned made her jaw drop.

"This is our most exclusive bungalow." Gaspar sounded proud as he waited for Isla to catch up. She didn't seem able to keep up with his freakishly quick pace. Slapping one hand on the side of the building, she leaned against the wood as she tried to capture her breath.

"It's...lovely." She knew that she seemed like a complete rube, but Isla couldn't help looking around her with wide eyes. The bungalow was larger than her entire apartment at home—an apartment that her mother and sisters lifted their noses at—and was built right *over* the water. She swallowed thickly, regarding the stilts that, though they appeared sturdy enough, had the opening credits of *Jaws* running through her head.

"You have not seen the inside yet." With a wide smile, Gaspar opened the door wide and ushered Isla inside. As Gaspar pointed out the Egyptian-cotton sheets, the Jacuzzi bath overlooking the ocean and the breathtaking view of the horizon, Isla felt something uncomfortable skitter over her skin. Her attention had been caught by the thick panel of glass in the floor that allowed her to see the dark water beneath the structure.

"Breathtaking, is it not?" Isla started when Gaspar spoke from right behind her. She had thought he was across the room. She turned and found him staring into the depths of the water beneath their feet, entranced.

"How thick is this glass?" She could hear the nerves in her words, and Gaspar's soft chuckle and reassuring smile did nothing to alleviate the sensation of being... well, exposed was the best thing that she could think of.

She imagined that the glass had been put in place as a novelty, for visitors to watch schools of tropical fish and to admire the jewel-toned waters of Tahiti. She couldn't help but think, however, that the opposite could be true, too—that something from beneath could be watching *her*.

Isla shuddered lightly, then reprimanded herself for her overly active imagination. She looked up to find Gaspar's pale blue eyes trained on her intently. He seemed to be searching for...something, but she couldn't tell what.

"You are different than most." At Gaspar's words, Isla shifted uncomfortably. "Most see nothing but the beauty of an island such as this. They do not recognize the danger beneath such beauty."

"Right." What was she supposed to say to that? "Is there someplace where I can get some lunch maybe?"

Isla was feeling peckish after her long day of travel, and she grabbed at the opportunity to distract her intent concierge. "Nothing fancy. Just a sandwich or something is fine."

Gaspar still seemed fixated on her. His head was cocked to the side as he examined her, and Isla swallowed thickly, not sure what to say or do.

"I will have an assortment of lunch foods delivered to the suite." An emotion that Isla couldn't quite identify flickered over the man's face, but then it was gone before she could study it further. If she had to label it, she would have said that he was perhaps a bit sad.

"Thank you." The thought of staying in the bungalow, however exposed she felt there, was highly preferable to leaving and exploring the grounds by herself.

Irritation washed over her skin, and it was all directed at herself. The whole purpose of accepting this trip was to nudge her way out of her comfort zone, yet here she was, thwarting her own efforts.

"That's very kind of you, but I think I'll take a walk and explore a bit." Another expression that she couldn't quite interpret flickered over the man's face.

"As you wish, Miss Miller. You will find a small sandwich bar by the pool." Gaspar nodded, then hesitated, seeming on the edge of saying something that he wasn't sure he should say.

"Thanks, Gaspar." After assuring him that she had her pager in hand, she followed him back out into the sunlight. He was silent as he walked her to the end of the dock, speaking only when they were about to part ways.

"The owners of the resort prefer that guests stay within the grounds. Liability issues, you know." Isla nodded in agreement, distracted by her new surroundings. When her concierge snapped her name she looked toward him, and she was startled to find that his expression was deadly serious.

"Whatever you do, Miss Miller, please be careful. The owner of the suite would be most displeased should anything happen to you."

Isla decided that her adventurous new attitude had perhaps been a bad idea.

Sucking nervously at the remains of her watered-down lemonade, she felt conspicuous. Perhaps there was some Tahitian custom that she was unaware of. Why else would the others who had gathered around the pool in the space of time she'd been there be so obviously interested in her?

Even the ones who were obviously couples seemed interested in her. One woman had even winked when she'd caught Isla's eye.

All of the unexpected attention made Isla feel as though she were caught in a dream, one of the ones in which she was naked in public and surrounded by mocking people. These people, however, weren't mocking her. No, many seemed…attracted, for lack of a better word. And that, she reminded herself as she got off her lounge chair and moved away from the pool, was ridiculous.

"Oh!" Having turned back quickly to see if she was still the subject of curiosity, Isla found her way blocked by a wall of solid flesh. Fright shuddered through her as she shrieked and turned around.

Cursing herself for her rudeness, she shook the nerves away.

"Oh, I'm so sorry. I'm so clumsy." Stepping back to

smooth her dress, Isla found herself looking up at one of the most handsome men that she had ever seen—and that included Mr. McConaughey himself.

The man nodded, saying nothing, and Isla swallowed around a suddenly dry throat. Gorgeous as he was, he was looking at her as if he was a predator and she was his next meal.

Despite that, she felt an attraction tug at her, one more intense than anything she had ever felt.

"Is everyone here gorgeous?" She didn't realize that she had said the words aloud until the ghost of a smirk appeared on the man's lips. She cringed and looked at her toes, which she had painted bright coral for the trip.

She couldn't resist looking back up at the man. And then there it was, that feeling that she had been waiting for so long. That tug, right in the depths of her belly.

Desire. Something about him was…magnetic.

He wasn't at all the type of man that she usually gave a second glance to. He was tall, over six feet if her guess was correct, and his muscles pressed against pale skin. His hair was raven dark, a mess of silky curls, and the eyes that regarded her with something dangerous in their depths were the color of a cappuccino.

More than that, those muscled arms of his were painted with intricate, sapphire-blue tattoos, something that she had never particularly cared for before. She found the ink fascinating, however, and the small silver studs that winked on his earlobes intrigued her, too.

"Ahem." The man still hadn't spoken, but he was watching her intently, just as people by the pool had. His attention, however, didn't set her on edge or make her want to flee.

No, instead she had to resist the urge to jump straight into his arms.

"I...I'm Isla." When in Rome, and all that.

The man blinked, as if she had surprised him, though he swallowed down the emotion quickly.

He seemed skilled at presenting an expressionless face.

"My name is Sloane Goldhawk." Narrowing his eyes, he cocked his head to one side as he studied her as if he were trying to figure something out. "I am the mechanic on the island."

"It's—it's nice to meet you." She held out her hand, and the man stared at it like he'd never seen the gesture before, so she quickly pulled it back. Though she'd had limited interactions with mechanics—she rode the subway to work—something about the information didn't jive with what she saw in front of her.

He seemed...powerful. Charismatic. Someone who should be covering his tattoos with a business suit every morning before heading to work to run his international corporation.

"Are you settling in all right?" Isla looked up at Sloane with wide eyes.

"How did you know I'd just arrived?"

That whisper of a smile appeared on Sloane's lips again, and he leaned in, just an inch, but it was enough to set Isla's pulse skittering through her veins.

"I was working on the boat that was supposed to pick you up from the airport." She inhaled deeply without thinking about it. Sloane smelled of an exotic and delicious mix of herbs and soap.

"Also, we don't have many reservations this week. It's a small resort. It would be hard to miss you." Isla looked up, dazed, as Sloane drew back, amusement fully visible on his face by this point.

"Oh." That must have been why she'd gotten so much attention at the pool—hers was a fresh face.

At that moment, she couldn't have cared less. Sloane was...teasing her?

Maybe even flirting with her?

Isla bit her lower lip, inhaling sharply. No. No way was this gorgeous man attracted to her. He was an employee of the island.... It was probably part of his contract, to make the female guests feel special.

She watched as his stare tracked over cheeks that she knew were flushed and eyes that she could tell were wide with the beginnings of a crush.

She felt like an idiot.

"Um. It's nice to meet you, Sloane. I...I'm going to go finish my walk now." Cheeks burning, Isla nodded awkwardly, then cast her eyes to the ground as she hurried away.

Sloane watched as the petite woman hurried down the tiled path to the gates of the resort. Though she seemed as if she couldn't wait to be outside the resort, she paused and looked around guiltily before she slipped out of the grounds.

Sloane wrestled for a long moment with feelings that he didn't want to have. Clearly she didn't care that it wasn't safe for the humans on the island to venture off the resort property—not only was the rest of the island a tangle of wild, overgrown jungle, exotic wild animals and all, but the verdant foliage hid the occasional rogue vampire, one who had tired of Lucian's rules and who had fled the confines of the resort to make it on their own. These rogues subsisted almost entirely on animal blood, and an unaware human would make for a celebratory treat for any of them.

Or perhaps the seemingly shy, mild-mannered woman was simply overwhelmed by the vast amount of attention that she was attracting and wanted some room to breathe.

Still...why should he care? No matter what her demeanor seemed to suggest, if she was on the island, she had to have some knowledge of the vampire population that inhabited it. Those same vampires were responsible for her well-being, not him.

Although there was something...different...about this human. It started with her smell, which, while delicious, held a note of something that he had never before smelled on a human.

It didn't matter, he reminded himself. He was done with humans. They were too fragile, their lives too easily lost.

Or turned, and the turning could be yet another way to break them. He shuddered at the memory of Ana. The sweet human he had known had died in the change, leaving behind a feral animal who wouldn't be controlled.

The past was in the past, he reminded himself. He needed to focus on the present. He knew better now.

Sloane watched as Isla inhaled a deep breath that he heard even from where he stood, nearly the length of a football field away. She seemed to brighten, away from the scrutiny of others, and though he was cursing himself for having noticed her at all, he found her shyness intriguing.

Alluring.

With a muttered curse, Sloane trudged after her, slowing his pace to that of a human's.

Even if she was the kind of woman who didn't believe in the paranormal, this resort didn't seem like the kind of place that she would choose to vacation in. Simply put, there was more to her, to her story, than met the eye.

And she clearly needed some time alone. Sloane sighed heavily as he slipped out the gates behind her. She walked blithely along ahead of him, growing more sure with every step. She moved with a grace that he had never before seen in a human. Sloane reminded himself that it was none of his business what the woman did—none of his business if she wanted to wander off into the depths of the jungle. He shouldn't be concerned that, as she'd eaten her sandwich by the pool, the vampires just waking from their day's sleep had been inhaling the tropical scent of her blood and looking at her like she was dinner. He shouldn't have cared that the human fangers had eyed her suspiciously, jealous of their paranormal attachments.

Something about the woman pulled at him, and it was more than her fresh beauty or the alluring scent that wafted off her skin. Maybe it was the human fragility that he saw.

Maybe he so badly felt the urge to protect her because he hadn't been able to protect Sully from his ultimate death. Hadn't been able to protect Ana from the insanity that had swallowed her. And wouldn't a shrink have a field day with that little bit of introspection.

"Get with it, Goldhawk." Sloane scowled at himself as he followed Isla through what had possibly, maybe, once been a path and now was long overgrown.

He was a vampire. He was, by nature, supposed to be hedonistic, interested only in things that he wanted and needed. Right now he wanted to keep an eye on the attractive human.

Why did he need to ponder it beyond that?

He heard the water before he saw it. He smelled the minerals that saturated the liquid, a scent that reminded him of his home—his original, human home—in what was now the Rocky Mountains in Canada. Breathing it deep into lungs that no longer needed air, Sloane observed Isla's obvious pleasure in the discovery of the small tropical waterfall, the one that had carved a small, cool pool out of the rock below it.

"Oh!" He couldn't help but smile at the small exclamation of delight that slipped from her rosy lips. Thinking to keep an eye on her while she sat by the small pool, he bent his knees in preparation, then jumped up to the top of one of the trees that bordered the small pool. He settled into a crouch on an outstretched branch, his movements barely disturbing the heavy, waxy leaves.

He refused to ponder the fact that, deep down, he knew he was watching her to make certain she stayed safe out here in the wild. He could try to convince himself that it was simply because he liked to look at her—liked to watch the beat of her pulse against the tissue-thin skin at the base of her jaw—but it was a lie.

Having settled himself high up in the tree, where he could see approaching threats but where Isla could not see him, Sloane looked back to Isla.

When he saw what she was doing, he nearly fell out of the tree, vampire athleticism and all.

"Damn." He had assumed that shy Isla would simply sit by the pool, contemplating the crystal depths as she savored the solitude that she had so clearly craved.

He had been wrong.

While he had been arguing with himself, the woman he had pegged as reserved had slipped her sundress over her shoulders and down, where it now pooled around her ankles. Now she stood in a skin-colored strapless bra and bikini panties that gave the impression that she was completely naked.

Sloane felt his fangs begin to slowly descend from his gums as his eyes raked over the expanse of skin she had bared. It put him in mind of roses and cream, the pale expanse already flushed from exposure to the sun.

It was smooth and perfect and made him want to take a taste.

Her hands fluttered at her sides nervously as she looked around her, and Sloane found it enticing that she was so nervous, so self-conscious, even though she was completely alone. At least as far as she knew.

"Man." He watched as she tentatively stepped toward the pool that had been carved out of the slick rock, dipping her toes before diving straight in, as he would have done. He had ample time to gaze upon the ripe curves that made up her small body—the curvy legs, the swell of her hips, the slim waist, the delicious mounds of her breasts.

"Fuck." Sloane's cock hardened painfully when, at the last moment, Isla reached behind her back and quickly unhooked her bra. She flung it behind her as she slipped into the pool, which was surprisingly deep.

He had a quick but vivid impression of full, plump breasts with nipples the color of rose petals.

This wasn't good. Swallowing thickly, Sloane closed

his eyes against the vision of Isla rising back out of the water, the clear liquid coursing in streams over her slender shoulders and down into the crevice between those heavy breasts.

The lust riding him wasn't normal. And with lust came the need to feed, to mark her as his own so that no one else would touch her.

He had no delusions about what would happen to him if he marked a human so pretty that she obviously had to be for Lucian.

He would be dead. And likely, so would she. When Isla lay back in the water, letting it buoy her weight as she floated on her back, he groaned.

Her entire frame was bared to his gaze, and for the first time in memory he found that desire overruled his thirst. He wanted to sheath himself inside of her, wanted to mark her with his scent.

The voice telling him that he couldn't was growing quieter and quieter, fading away into the recesses of his mind.

So wrapped up was he in the vision before him that he didn't immediately snap to attention when the scent crossed his consciousness. He turned his head to the side, not sure if he had sensed what he thought he had.

Yes…there it was. The vinegar smell unique to vampires. It was a scent he was well familiar with, yet this one seemed…different. Stronger than it should have been when the vampire wasn't yet close enough for him to hear.

The only thing that Sloane could think of was that there were two vampires prowling around Isla as she swam. But rogue vampires rarely traveled together.

His fangs descended the rest of the way in a heated

rush, and possessiveness washed away the lust. One or two, it didn't matter. He was feeling protective of Isla, and although he didn't know who—or how many—vampires were stalking her, he found that he didn't care. The sudden invasion, right while he was lusting after the woman, turned a switch in his brain and he growled, determined to protect what his instincts decided was his.

Though he heard nothing, the scent failed to strengthen, which told him that the intruder had heard his growl and had stopped moving. He growled again, low, an animalistic sound that told the other vampire that this area was his territory…and that everything in the territory was his.

He would pay later for declaring this strange woman as his own—that much he knew even through the impulse-driven fog of his mind. But he couldn't seem to help himself, an alpha animal who had found his mate.

Sloane checked to make sure that Isla was still swimming in the pool below, blissfully unaware of any threat. Bunching his muscles, he leaped to the ground like a wildcat, landing in a crouch.

The dry scent of the other vampire began to fade. The other was drawing back. Sloane felt the adrenaline rush into his stagnant blood, the thrill of having won a face-off, but it was twined tightly with a mix of emotions that he did not want to feel.

What had he just done?

Chapter 3

Sloane let himself look at Isla one last time. She was standing in the pool now, the cool water kissing her rosy nipples, forcing them to sharp points. Despite what had just happened, he felt his cock again begin to rise, thickening with the almost desperate lust of a second erection.

He needed to get her the hell out of the water and back to the resort, where he could avoid her for the rest of her stay. But his instincts and the hormones that still shot through his body wanted him to slide into the water with her and tear the last tiny scrap of fabric from her body. He wanted, more than he'd ever wanted anything, to hilt inside of her in one hard thrust, at the same time sinking his fangs into the delicate pulse at her neck, drinking from that ambrosial mix that smelled of mangoes and copper.

Drinking until all of his hungers had been sated.

With a will that he hadn't needed to put to use since his time on the battlefields of World War II, Sloane swallowed down his instincts, his need. Retracting his fangs before he was ready was painful, but he had no choice.

He made sure to make a lot of human noise as he stalked through the last bit of undergrowth toward Isla to let her know someone was approaching.

"Stop!" Isla's voice was full of nerves, and she whirled in the water to face him, her hands clutched protectively in front of her naked breasts. "I'm…I'm not dressed. Please, just give me a minute."

He watched a spark in her eyes appear when she laid eyes on him, recognizing him. He heard her pulse quicken and wished that he hadn't.

She wasn't immune to him. She felt the same heat that he did.

"It's you." Relief was evident in her voice, and Sloane shook his head at her naiveté. She had met him all of once, and he knew better than anyone that he was not a creature to be trusted. "I'm so silly. I'm…I'm skinny-dipping. Please, just turn around. Let me get my clothes on."

Isla waded to the rock where her bra and dress lay. He could smell the cotton scent that had been teased out by the sun.

She faltered when he deliberately turned the corners of his lips up in a feral grin.

"What are you doing, running off outside the gates of the resort?" Stalking to where she blinked up at him from the water, he bent at the waist and clasped his hands under each elbow. "Didn't anyone tell you that guests of the resort are supposed to stay on the grounds?"

"What—" Isla let out a sound of indignation as Sloane easily lifted her by the elbows, hauling her from the water.

He set her down on the rock abruptly, squashing the need to pull her to him, to consume her lips, to wrap those shapely legs around his waist.

He schooled his face in a scowl, trying to look menacing.

"What the hell do you think you're doing?" Her voice vibrated with temper. Instead of trembling in front of him, she surprised him yet again, glowering up at him, anger bringing her blood to the surface of all of that luscious, naked skin.

"This is the jungle, sweetie." Sloane tried to sound condescending. The way that she narrowed her eyes at him told him that he had succeeded. He heard the grating sound of her teeth scraping together as, with one arm still clasped over her naked breasts, she bent at the waist and scrabbled for her sundress.

Forgoing the bra, she pulled the thin cotton over her head. He didn't have the heart to tell her that the thin fabric clinging to her damp skin was an even more erotic sight than her naked flesh had been.

"Thank you ever so much for pointing that out." Well, damn if the woman he had pegged as meek and mild didn't have a fiery temper to match her hair.

He supposed that it was contrary of him to find her anger arousing, but he did. At the same time, he could have shaken her for her thoughtlessness.

"You're not listening." Bending until his face was right in hers, Sloane caught her stare with his own, making sure that she was paying attention. "Those gates around the resort? They're there for a reason. Tahiti is beautiful, sweetie, but beauty often hides something sinister."

"I'm sorry." Obviously uncomfortable, she crossed her arms over her torso, running her hands up and down her upper arms. "Is that why you're here? To retrieve me? Am I in trouble?"

Sloane smelled the champagne fizz of adrenaline as her pulse stuttered, then began to beat again, double time. She was nervous. *He* made her nervous.

Part of him hated that, and the other half was simply glad that she was finally paying attention.

"I saw you leave the grounds. I followed you because I wanted to make sure you were safe." This wasn't a lie, though he still didn't understand what, exactly, had drawn him to her from the beginning.

"Why do you care?" Hands on her hips, Isla didn't retreat, even though he could sense the tiny trembles that ran through her small frame. She stared right back at him, and the predator inside of him recognized its equal. "For that matter, if you saw me, why did you let me leave?"

"You seemed like you needed some time alone. You've clearly had a long day, and you seem like you're maybe a little bit out of your element." The fire in Isla's eyes flickered and then was banked as she seemed to think through what he said. He knew that he had hit home, but it didn't bring him any closer to understanding her.

"Thank you, then." Isla ducked her head, and the heavy curtain of her damp, tangled hair hid her face, but he heard that irregular murmur in her heartbeat again. He watched, still wondering what the hell it was about the woman that he found so damn enticing, as she slipped her damp feet into her leather sandals. Decent again, she looked up at him almost shyly, tucking a long strand behind her ear.

"Taking a trip like this is not something I would normally do. My friend was supposed to go, but at the last minute she couldn't. She offered the trip to me, and I…I guess I'm trying to prove a point to myself." Sloane schooled his face into a mask of indifference. Her revelation had shed a whole new light on his understanding of her situation.

He would have bet his boat that she wasn't a fanger. He also knew that, if her friend had secured a trip here, that same friend likely *was*.

"Is stripping naked in the middle of the jungle not something you would normally do either?" His voice was wry, and he deliberately kept what he was thinking out of it. He would sort through that later. Still, he couldn't help but be amused. Isla seemed to have a much different image of herself than what he saw in the woman in front of him.

Isla flushed, and she looked down at the ground. He could see the beginnings of a smirk forming at the corners of her lips, however, and he knew that she was proud of herself.

"Come on." He nudged gently at the small of her back. The sensation of heat that washed from her warmer skin into his own was addictive. He wanted to press against her, skin to skin, and experience the same thing all over. "Let's get you back to the resort. I wasn't kidding—it's not safe out here."

Clearly uneasy, Isla looked around. "I did some research before I came." Her words were mumbled as she followed him back to what could remotely pass for a path. "I thought that the Tahitian islands had very few natural predators. Other than those mythical vampires."

"Very few doesn't mean none." Sloane ignored her comment and sniffed the air around them, searching for that dry smell of vampire again. He kept his mouth shut about the not-so-natural predators that hunted the island, certain that that knowledge would scare the wits from Isla.

"Why did your friend decide on Ile de Nuit?" Sloane tried to make the question sound casual as they walked.

Isla looked around her nervously, probably on the alert for the dangers that Sloane had mentioned. He wasn't entirely opposed to the fact that she stayed closer to him than she likely would have had she felt safe.

It was good for her to be on edge. He was now suspecting that the woman truly had no idea what she had gotten herself into.

"When she told me about the legends, she said that she found the local history behind it fascinating." They walked through a shaft of sunlight that had speared through a gap in the canopy of foliage, and Sloane found himself fascinated by the play of gold on the red of her hair. "Jessie's kind of quirky that way. I know her from work—I'm a paralegal. She's this buttoned-up lawyer by day, wild child by night. She's fascinated by all things paranormal and was so excited about this trip. She didn't buy travel insurance. Since she was super disappointed that she couldn't come, and she couldn't get a refund anyway, she insisted that I take her place. And I needed to get away. I mean, I thought that it would be good for me to go."

Sloane noticed the slip of the tongue and wondered what was haunting her so badly that she would go on someone else's vacation. But if he had only had suspicions a few minutes ago, he was now certain.

Isla Miller had no idea that Ile de Nuit was really inhabited by vampires.

Isla was mortified. Not only had she acted recklessly when she set off for her walk in the jungle, but the one time that she had cast caution away and done something spontaneous, she had been caught red-handed.

The sun had been so warm, the air so moist and welcoming, that she had simply felt the urge to feel it on her skin…on all of her skin. She'd thought that she was completely alone, so what was the harm in it?

Now she had no idea what to do or to say. The gorgeous man she had tried to flirt with, until she'd gotten completely tongue-tied, had been kind enough to make certain that she hadn't come to harm, and for his effort she'd treated him to a peep show that he couldn't possibly have wanted.

Looking down at the sundress that was now clinging to her sweaty, still-wet skin and to the bra that was wadded up in her right hand, she grimaced.

She would be avoiding the man as best she could for the rest of her trip. For heaven's sake, it was just so typical of her that she couldn't even do a vacation properly.

"Don't be so hard on yourself." Isla looked over at the simply spoken words to find Sloane studying her as he walked. His steps were sure and steady on the uneven ground, even though he was looking at her and not at where he was going.

If she'd tried to do the same, she would have wound up flat on her face.

"Oh, it's nothing." She waved her hand in the air as if she was dismissing the entire episode, but she knew very well that she hadn't.

The only one in a family of overachievers, one whose job as a paralegal had been viewed as the easy road when she could have been a lawyer, the inferiority complex was lodged deeply in her psyche. Nothing she did ever felt quite good enough.

Not that she was about to tell that to the gorgeous stranger.

"Isla. Look at me." She did and tripped as soon as her eyes locked with his. Man, but he was gorgeous. And nice.

So obviously he wouldn't be attracted to her. Men like that never were.

"You clearly didn't know how serious the owners are about resort guests not leaving the grounds." His expression darkened, and Isla shivered a bit. She wasn't afraid of him—which was strange because there were days when she was afraid of her own shadow. Still, she didn't want to be on the receiving end of that look, ever.

"It was stupid." She wiped the palm of her empty hand on the skirt of her dress. The humidity was like a wet blanket, heavy and suffocating and above all wet.

The sounds of the jungle went silent in the blink of an eye, causing that humidity to almost vibrate in the thick air. Isla registered the change in noise only a second before Sloane growled—actually growled. Moving quickly, he pressed Isla behind him.

She froze. "What's wrong?" Sloane was looking

around them quickly, as if assessing the situation for danger.

Isla's stomach sank. If her ill-advised walk got them both in trouble, she would never forgive herself.

Sloane growled again, and Isla blinked at the hard muscles of the man's back. The sound was so animal-istic, so primal, it made heat flood through her...right through her. It was a totally inappropriate response to the situation, but she found that she liked the sensation of being protected.

A man stepped out of the foliage and onto the path in front of them, as if he had materialized from thin air. Beneath the fingers that she discovered were clenched into the muscles of his back Isla felt Sloane's tension go from full throttle to simply being on alert.

"Marcus." Sloane still sounded wary, and Isla wasn't sure why. She had seen this man briefly already, stand-ing on the end of the dock when she had arrived. Like nearly everyone else she had seen so far that day, he was attractive, with creamy skin and neat gold hair.

Despite the heat and humidity, he wore a tidy black suit, one entirely unsuitable for walking around the jungle.

Isla found it incredibly strange that he didn't seem to be affected by the heat at all—his suit was unwrin-kled, starched even, and everything on him was tidy. It made her feel sloppy in comparison, but then, she al-ways felt as though she'd been thrown together rather than neatly organized.

"Sloane." The two men eyed each other warily, and Isla was put in mind of two lions facing off over a fresh kill. Then the man Sloane had called Marcus turned to look at her, and her heart jumped as she found herself on the receiving end of his intense stare.

"I was informed that a resort guest had wandered off the property." Marcus smiled at her, but Isla noticed that the pleasant expression didn't quite reach his pale eyes. "I have been searching for you, Miss Miller, to make certain that you were okay."

"I saw her leave. I've been with her the entire time." Isla had opened her mouth to speak, but Sloane did so before she could, the growl still evident in his voice. What was wrong with him? The other man had simply done the same thing that he had—namely, tried to save her from her own stupidity.

"If you two are quite done." Her words were quiet, and when both men turned to stare at her, she felt herself shiver with nerves. Swallowing thickly, she lifted her chin with more bravado than she felt.

"I don't need to be spoken for." Sloane scowled, and though her instinct was to hush, she continued, "I'm sorry I broke the rules—I wasn't trying to be troublesome. It was thoughtless. Now, if you don't mind, I'd like to get back to the resort and try to enjoy at least part of my vacation." Head held high, she marched off in the direction of the resort.

At least she hoped it was the direction. Because neither man stopped her, she figured that she was okay.

She felt their stares boring into her back as she went.

It took fifteen long minutes to reach the gates of the resort from which she had so easily slipped out not more than an hour earlier. The return trip was much less pleasant than the walk there had been—she was hurrying, for one thing, instead of strolling, and the extra exertion made her perspire and wish desperately for a huge glass of ice water. Also, gone was the pleasant sensation of freedom, replaced by the nagging feelings of self-doubt twined with confusing feelings about Sloane…feelings that she had no business having at all.

"Stop it." Inhaling deeply as she placed a hand on the wrought-iron gate, Isla tried to shake the negative feelings away.

Scowling to herself, Isla decided that she was going to go back to her bungalow, cover up the creepy window in the floor and regroup. Maybe she would take a bath in that beautiful, large tub and then she would go to bed.

Surely in the morning things would be better.

Slipping through the gate, Isla turned to close it again behind her. She screeched and jumped when she found Sloane standing right behind her.

"What the hell are you doing?" Placing a hand over her skittering heart, she tried to catch the breath that had been startled right out of her. "Why are you following me?"

Sloane merely raised an eyebrow, though he didn't look happy. "I'm making sure that you get back safely." If she didn't know that he was a stranger, she would have thought that he was upset with her attitude toward him.

"Well, I'm back. Thank you." Tired of it all, Isla wiped the sweat from her forehead with the back of her hand. She was tired. She wanted that bath and some sleep. "Next time I decide to go skinny-dipping in the jungle, I'll let you know first so that you can talk me out of it."

Suddenly near tears, frustration slicing through her veins like razors, Isla stalked off in the direction of her bungalow. She paused and turned back when she heard Sloane call her name.

"Skinny-dipping means that you're completely naked." His glower melted into a lazy, nearly cocky grin, and he swept his eyes up her and then back down, leaving her gaping and with no way to interpret the action except for what it was.

"And if you're going to be completely naked then yes, please do let me know."

Sloane enjoyed the flush that spread over Isla's skin as she realized that he was flirting with her. Seemingly at a loss for words, she spun on her heel and marched off.

The woman had horrible self-esteem, and he couldn't imagine why. She was beautiful, funny and bright, if a little naive. He had meant only to coax her from her bad mood, which he knew was partially, if not entirely, his fault.

But he knew that he had only spoken the truth. The thought of being near a fully naked Isla made him groan softly with need.

He shook his head, trying to rid himself of the haunting visual. He had other things to think about.

Had Marcus been telling the truth when he'd said that he was in the woods looking for Isla? As Lucian's right-hand man, it was entirely plausible.

Equally possible, though, was that Marcus had been the vampire he had warned away from Isla. And if that was the case, then Sloane could be in a world of trouble.

Or maybe he wouldn't be. He had no idea why her friend had been invited to the island by Lucian, nor why the vampire had allowed Isla to take Jessie's place. The ancient vampire usually kept those who he brought on his personal whims close by, and he hadn't yet seemed to show any interest in Isla at all.

The part of the beast inside him that had decided that Isla was his roared at the thought of Lucian even looking at her, and Sloane groaned at the realization. She had been invited there for a purpose, that much was certain, and because of that he should stay away. But the primitive part of him now viewed her as his alone, which made staying away very difficult indeed. His instincts screamed at him to follow her, to make sure that she got to her bungalow safely.

He couldn't. She wasn't his. And he had sworn off entanglements with humans not six months earlier. Sloane's heart clenched in his chest at the memory of Sully, who had been twenty-two when they had met and the one friend in whom Sloane had been able to share his true nature. That friend had died at the age of ninety-three, gray and frail and so utterly human that it broke Sloane's heart.

No. He couldn't go through that again. Moreover, he wouldn't. Not only was it his grief that he was thinking of, but also that of any human he would be involved with romantically.

How would it feel to age when your lover stayed frozen at thirty-four, before the prime of his life had even hit him? It was a disastrous situation to imagine all around.

With more effort than he could recall ever making, Sloane turned deliberately away from the direction Isla had gone. It was like walking through quicksand, but he did it.

He walked away.

* * *

"The woman is back on resort property." On the other end of Lucian's phone, Marcus sounded weary. "She is safe. She was with Goldhawk."

"Goldhawk?" Lucian scowled, even as his mind began to turn over how he could work that to his advantage. The only reason that Goldhawk had been allowed to live on the island without joining the clan was because they had a history. The fact that Goldhawk wasn't aware of that shared history, and wouldn't see his revenge coming, made Lucian's plans all the sweeter.

"There's more. Goldhawk scented me, and he warned me off." Lucian's eyebrows rose in surprise, and then he began to laugh, the sound mirthless even though he was pleased.

This was too perfect. Sloane Goldhawk had just tied everything up in a neat bow and delivered it right into his lap.

"He warned you off Isla Miller?" That meant that the beast inside of Sloane had claimed Isla as his own. That made two women for whom they had both had feelings. As Lucian thought of Ana, and of how Sloane had broken the once-sweet beauty, fury began to haze his vision with red.

Yes, it was too bad for Sloane that Lucian would win this round. And Sloane would never see it coming.

Chapter 4

As Isla's ancient laptop booted up, she started the water for her bath. Wishing for some kind of fruity, girly bubble bath, Isla logged on to the resort's wireless network and opened up her email. She wasn't expecting anything in her in-box besides an email from Jessie, nagging her for not checking in yet.

That email from her friend was surprisingly not there, but one from her mother was. Her mother harbored none of the same warm feelings toward Isla that Jessie did, so Isla wasn't too excited to see the waiting message.

"Crap." Isla was tempted to just delete the message without reading it—it was only going to make her feel bad—but she couldn't just disown her sisters and ignore her mother.

The email was a response to the phone message that Isla had left before she had left, telling her mother where she would be and what she would be doing. The email was short, to the point and hurt like hell.

Isla,
I am very disappointed that you have decided to run off to some tropical island without discussing it with me first. More, I am appalled that you have chosen a destination called *Vampire Island.* Vampires? Isla, you know how I feel about this. It isn't good for you to socialize with people who are fascinated with those things.

I want you to come home right now. If you need a vacation, surely we can find a more suitable spot.
Mother
PS: How can you afford a holiday in Tahiti right now? I hope you aren't dealing drugs.

Isla barked out a laugh that sounded strangely, even to her ears, like a wail. Setting her laptop down gingerly on the bathroom counter, she then turned off the faucet to the tub with a hard wrench of her wrists and stared at the small drip that remained, disturbing the clear and otherwise smooth surface of the liquid.

She didn't know why these kinds of interactions with her mother still upset her. They were nothing new, after all—they'd been occurring ever since Isla's teen years, when she hadn't shown the wicked intelligence and drive of her two sisters, one of whom was a plastic surgeon, the other an astrophysicist. Isla's mother— a single mother since the death of Isla's father nearly twenty years earlier—was a hugely successful prosecutor, and her attitude to her least impressive daughter was only slightly different than it was in the courtroom.

Isla restrained the urge to throw the laptop into the bath or, better yet, right into the ocean right beneath her feet. Every bad feeling that she'd ever had about herself came swimming to the surface as her mother's words circled through her brain.

But an image of Sloane—tall, tasty Sloane—flashed through her memory, and with it came a wave of heat. He had flirted with her—if she went out on a limb, she would even say that he wanted her. And because she found that she wanted him right back, that was actually quite a spectacular aspect of her trip right there.

If she went home, she would lose the chance to explore that.

If she stayed here, would she explore it anyway?

Suddenly Isla's feelings shifted from guilt to anger—anger at herself for letting her mother make her feel this way yet again, and anger at her mother for doing this to her.

Before she lost her nerve, Isla swung her feet out of the tub. Maybe she'd gotten too much sun that day, but she was feeling…different. Sexy. Braver. She had no idea where the feelings had come from, but she was going to follow through with them while she still felt bold enough to follow through.

Hastily she brushed her teeth and ran a comb through the long tangles of her hair. Flinging open her suitcase, she pulled out a fresh sundress and tugged it over her head, deciding to forgo any underwear at all.

She was going to be brave and seduce Sloane Goldhawk into a holiday fling—or at the very least a hot one-night stand. What did she have to lose?

Slipping her feet into rubber flip-flops, Isla flung open the door of her bungalow and blinked. It was now full night, the dock lit with torches. In the distance she could see the resort bustling with far more activity than it had been earlier in the day.

Instead of shrinking from it, she found it comforting. She could hide among the crowd rather than feeling singled out as she had that afternoon.

At the point where the dock met the water she met Gaspar. He held a bucket of ice and a bottle of what appeared to be champagne.

"Just the lovely guest that I was looking for," he said with that same flirtatious smile.

Half of her felt the need to acquiesce, to follow Gaspar back to her accommodations and accept the wine with a polite smile and whatever conversation was needed to get him out of her hair. The other half was feeling a bit wild. That overwhelming need to bare her teeth again overcame her, and she actually did it. She hissed.

Even without the champagne, she felt drunk on her boldness and smiled widely, aggressively, at the man, who seemed a bit taken aback by the change in her attitude.

"May I?" Gaspar didn't seem overly pleased to do so, but he passed the bucket and bottle into Isla's extended arms. The chill of metal caused gooseflesh to prickle her skin.

With a nod of thanks, she walked as fast as she could in the direction of the beach, toward the lone houseboat that she could see anchored in the distance. Her gut told her that that was where Sloane lived.

Nerves skittered through her frame as the reality of what she was about to do hit her. She clutched the bottle of wine ever more tightly to her chest as she walked.

She had a feeling that she was going to need it.

* * *

"She hissed at you?" This was music to Lucian's ears. Gaspar babbled on, but Lucian only half listened.

He had already known, but the knowledge that Isla's vampire blood was coming to the fore in this environment thrilled him.

It was rare for a vampire to bear young. When they did, their offspring all carried their vampire heritage in their blood. But it was rare—very, very rare—for a vampire to be born rather than made.

Still, it happened. Isla was one, and all she needed was a vampire's bite to activate the rest of her powers in her blood, locked as they were beneath her human DNA.

Born vampires were stronger, faster. Better. And this one carried his genes within her. He needed her blood to become well again.

"That will be all, Gaspar." He pressed a button on his phone, and a buzzer sounded. Moments later a naked young man entered his office, his hands bound behind his back. His skin was pale, littered with red scars from bites.

His eyes, when he looked at Lucian, spoke of his hunger to be fed on.

"Come here, boy." Hunger and arousal stirred in Lucian's gut. He wanted to celebrate the news that Gaspar had just given him. He could smell the boy's excitement as he crossed to the desk and sat on Lucian's lap.

Lucian's fangs slid through his gums, and he bit into the boy's neck without preamble. The young man shuddered as the pleasure of the bite washed through his frame.

Lucian sucked, drawing the life force into his veins. Soon, he reminded himself, soon.

Soon he would drink from the neck of Isla. Soon he would again be well.

Sloane sat on the upper deck of his houseboat, a glass of icy-cold sipping tequila in his hand. After the day that he had had, he wanted nothing more than to have a drink, or maybe two, and obliterate all thoughts from his head.

As the smooth, cold liquid slid down his throat, burning a fiery path straight to his gut, Sloane inhaled deeply, a habit that he had never managed to break himself of. When the indescribable smell of Isla filled his nostrils, he froze, not sure if it was real or a memory that was haunting him.

That tropical, sweet scent intensified, and Sloane knew that she was near. When he heard her tentative tread on the deck of the boat, he tossed back the contents of his glass and stood, looking down to the deck of his boat.

"Hi." The woman's eyes as she looked up at him were wide and a bit wary, as they should be. He knew why she was here, and though half of him thrilled to it, the other half wanted to warn her away.

"What are you doing here?" Sloane felt the prickle of his fangs at his gums. She wore another thin sundress, this one a pale pink, and she looked so sweet and innocent that he had to clench his fists against the urges rioting through him.

"I don't entirely know." Her honesty caught him off guard, a rare sensation for him. Before he could formulate a response, she was climbing the ladder to the upper deck, a bottle clutched tightly in one hand.

Once on level ground again, she stood in front of him, her posture more open than shy, as it had been earlier in the day. He could hear her heartbeat skitter, speeding up and then slowing down, and knew that she was nervous.

It added a delicious note to the scent of her blood, and it made his mouth water.

"Here." Isla held out the bottle. Sloane didn't move, and she huffed out an impatient breath.

"You shouldn't be here." Isla's eyes narrowed, and he saw a hint of the fire that she had teased him with earlier. "Were you just leading me on when you were flirting with me earlier, then? Is that all it was?"

He might have had the strength to play the arrogant asshole if he hadn't heard the thread of vulnerability that ran through her voice. "Hmm." For a long moment she simply stood there, assessing him. He could still sense the nerves that rioted within her and wondered if she was going to stay or go.

"You have a hot tub on your boat?" Sloane wasn't sure what to do with that abrupt change in conversation, so he began to peel the foil off the bottle of champagne she had handed him. Maybe more alcohol would calm the need that was pumping through him—the need to completely possess the beautiful woman who stood in front of him, silhouetted in the moonlight.

"It's a pretty common feature on houseboats these days." He watched as she wandered over to the hot tub and, bending, dipped her hand into the warm water. "I don't use it often, but I felt the urge to tonight."

"You must have read my mind." Isla inhaled deeply,

drinking in the night air, then turned away from him. His gaze raked over her shapely backside and then up, watching as she pulled her long ropes of hair up, twisting them into a knot on the top of her head.

"What are you doing?" He growled at the sight of her neck, slender, naked and soft white. She looked back over her shoulder, free of pretense, and he could tell that she felt just as much of the deep desire, the connection, that ran between them.

"You said I wasn't skinny-dipping properly this afternoon." He heard her heart rate kick up yet another notch as she climbed up the two steps to the hot tub, then kicked off her flip-flops. She stepped delicately into the tub, humming with pleasure as the warm water hit her skin.

"Isla." Sloane's mouth grew dry, and he couldn't stop his fangs from poking through his gums. "I…I thought I had better give it another try."

Facing away from him and crossing her arms at her waist, she bent and clasped the cotton candy–colored hem of her dress in her hands. Sloane couldn't take his eyes off her as she lifted the fabric up over her head and off.

"Fuck." The woman wasn't wearing a thing underneath her dress. His erection was sudden and painful, pressing against the waistband of his shorts uncomfortably. "Isla. What do you want from me?"

She looked back over her shoulder at him, her eyes luminous. He cursed himself when he saw doubt begin to form there. Surely she knew how beautiful she was, naked and gleaming in the moonlight.

"If you don't know by now, then you need to get out more." Her words were humorous, but Sloane sensed that they were a cover for that doubt. He couldn't bear the idea of her thinking that he didn't want her, especially when it was all that he could do not to bend her over the tub and thrust deep inside of her with both his cock and his fangs.

"You're so beautiful." Crossing to the hot tub, he set the bottle of wine on the ledge and pulled his T-shirt over his head, hearing her quiet sigh of relief at the same time.

"You don't have to say things like that, Sloane." Her voice was quiet, and she sank down until the water hit her hips. He couldn't see her face, but he heard the sadness in her voice. "As long as you want me, that's enough."

"Fuck that." Ripping his shorts off with one hand and painfully retracting his fangs so as not to scare her, he slid into the tub behind her and clasped his arms tightly around her waist, pulling her back against his raging erection.

"If I say that you're beautiful, it's because I think that you are." Clasping her tightly, he arched his hips, pressing his cock into the crevice between her buttocks, savoring the shiver that passed over her skin. "Does this feel like I'm not attracted to you?"

"N-no." Could he do this? Could he take her without biting her? The hunger was so tightly entwined with sex for all of his kind.

He had to try, had to possess at least some aspect of this beguiling, titian-haired human.

"Remember that then." Releasing his tight grasp, he created mere inches of space between them. Bending down—she was so small—he placed a hot, moist, openmouthed kiss at the base of her spine.

"Oh." That tiny syllable, fallen so innocently from her lips, was full of wonder. Sloane was suddenly sure that she had never before been treated properly—never been shown how incredibly sexy she was.

He was a goner. No matter the consequences, he had to have her. Had to have her now.

Focusing hard on keeping his fangs in check, he kissed his way up her spine, pausing to nip at the nape of her neck. His slid his hands from her waist up to cup her breasts, massaging their heavy weight, reveling in the responsiveness of her nipples, which contracted beneath his touch.

"Do you like that?" Slowly, sensually, he played his fingers over her breasts. She moaned and arched her back, pressing her flesh into his hands.

"Oh. How are you… Oh." Sloane was nearly undone by her response. He had barely touched her and she was already writhing against him. He hissed when her curvy behind made contact with his pelvis, pressing against the solid length of his erection.

"Shh. Just relax and enjoy." Arching his hips into her bottom once, Sloane groaned and forced himself to pull back. It was too soon, though he suspected that she was already ready for him.

She groaned when he slid his hands back down to her waist, moving her until she knelt on the seat of the hot tub, her breasts pressed against the side.

"Do you want to stay here?" He nibbled on her earlobe as he again began to strum her nipples, his movements slow and designed to torment. "We can be inside, where no one can see us in just a minute. You can be underneath me, my cock deep inside of you, seconds after that."

He felt her stiffen against him, and he stilled, letting her adjust. He knew that she hadn't considered that they were outside, that someone could happen upon them at any moment.

Now that she had tapped into the fiery little temptress that lay beneath her shy exterior, though, he suspected that he knew which option she was going to choose.

"Can you be inside me in seconds if we stay here?" Her voice was breathy with need, and he groaned as she teased him right back. Her words tempted him to position his cock in the slippery cleft between her legs and take her, right that moment, but he wanted to draw more heat, more passion from her first.

"We can stay here. But we do this my way." With one last pull on her nipples, Sloane slid his hands back over her shoulders, down her spine and through the crack of her buttocks again.

When he drew a stripe through her slippery lower lips she cried out, pushing into the touch.

"Do you like the idea that someone could see us?" Sloane wasn't all that concerned that someone would— in the past six months he had encouraged his reputation as a loner. Vampires were predominantly interested in a good time, and the party was up at the resort, not down here in the quiet.

But it gave him a little edge, too, knowing that they were in the open. For someone so unsure of her passions, like Isla, he suspected that it was a newly discovered kink.

"I—I do." With one finger he pressed inside of her, submerging the tip into her heat, groaning aloud at how good it felt.

She was so tight, so hot, so wet. He couldn't even imagine what her pussy was going to feel like around his cock.

"Oh." Isla arched like a cat as Sloane began to move his finger in and out of her. Her breath started to come in quick little pants, and as she bent over the edge of the tub, she buried her face in her arms, seemingly overwhelmed by the sensations.

"I want you to remember this." Sloane was hit momentarily by the fragility of the woman beneath him, and surprisingly, it didn't appeal to his predatory instinct. Rather than smelling weakness, he found that he wanted to make an impression on her life, fleeting as it was when compared to his own.

He stilled for a moment, waiting for his words to sink in. Only when she calmed beneath him, when the words whispered from her lips, did he again begin his caresses of her body.

"I will." A rush of satisfaction moved through Sloane as Isla reassured him. He felt drawn to protect her, to cherish her, something that he didn't understand but couldn't seem to fight.

"Good." Only then did he cover her with his body, positioning his cock at the entrance to her cleft. He could feel her heat, could tell that she was ready for him.

When he began to slowly press his length inside of her, his fangs again descended. Try as he might to retract them, he couldn't bring enough focus to the matter, not when his slow entry into Isla's slick, welcome heat was the single most pleasurable sensation that he had ever felt in his long life.

"Oh. Oh!" Isla's fingers scrabbled for purchase against the slick side of the hot tub as Sloane seated himself inside of her fully. Afraid that he'd hurt her, he stilled, allowing her a moment to adjust to his size stretching her tender flesh.

She whimpered, but it was not a noise of pain. Inhaling deeply, she then pushed back against him, forcing him inside of her just a tiny bit more, and a strangled groan escaped his lips.

"Isla." He wanted to taste her so very badly. But he settled for running his tongue down the nape of her neck. He halted abruptly when his fangs grazed her skin harder than he had meant for them to. A trickle of ruby blood welled up from the scratches, and then that intoxicating scent was there, right there, begging him to take a bite.

"No." He barely whispered the word, a verbal reminder to himself that he was more than a slave to his animal instincts. Burying his face in the tender skin that stretched tightly over her shoulder blade, Sloane stilled, every muscle in his body tensed, waiting for her to whip around, see his fully extended fangs and scream.

Though she paused as she felt the scratch of his teeth, it was brief, and then she was arching into him again, sliding her hips back and then forward, begging him without words to move.

The movement made the rich scent of her blood travel to his nose. His throat dry, he swallowed thickly.

He had to have just one taste, had to have that essence of her inside of him.

Sliding his hands down to her hips, Sloane pulled his cock nearly all the way out of her heat, then pushed back in. As he did so, he bent his head and swiped his tongue over the droplets of blood that spilled bright red against her pale skin.

"Shit, that's amazing." She tasted as she smelled—mangoes and vanilla, sweet and delicious. Denying himself more to drink, that small lick ramped up his carnal hunger, and he began to move faster and harder, sliding in and out of her with purpose.

"Sloane!" His name was a strangled cry on her lips as she bent as far over the edge of the tub as she could, allowing him as deeply into her body as possible. Knowing that he wasn't going to be able to last long, he slipped one of his hands into the waves of warm water, down the softly curved expanse of her belly and between her legs. His fingers delved between the soft curls there, finding the hard nub of her clit.

"Fuck!" He would have chuckled at sweet Isla's profanity had his own need not stretched every bit as tight. With a firm finger and thumb, he rolled that tender spot between her legs, judging from the irregular jerks of her hips that her orgasm was close.

He groaned long and loud when Isla tumbled off the edge, her tight heat milking the length of his cock. He wanted to give her more but was so drunk on the pleasure that both her body and her blood had brought him that he lost control in nearly the same moment.

Around them the water of the tub calmed, as did the racing heartbeat that he could hear pounding through her veins. Somewhat stunned by the intensity of what had transpired between them, Sloane began to withdraw his cock.

"Don't." Isla protested as he slipped from between her legs. He knew that he should be kicking himself for getting involved, even this far, with a human, but he was very nearly drunk on the taste and feel of her.

More relaxed than he had been for years, Sloane settled onto the seat of the hot tub, wrapping Isla in his arms.

He watched her lift her head to the cool, moist night breeze and thought that she looked happier than he'd yet seen her.

"I don't normally behave like this." Isla started to speak, then halted again. She wasn't embarrassed, exactly—what had just transpired between herself and Sloane had been too intense for that.

Still, she felt the need to explain to him that she wasn't the kind of woman who went around having kinky hot-tub sex with men she barely knew. Except that it seemed like, actually, she was.

She didn't know what had come over her since she had arrived on the island. Nervous as she had been, the longer she was here, the more it felt...right. Like she was where she belonged.

She hadn't felt so sure of herself...ever. Even if it was still layered with her habitual uncertainty.

She tried again. "I don't... I mean... The whole point of this trip was for me to step outside of my comfort zone. To break out of my shell." She squirmed in the thick silence that followed, unprepared when Sloane began to laugh and pulled her onto his lap.

Isla sputtered as the water rocked around them with the movement. Sitting on Sloane's hard thighs meant that her breasts rose above the line of the water, and the tips puckered in air that was cooler than the liquid heat.

"What's so funny?" She squirmed, not sure how she felt about her torso being bared to the eyes of anyone who might pass by. It had been exciting in the heat of the moment, but now she felt as though she ought to cover up.

"You fascinate me." Isla heard that chuckle again and scowled as she wiggled, trying to extricate herself from the arms that were banded around her naked waist.

"You don't have to be sarcastic." Embarrassed now, her face flushed a bright red, Isla rapidly tried to calculate a method to get out of the hot tub and get her clothes on without becoming even more mortified.

She wasn't hopeful.

She gasped when she found herself lifted and spun in the water, turned so that she faced Sloane, one of her knees on either side of a muscular thigh on the bench. His face was deadly serious, even a bit ferocious, and Isla sucked in a breath when she took in the expression on his face.

He looked like he was about to eat her alive.

"You fascinate me," he began, and Isla inhaled sharply again, this time because she could feel his cock becoming hard, pressing heavily into the tender skin of her inner thigh. "You fascinate me because you are beautiful and sweet and funny. You have a wild streak beneath the innocence. And you have no idea how intriguing you are." He leaned in, nuzzled his nose into her neck and inhaled deeply, and Isla shivered as his lips moved along the tender column of her neck.

"I—I'm not very interesting." Those lips moved from her neck, and she tilted her head to the side, hoping that they would return.

They didn't. Instead Isla turned to find a very irritated Sloane looking at her.

"Why would you think that you aren't interesting?" He studied her face intently, then reached to the steps beyond the edge of the tub, where he had left the glasses of champagne. Handing one to Isla, he waited for her response.

Stalling for time, she gulped at the liquid courage.

"Isla." Lacing one finger against her jaw, he turned her face until she had no choice but to look him in the eyes. She was terrified of what she would see there—judgment over her actions, certainly, and most likely laced with a healthy dose of contempt.

She saw none of those things. Instead she found the pools of copper that were his eyes reassuring, even a bit hypnotic.

"I don't for a moment believe that you are the kind of woman who does this regularly. That's part of your allure. However, I wouldn't judge you if you were." Isla cocked her head to one side a bit, searching for the truth in his words.

"I...I just felt like I needed to..." Her words broke off, and she stared down into the dark water, where she twisted her fingers together nervously.

"How you choose to live your life is no one's business but your own." Sloane's face was stern, but after one heart-clenching moment, Isla understood that the anger that he felt was directed not toward her but toward those would dare to judge her.

"Now. What made you come here tonight?" Instead of feeling shame, when Sloane showed no disapproval over her brazen behavior, Isla found herself drawn to tell him about the email from her mother.

"My... I..." The frustration that Isla always felt whenever she thought about her mother and her sisters washed over her, and she bit her lower lip in consternation. As she did, she felt Sloane hiss in a breath from where he rested his chin on her shoulder.

Heat simmered inside of her, helping to extinguish the uncertainty that always accompanied thoughts of her mother. Because she was quite happy to simply forget all about the woman, she moved quite deliberately against Sloane, rubbing herself against his erection.

"Tell me." Though his voice was rough with lust, Sloane clamped his hands tightly on her waist, halting her provocative movements. "I want to know."

Isla considered refusing, not wanting to share something so private with someone who was only asking so that he could get into her pants. However, there was a note of truth in Sloane's voice.

Also, her pants had come off more than an hour earlier. He was still here, and so was she.

"I don't get along very well with my family." Isla swallowed the rest of her fizzy drink in one large swallow, and when the warm aftereffect hit her mind, she found bravery along with it.

"I don't know if you're close to your family," she started and noted that he tensed beneath her. Regardless, she continued, "I guess I'm close to mine, but I'd really rather not be."

"Why is that?" Sloane slid his hand from where it was splayed over her belly, tracing up the stripes of her rib cage to skim over the underside of her breast.

"I'm not good enough for them." The words came out in a heated rush, and it was a relief to finally speak them to someone. "My mom is a judge. She's so strong, like a superhero. She raised us alone. She's done well for herself. Her daughters—at least two out of three— are very successful."

Isla waited for Sloane to agree with her mother. He
did not, instead cupping her breast in his large hand
and gently squeezing, forcing heat to radiate outward
from his touch.

"My sister Angela is an attorney. My other sister,
Madeline, is a doctor. They're both married to successful men. I've always been...different. My mother has always treated me differently. Sometimes I really wonder
if she loves me at all. And today she sent me an email.
She's very upset that I've decided to go on holiday to an
island that is littered with vampire legends. She hates
all things supernatural. If her friends found out I was
here, it would embarrass her to no end."

Isla knew that frustration was apparent in her voice,
even as she arched her back, pushing her breast into
Sloane's touch.

"You're an adult. You chose this resort." Isla stiffened at the words until she became aware, again, that
he wasn't expressing disapproval.

She hadn't realized quite the extent to which she
had been conditioned to her mother's expectations of
behavior.

"Yes. Well...not exactly. It was my friend's trip.
Something came up and she wasn't able to go, so I
came instead. But...well, yes, in the end I suppose I
still made the decision to come." Sloane bent his neck
and traced his lips along the nape of her neck, and Isla
shuddered at the sensation.

"I... I... Oh." She felt a scratching sensation and
assumed he had nibbled on her neck. It didn't hurt—
on the contrary, she wished that he would do it again.

"I don't particularly like my mother. And she doesn't
care for me either." Isla had never acknowledged this

out loud, and although she felt as though she should feel guilty, she didn't. "I'm sick of doing what she wants when she doesn't even seem to love me. And all this fuss over vampires—something that's not even real. It's silly."

"Well, then." Sloane shifted Isla until she again straddled his hips. This time he positioned his cock right at the heated entrance to her cleft. She wanted—craved—that moment when he slid inside of her, filled her.

Made her forget everything else.

"You are your own woman. Now it's time for you to live your life the way that you want to. Step outside the shadow of your family." Again picking up the bottle of champagne, he suddenly upended the remaining contents over Isla's breasts.

"Sloane!" Every muscle inside of Isla clenched at the unexpected coolness of the liquid that now ran in rivulets over her torso. At the same time, Sloane began to inch inside of her with excruciating slowness, and Isla groaned as sensations overwhelmed her.

As soon as he had seated himself fully inside of her, Sloane lowered his lips to the cleft between her breasts and licked up a stream of champagne. Pressing his forehead to hers so that she could not look away, he grinned at her, and Isla shivered at the carnal promise demonstrated in his devilish smile.

"If this is the way that you want to start living your life, beautiful, I'm not going to complain."

Sloane had no idea what the hell he had gotten himself into.

He watched as the last trace of strawberry-colored hair disappeared behind the heavy door of Isla's bungalow. After spending the past few hours in her company, he was more convinced than ever that she knew nothing about vampires.

He was also certain that he had found a human whose eventual death could tear him in two.

He would never consider turning her. He couldn't, not after what he had done to Ana.

Furrowing his brow and scowling, he stuffed his hands in the pockets of the shorts he had pulled back on to walk Isla from his boat back to her bungalow. He didn't like that her accommodations were so remote any more than he liked wondering why Lucian had allowed her onto the island.

He couldn't do much about the wondering and the concern. He could, however, extricate himself from the situation before getting in any deeper. For reasons that he couldn't quite explain, he knew that eternal separation from the sweet little human who had just kissed him good-night with enough heat to make his head spin would be far worse than it had been with Sully.

The stench of dry vinegar accosted his nostrils as soon as he stepped from the wood of the dock to the sand of the beach. He stilled, lifting his head to draw the scent deep. Though he had never been a vampire particularly gifted with tracking, he was certain that the vampire whose presence he was detecting was the same one he had first smelled in the woods that afternoon.

On a hunch, he kept his senses attuned to the smell. As he had suspected, it intensified, and now that he was expecting it, he could discern the change in the smell.

It was indeed a second vampire joining the first. The proximity to Isla was not a coincidence—he didn't believe in chance occurrences.

Something in the second scent seemed vaguely familiar, though he didn't think it was one that he'd smelled before. Sloane waited, still and silent, at the edge of the dock. The hiding vampires would certainly know that he was there and would know now that he was the one who had staked a claim on Isla earlier that day.

As he waited he growled, just once—a warning to those hiding in the shadows. As he had predicted, the scents soon faded, the interlopers acknowledging the warning.

After his behavior that afternoon—primal behavior that Isla had somehow managed to drag from him—it was too late for him to pretend that he hadn't claimed her as his own. Though he had no intention of pursuing her further—no matter that he felt a sharp pang lance through him at the thought—perhaps that claim would keep her safe until he could persuade the innocent woman to leave.

Chapter 5

When Isla had first perused the activities listed in the resort brochure, she had thought that sunrise yoga sounded mystical and wonderful. She was now having second thoughts.

The resort was alive with the sound of birds and fresh air, but she passed very few people on her way to the recreation building. Shrugging, she surmised that she shouldn't be all that surprised, given the early hour.

A white tent stood beside the white stone building where yoga sessions took place, and it swayed slightly in the early morning breeze. Though no one else was there yet, Isla could see rolled-up yoga mats, foam blocks and blankets stacked neatly inside the tent. She assumed that this was where she was supposed to be.

Inside the tent, she looked around tentatively, then slowly unzipped her hooded sweatshirt and, throwing it aside, she took one of the mats in hand. When she went to unroll it she found that it was still bound with plastic—it was brand-new. Pursing her lips, she put the mat back and picked up another one.

It was the same—brand-new, still in its packaging. A quick survey told her that all of the equipment in the tent had never been used, which she couldn't think of an explanation for.

Maybe yoga was something new that they offered at the resort?

Regardless, the equipment was here and she was here. The instructor hadn't arrived yet, but Isla didn't want to waste a moment of this perfect day. Spreading out her mat, she dropped to her knees and stretched her neck from side to side calmly. Though far from an expert, Isla had practiced yoga for several years.

Sinking into child's pose, Isla tried to empty her mind of thought, but she couldn't help but grin into the yoga mat as the stretch eased the stiffness from Sloane's attentions the night before.

Inhaling deeply, Isla eased herself farther into the pose. Instead of the relaxation that typically accompanied it, however, she felt a chill waft over her skin. Frowning, she shivered, feeling as if cold fingers were dancing over the nape of her neck. Ever since she had set foot on the island the day before, her sixth sense had been running wild, making her imagine spooks around every corner.

She was being foolish. But...

Drawing up until she sat back on her heels, Isla looked around the tent quickly. She had almost convinced herself that she was letting her imagination run away with her when her eyes darted past the still figure, then swung back.

At the front of the room, facing her, was a woman holding the impossibly difficult dragonfly pose. Startled, Isla lurched to her feet. She hadn't heard the woman enter the tent, nor had she heard the heavy exhalations of breath that usually accompanied the difficult pose.

The woman balanced on her hands, one leg tucked behind her rear and one extended to the side, her foot flexed. Her face was turned to the ground, the length of her incredibly long, inky black hair sweeping the ground.

Isla's mouth fell open slightly as she took in the spectacle. She had seen many experienced practitioners hold the dragonfly pose before, but never with such ease. The woman before her was so still that she could have been carved from stone.

Suddenly very uncomfortable, and certain that this session would be far out of her league, Isla stooped to pick up her mat. She paid a lot of attention to rolling it up precisely, and when she again stood, the neat roll in her hand, she started.

The woman was still in the dragonfly pose, but she had lifted her head and was staring right at her.

"Hello, little one." The woman's voice was melodic, and she showed no shortness of breath at all as she twisted her body effortlessly into a handstand. Instead of demonstrating how difficult it must have been, her lips twisted in an eerily calm smile.

Isla shivered, though she couldn't quite understand why. Isla swallowed down her own feelings and smiled brightly at the strange woman.

"Wow, you're so strong." The woman seemed amused at the comment. Isla had to fight back the urge to hiss in response—and what was with this new hissing habit of hers? No matter the expression that crossed the other woman's face, she was an incredible beauty, her skin pale olive, her hair shiny as silk. As she fluidly swung herself from the handstand to her feet, nearly bending herself in half as she did so, Isla noted that the woman was tall, slim and lithe in a way that Isla would never be.

"Yes, I am very strong." The woman smiled, standing unnaturally still as she stared at Isla. Isla decided that, for once, instead of listening to the voice of her mother that always sounded in her head, she was going to listen to her own gut. This woman made her very, very uncomfortable, though the woman had done nothing overt to distress her.

No matter how appealing the prospect of sunrise yoga had been, she knew that she would never be able to relax if this woman was the instructor.

"You know, I'm not feeling very well." Isla smiled tightly at the strange woman. "I think I'm going to head back to my room."

Keeping her stare on the ground, Isla returned her rolled mat to the group of mats that were still wrapped in plastic. Grabbing her sweatshirt, she headed to the exit of the tent, not bothering to cover her shoulders again.

Nervous perspiration had broken out over her skin.

She jumped when she looked up and found the woman standing in the entrance of the tent, blocking her way. The woman smiled—a kind smile on the surface, but Isla just couldn't shake the discomfort.

"You're a pretty little one, aren't you?" The woman tilted her head, staring at Isla with unabashed curiosity.

"Excuse me." Isla tried to skirt past the woman, her

nerves now screaming, though she still couldn't have said why. The woman didn't move.

Isla opened her mouth, and there was that damned hiss again. Her fingers curled, and she felt the overwhelming urge to launch herself at the other woman, to attack.

Her mind overruled the urge, thank heavens. She was well and truly intimidated by this woman and had no illusions about who would win this chick fight.

Isla's growl was cut off by the sound of an unfamiliar male's voice, stern and full of repressed anger.

"Luana!" The woman didn't jump, rather acted as if she had expected the man to show up. Instead she smiled down at Isla, and though this smile was the closest to genuine yet, Isla saw that Luana's eyes were deep black and extremely cold.

"It seems that yoga is cancelled for today." A tall, thin man with golden hair appeared on the grass by the tent. Moving quickly, he was behind the woman he had called Luana, his hand on her arm.

"Am I in trouble, Marcus?" She tilted her head provocatively, but she didn't look at the man behind her. Isla distinctly saw the intimacy between the pair, though there seemed to be more to it than that.

"Luana, Mr. St. Baptiste has requested your presence." Marcus's face twisted with consternation as he turned to Isla. "I'm so very sorry, Miss Miller, but sunrise yoga has been cancelled today. Please, feel free to stay and use the tent. I think you'll find the equipment is to your taste. Your friend mentioned, when she was transferring her tickets to your name, that yoga is one of your interests."

Isla jolted. She couldn't recall telling Jessie—telling

anyone—that she practiced yoga, but she must have. It wasn't that she kept it a secret, it was just that the activity was something she preferred to practice alone. Still, it niggled at her.

Her love of the exercise was something she liked to keep just for herself.

"Thank you, but I...I'm not feeling very well. I think I'm going to go lie down." Though Marcus didn't alarm her in the same way that Luana did, and though she no longer felt quite as nervous or aggressive as she had, she wanted to get out of there.

Pushing past the pair—Marcus drew Luana in close to him to allow Isla to pass—Isla all but ran out of the tent.

Her discussion with Sloane the night before had clearly opened some of her neuroses up. Halfway back to her bungalow, Isla had a change of mind and veered her course to the boat where Sloane had awakened all kinds of carnal pleasure for her the night before.

She wasn't a virgin, but her experiences were few... and none of them had been particularly wonderful. Not only was Sloane skilled as a lover, but he had made her feel special in a way that she'd never felt before.

It occurred to her that he may not be up yet—though she imagined he had to work today, she had noticed that the resort didn't really seem to wake up until early afternoon.

She was unsettled enough by her encounter with the eerie woman named Luana that, although aware of the beauty of the pale, early morning sky and snowy sand, she didn't take the time to appreciate it.

The houseboat was still, rocking ever so slightly on the water. Sucking her lower lip between her teeth, she studied it, suddenly uncertain. She wanted to tell him about her strange encounter. Still, no matter how intimately acquainted she now was with his body, she realized that she didn't know him well enough to anticipate his reaction to an early morning wake-up call.

Halting at the edge of the sand, Isla argued with herself over what to do. Then she looked up, to the upper deck of the boat. What she saw there made her mouth go dry.

Sloane stood still, his large frame silhouetted against the blue of the sky. He was wearing nothing but a pair of white boxer briefs.

Clearly having seen her before she saw him, he was watching her intently.

He did not look happy.

The scent of Isla was permanently imprinted on his brain.

After the previous night, the smell of mangoes and vanilla had haunted his dreams. Upon waking, Sloane had found his throat dry with a thirst that he hadn't experienced since his adolescent years as a vampire.

The single taste he'd had of Isla's blood had awakened his hunger. He wanted more.

Instead he warmed a mug of prepackaged animal blood and chugged it back. He chased it with strong black coffee that he drank from a chipped old mug.

When the scent that had laced highly erotic dreams all night intensified, he thought that it was just his imagination—his desire for more.

"What have I done?" He cursed as soon as he realized that she was near. After ascending the steps to the upper deck, he braced himself to do what he knew he had to.

She stood on the beach, looking up at his boat, uncertainty painted over her features. The way that she nibbled on her lower lip made him want to bite it until he could taste the nectar that was her blood.

Her skin showed the slightest hint of gold from her time in the sun the day before. A lot of her skin was on display, clad as she was in a fitted athletic camisole and tight black shorts.

When she looked up and her stare locked in on him, he swallowed back the intense connection that he felt with her, making sure that his expression was blank.

"What are you doing here?" As if she had rudely interrupted his preparations for the day, Sloane scooped to pick up a towel, running it over his shower-dampened head.

It was a mistake. It was the towel she had used the night before, and it was saturated with her delicious scent.

His fangs prickled against his gums. The beast inside of him had had a taste of the woman he had claimed, and it was not happy at being denied.

"I… Good morning." Isla lifted a hand to shield her eyes against the sun that was moving ever higher in the sky. The movement arched her spine and thrust her breasts forward, and Sloane stifled a groan.

He wanted to jump down to the sand, to press her to the ground and take her right there, tasting her life's essence as he thrust inside of her.

Instead he felt like a major dick as he deliberately stayed silent. Much as he wanted her, and much as he knew that she wanted him, this—whatever this was—between them was not good.

He was immortal. She was a human. By pushing her away, he would protect his own sanity…and her own because the one human he had turned had lost her mind. He would also, if he did things right, drive her away from the island and from the danger that he knew she was in.

"I…I wanted to see you." Sloane squeezed his eyes shut at Isla's words. She was so naive, so innocent. She so earnestly displayed her feelings.

He hated to crush that sweetness, much as her mother and sisters seemed to have tried to do her entire life. He just couldn't see another way out.

"I have to get to work." This wasn't a lie exactly. Sloane didn't have a supervisor, having made his thoughts on the matter quite clear when he had first come to the island. Boats and other vehicles that needed fixing were brought to this stretch of beach, and he fixed them as he was able. So far the agreement had worked well for both himself and the mysterious Lucian St. Baptiste.

So, he could have taken the time to listen to her, to steal a kiss from her lips, to inhale that magnificent scent. But that would only have prolonged the inevitable.

He wanted her off this island.

"Oh. Well. Maybe I'll see you later?" Sloane hated himself for making that sad acceptance cross her face. If anyone else had treated her this way, he would have wanted to tear them limb from limb.

Two vampires were following her. His heart was still sore from the loss of Sully.

"Look, baby, we had fun last night. Let's not make it into more than it was." He saw her eyes go wide, saw the flash of pain and then that dreadful acceptance.

He was an ass.

"Right. Well." Isla whirled on her heel and started to leave. After two steps she turned and stomped back, her fists clenched with anger.

He could smell the warm syrup that temper added to her blood. He wanted to wrap her in his arms and never let her go.

"Screw you." Isla glared up at him, her eyes widening as if she couldn't believe that she said the words before again spinning and walking away. This time she didn't come back.

Sloane watched until she disappeared from sight before jumping from the upper to the lower deck, landing in a crouch. The confrontation had made him tired. Quickly slugging back the rest of the contents of the coffeepot, Sloane pulled on a pair of battered jeans and a black T-shirt. A boat that needed work was already anchored a half mile away down the strip of sand. He had never tested how long he could go before fixing something without irritating the powers that be. He also had several emails in his in-box, messages from the board of his massive corporation.

He had started his real estate empire several centuries earlier. It had changed names and forms many times over the decades, but he had had the benefit of time when it came to turning a profit on properties. He had even held on to one small Irish castle for nearly a hundred years before selling it.

He considered the advantage as karma's payback for the fact that he now had to drink blood to survive.

When he'd decided to take some time off, he'd left the decisions of the company in the board's hands. He trusted them implicitly, but right then they could have run the business into the ground and he wouldn't have cared.

They could wait, and so could the boat. He intended to make sure that Isla remained safe until she left the island.

Isla stormed across the resort in the direction of her bungalow. Though her first instinct had been to question why she wasn't good enough for him, and to wonder what she could have already done to drive him away, the feelings faded quickly.

He wanted her. Dammit, he liked her. She felt the same way. So what was his problem?

Isla ground her teeth as she pictured shoving Sloane off the upper deck of his boat and into the surrounding Tahitian waters.

In her mind's eye he looked like a drowned rat when he emerged.

Sighing as she admitted to herself that he wouldn't look like anything of the sort, Isla slowed her pace and tried to calm down. She considered it progress that, instead of falling to pieces over the rejection, she had gotten mad.

Feeling somewhat shortchanged by the aborted yoga session that morning and now craving the peace of it more than ever, Isla decided to return to her bungalow and work through some postures on her own. In no mood for company, she grimaced when she found Gaspar waiting at the end of her dock in one of the sleek black golf carts.

"Miss Miller." She nodded stiffly, not sure how to behave around the man after his flirtatious overtures the night before. Though she saw the man's eyes roam over the expanse of skin visible in her yoga spandex, he made no comment on her appearance.

"The owner of the resort has invited you to brunch in his chambers." Isla noted a hint of something she thought might be reverence in Gaspar's words, which she found odd. Exasperated with the drama that had surrounded her ever since she had set foot on the island, Isla was tempted to just pack her bags and leave.

That was what the Isla of two days ago would have done—she would have called Jessie to commiserate, then she would have retreated to something familiar and safe.

She wouldn't give in. She was going to enjoy this vacation if it was the last thing she did.

"Thank you, Gaspar, but I'm really not in the mood." With a tight smile, Isla brushed past the man and the cart and stepped onto the wood of the dock.

She turned when he called out her name. He had stepped out of the cart and was frowning slightly.

She knew that she wasn't imagining the way that his eyes slid over her body.

"Miss Miller, not very many people get the chance to visit Ile de Nuit." The tone of Gaspar's voice was reproachful. "Mr. St. Baptiste is very selective about those he invites to the island. He invites even fewer to visit him personally because his health is so fragile. It is an enormous honor."

There it was, the guilt that shadowed so much of Isla's life. She closed her eyes against it, vowing that she wouldn't let it drown her like it so often did.

When she opened her eyes, Gaspar was watching her with a textbook sympathetic smile. She pursed her lips, not sure she could push back against the impulses that were second nature to her.

"His personal chefs will provide a meal unlike anything you have ever tasted." Isla sighed, knowing that she was beaten.

She might have had the strength to refuse, but the uncertainty from her encounter with Sloane chose that moment to rear its ugly head.

She didn't know much about him, just what Jessie had told her—that a reclusive billionaire named Lucian St. Baptiste owned the Tahitian island and the resort that sat on it and that he was rumored to be ill and fairly eccentric.

Well, recluse or not, maybe breakfast with someone who had singled her out—someone who might make her feel special, even for an hour—might ease the sting of Sloane's rejection.

Chapter 6

Rage slid through Sloane's body. Mixed with it was dread, an emotion that he hadn't felt for centuries.

Lucian wanted to get Isla alone. Sloane knew this without a doubt. What he didn't understand was why.

He couldn't just barge into the compound where Lucian lived—it was heavily guarded, keeping the recluse in and curious onlookers out. He didn't for a moment believe that he could sneak in under the guise of being one of his servants.

Lucian undoubtedly knew what he looked like. He hadn't become a billionaire, hadn't become powerful, by being dumb.

Sloane would be damned if he would just let Isla go. He'd followed along behind the golf cart, his mind trying frantically to come up with some way to plausibly accompany her.

After his performance earlier that morning, Isla certainly wasn't going to invite him. In trying to protect her, he had shot himself in the foot.

He didn't smell the distinct signatures of the two vampires who had been following Isla. Perhaps Lucian had had nothing to do with them after all—perhaps he truly was just curious about this innocent, delectable human.

With a low growl, Sloane made his decision and let Isla follow Gaspar into the compound. All he could do now was make sure that she left the compound unscathed.

The interior of the building to which Gaspar led her was a gothic masterpiece.

Isla stood just inside the entryway, staring around at the massive stone columns, the arched ceilings, the sconces that shone with the light of pillar candles despite the early morning hours.

It was as if she had stepped through a portal that led from Ile de Nuit to an ancient European cathedral.

"He is eccentric." Gaspar rolled a shoulder in a small shrug as he caught her openmouthed stare. He smiled, a mischievous curl of the lips, as he spoke.

"Right." Isla tugged self-consciously at the hem of her shorts. Her outfit was entirely inappropriate for the ornate home in which she now stood.

Gaspar noticed her gesture. "Mr. St. Baptiste will be happy to make your acquaintance, no matter your attire." He smiled at Isla again, but the way that his eyes lingered on her flesh made her shiver.

Sloane hadn't looked at her like that. No, his stare told her of his arousal without making her feel as though she was about to be eaten.

"Come." Isla had opened her mouth to make excuses about going home to change and possibly never returning when Gaspar again spoke. She found herself following him apprehensively through the castle-type structure, intrigued despite herself.

What kind of man would build something like this on a tropical island?

Two massive flights of stairs later, Gaspar pushed his way into a room so grand that it appeared to be a ballroom. A massive crystal chandelier sparkled overhead, the light reflecting off the skin of...

Women.

Lots and lots of women.

"What the hell?" Isla didn't realize she had spoken aloud until she met the hard stare of Gaspar. She shivered at the coldness in his eyes. Still, she couldn't think of a good reason to leave that wouldn't make her look like a paranoid psychopath.

"Miss Miller." She turned to meet the lightly accented voice that spoke.

In the arched doorway across the ballroom was an incredibly attractive man. It had to be Lucian St. Baptiste.

For a man who was supposedly ill, he was remarkably charismatic. Slight of build and with very white skin, he had silky hair that fell past his shoulders in dark waves, a finely chiseled face and eyes so dark that it was hard to differentiate between the iris and the pupil.

Those eyes were fastened on her with the kind of appreciation that made a woman feel like she was the only female in the world of any importance.

"Hello." Isla had no idea how she was supposed to act right then, with a man who was openly flirting with her yet surrounded by other women—beautiful women, spectacular women who were staring at her with open animosity.

"When Gaspar told me about the beautiful new resort guest, I knew that I had to meet her." The man stepped toward her and caught her hand in his own. When he lifted it to his lips she repressed a shiver.

"Miss Miller, I am Lucian St. Baptiste." Isla didn't like the man's touch, yet...he seemed somehow familiar to her. She was certain that she had never met him before, though. "I am the owner of this resort. Come, let us eat and...get to know one another."

The polite thing to do was to smile and go along with the meal, even though suddenly every cell in her body was screaming to get away from this man.

She thought of Sloane and everything that he had awakened inside of her.

"I'm sorry. I have to go." She thought she caught a glint in the man's eye as she pulled her hand from his grasp, but it was gone so quickly that she couldn't be sure.

She thought of Sloane, of how angry she was with him right then.

She thought of how much he could make her *feel*.

"Thank you for the invitation, Mr. St. Baptiste. What I have seen of the resort so far is lovely. But I have to go."

The smell of Isla when her blood was heated was intoxicating.

Relief that he didn't know he was capable of had punched him in the gut as soon as he saw Isla leave the gothic monstrosity that St. Baptiste called a house. Muscles taut, Sloane had watched as she blinked in the sunshine like a deer emerging from the woods. She had frowned, shaking her head sluggishly. For an infuriating moment he wondered if she had been drugged—though a vampire didn't need a roofie to do whatever he or she wanted to do.

Temper washed over her face as if she had consciously made a decision. He slipped silently from the tree as Isla walked away from the monstrosity of a building.

Wherever she was going, she had something on her mind.

He didn't need to be a mind reader to know what that was.

Following at a discreet distance until they were close to his boat, he then warped into vampire speed and ran, making sure that he was on the deck of his boat before she got there.

The confrontation might as well come now as later. The fire he had sensed deep in Isla burned a little bit brighter every time her saw her, and he knew that she wouldn't give up until she had said what she wanted to say.

Not bothering to wait for an invitation, Isla stormed right onto the lower deck of his boat and planted her feet.

Though he'd known where she was heading, he was still a little taken aback by the fiery temptress who looked ready to give him hell.

"Damn it, Sloane!" It took a hell of a woman to make him wary, and as he swallowed deeply, he acknowledged that Isla had done exactly that. "I know you're there!"

He still had to try. His instinctual claiming of her had

ratcheted up another notch as he had waited for her to exit the house of another man. He wanted this woman to be his own in every aspect.

That didn't mean that it was a good idea.

Trying to school his face into a mask of indifference, he sauntered from the inner quarters of his boat to the deck where Isla stood. He was careful to stay far enough away that he couldn't reach out and touch her, though her scent invaded his consciousness and made his fingers ache with the need.

He didn't speak; he simply raised an eyebrow at her.

"Lucian St. Baptiste just made it quite clear that he wants me." Though he already knew that he was in too deep, Sloane was unprepared for the tendril of fury that snaked through his gut at the words. Something he hadn't felt since Ana.

"I meant to ask earlier, why are you dressed like that?" He tried to distract her—and himself—with a change of topic. The reminder of the vast swathes of her skin that were still visible to the naked eye made his mouth water, and he didn't care for the idea that anyone and everyone else could see it.

Momentarily startled, Isla looked down at herself, then crossed her arms over her midriff self-consciously, and he hated that he had made her feel that way.

"I went to yoga this morning." She scowled at him, and he knew that it was a cover for her nerves. "And don't change the subject. You want me."

"I don't." The lie burned his throat as he spoke. "And the resort doesn't offer yoga."

"The hell you don't." Isla's expression dared him to argue. "And before you turned into a super ass this morning, I had intended to tell you about my strange almost session of yoga. Which the resort does offer, by the way."

Sloane puzzled over that momentarily as he studied her. His sharp sight noticed something strange about her appearance, something that took him a moment to place.

"Your bruises are gone." The shadows that had marred her skin earlier—the ones placed there by his eager fingers the night before—had completely faded. Her skin was back to smooth ivory, kissed with a hint of tropical sun.

Seemingly taken aback, Isla turned her head, craning her neck to look at her upper arms. Shrugging, she seemed irritated that he had changed the topic again.

"I've always healed quickly." Her brow was furrowed as she narrowed her eyes at him. "My whole family has. Even my sister, the doctor, hardly ever gets sick."

Alarm bells began to ring as he heard what she had said. And then she crossed her arms at the waist, clasped the fabric of her skimpy camisole in her hands and pulled it up and over her head.

Sloane had lived for hundreds of years, but he had never been as shocked as he was that very minute.

Isla stared up at him with defiance. Her fists were clasped tightly at her sides, and he knew that she was struggling against the urge to cover herself back up.

"You want me." She inhaled deeply, and Sloane couldn't help but look at the rosy tips of her nipples, puckering under his stare.

Sloane didn't respond. His throat had gone dry, and he had no words.

He, who had met millions of women over the course of his very long life, was completely bewitched by the woman who stood in front of him.

"I am going inside. I am going to get completely naked." Sloane squeezed his eyes shut at her words and uttered something that was halfway between an oath and a prayer.

"I'll wait for ten minutes. If you don't come in— and you know that you want to—then you'll never see me again."

Isla couldn't believe what she had just done. She hadn't planned it when she had left Lucian St. Baptiste's compound, but she had been confused by the man who had paid her such attention and the one who had rejected her so heartlessly that morning.

In the end, it was down to feelings. Never before in her life had she allowed herself to act solely on feelings.

She didn't know if what she had just done was a good idea.

Slowly drawing the thin shorts down until they hit the floor, Isla starting counting down the seconds of each minute as she stepped out of them. She thought about lying down on his bed, of arranging herself seductively with the sheet draped over her in tantalizing ways.

She decided against it. If he came to her, she wanted to know that he saw her as she was.

Her heart sank as her count approached the five-minute mark. Her cheeks flushed as she looked down at the shorts crumpled on the floor.

He wasn't coming. He truly didn't want her, and listening to her feelings had only led her to mortification.

Slowly Isla bent to pick up her shorts. Before she straightened all the way back up he was there, stepping through the sliding glass door that led into his bedroom.

He was the most dangerous-looking man she had

ever seen. Instead of frightening her, she found that with him, and only with him, did she feel completely and utterly safe.

She also found those bad-boy aspects of him—the ferocity, the glower, even the tattoos—sexy as hell.

Her lips curled upward as she realized that her mother would be appalled.

"You think that making me come running is funny, do you?" Sloane's words were gruff as he crossed the room toward her.

She shivered as his hands clasped her tightly around the waist and lifted. His palms were cool against her skin, which already felt hot and tight with need.

"I don't think there's a woman in the world who could make you come running." Isla wrapped her legs around his waist as he carried her the few remaining steps to the bed. Laying her down on crisp sheets that smelled deliciously of him, he then covered her body with his own, nudging a knee between her thighs intimately.

"You're wrong." Lowering his head to hers, Sloane kissed her, long and deep. Isla arched into the kiss, savoring the slow heat of the moment. When he finally allowed her a moment to breathe, she wondered if she'd actually heard him correctly.

"Sloane." His lips trailed from her own down the column of her neck. He paused at the spot where her skin was paper thin and pulsed with every beat of her heart.

She jumped when he closed his teeth over that pulse, then moaned when he soothed the bite with a warm swipe of his tongue.

"This isn't a good idea." Tugging the elastic from her ponytail, Sloane fisted his hands in the long tangles of her hair, dragging her head forward so that she had to look him in the eye. He stared at her unwaveringly, as if trying to tell her something important.

"Why does it have to be a good idea or not? Why does it have to be right or wrong? Can't it just be?" Beneath him Isla arched her hips. When her soft heat met the solid length of his erection he hissed, and a moment of triumph shot through her.

"So be it." Closing his eyes reverently, Sloane nuzzled his face into her hair, seeming to inhale the scent. Isla shivered, though she felt flushed all over.

She had never wanted anything more in her life than she wanted this man.

Moving away from her hair, Sloane again placed his lips on her pulse, lathing his tongue over the tender spot. Kissing a trail down the column of her neck, pausing in the hollow of her throat, he moved to the swell of one of her breasts.

The sensation when his lips closed over her nipples was sharp, like razors slicing through her veins. She cried out, the voice swallowed as Sloane again pressed his lips to her own, exploring her mouth with bold sweeps of his tongue.

Impatient, Isla bucked her hips against his. She wanted him inside of her, right that moment, and she didn't think that she could bear to wait.

She felt the vibration of Sloane's muffled chuckle as he denied her what she so badly wanted. She nipped at his lower lip in response. Drawing back, she took in the stunning visual that was his face—the face of a fallen angel.

His hand slid down her torso to the heated space between her legs—what he had in mind was clearly not of the angelic persuasion.

One finger slid in between folds that were already slick. She cried out again as he found the hard nub of her clit and circled the engorged flesh.

"Sloane!" Teasing her, he cupped her sex in his palm, then slid a finger inside of her damp heat.

It wasn't enough, and she moved frantically against him as he worked her sex with his finger. All the while he looked down at her, his golden eyes locked on her blue ones. The expression on his face did something to her heart, making it quiver in a way that was almost painful.

Her voice down to a whisper, she looked away, unable to bear the intensity of his stare.

"Sloane. Please. I need you." His free hand laced with hers, and his other left her slick heat and tangled in her hair.

Bending until his forehead was pressed against hers, he parted her legs wider with one muscular thigh.

"This is what you want." His words were not phrased as a question, but Isla sensed that he needed affirmation anyway.

Reaching up, she trailed fingers over the defined ridge of his cheekbone. His eyes glinted in response.

"This is what I want." She echoed his words, and as she soon as they faded, he thrust inside of her, one hard thrust that claimed her.

She gasped and clawed at his back, arching against him so that he could sink even deeper. Looking up into his eyes, Isla saw a look of such animal hunger that she shuddered, some primal part of herself responding to the call of her mate.

Then she could do nothing but hold on, her hands grasping at his back, his ass, the sheets, trying to gain purchase on something as he began to thrust, claiming her as his.

Her breath began to come in short pants, and she squirmed beneath him, close to the edge. As her cheeks flushed with pleasure, Sloane rolled, holding tight to her hips, until he lay back on his bed and she sat astride him, his cock as deeply inside of her as it had been yet.

Physical sensations overcame her at the same time as a wave of self-consciousness, and she reached her hands up to cover the flesh of her exposed breasts. Sloane growled and, reaching up, clasped her fingers in his, bringing them down to his chest and pinning them there.

"Don't you ever feel ashamed. You are beautiful." Glaring at her to make his point, he released her hands, sliding one to her hip, urging her to move.

Uncertain, Isla ducked her head, the curtain of her hair shadowing her face. Trying to call forth some bravery, she traced one of the tattoos on his chest with a curious finger, skimming his nipple as she did.

He hissed, and the hand on her hip became more insistent. Looking down at him with wide eyes, Isla balanced her weight on her knees, then rocked her hips back and forth.

Sloane groaned and closed his eyes. Emboldened, Isla moved faster, firmer. Her skin felt tight with pleasure as she found her rhythm. The edge that she had been balancing on only minutes earlier came into view, and she squeezed his hips with her thighs, trying to close her legs against the onslaught of sensation that was suddenly too much.

"Isla." Reaching between her legs as she rode him, Sloane found the center of her pleasure and began to roll it between his fingers. The sound that came from her throat as the intense pleasure finally washed over her was close to a scream, echoing off the walls of the small room.

Sloane held still, thrust as deeply inside of her as he could go, until her shudders quieted. She would have melted down against him, but he began to work her clit again. Impossibly, she felt pleasure begin to build again.

She shattered a second time only moments after the first, the shock short and intense. Astonished, she looked through the long tangle of her lashes at Sloane, wanting him to come with her.

He was watching her. She suddenly saw herself as if through his eyes, and as she did, she felt beautiful.

Emboldened, she knelt back until her long hair tickled his knees. Though it stretched all of her muscles tight, she snaked a hand behind her body and between their entwined legs. Tracing lightly over the heavy globes of his testicles, she found the impossibly rigid length of his cock, embedded inside of her, and circled her fingers against the root, squeezing him more tightly than her cleft would ever be able to.

One thrust, two, and Sloane's moan sliced the heavy, humid air in two. He thrust into her again and again, milking every last bit of pleasure for both of them. Clasping her by the waist, he pulled her back toward him and down until she was lying full length on top of him, his length still embedded inside of her.

Her face a whisper from his own, they stared at each other wide eyed. Isla didn't have much experience, but still she knew that what had just happened wasn't normal.

Entranced, she sighed and laid her cheek on his chest, surrendering to him completely.

Sloane could think of any excuse that he wanted for running, but he couldn't deny the honesty of what had just happened. He wanted her. She wanted him.

For the moment, that was enough.

Chapter 7

Sloane hadn't run.

Isla couldn't help the dreamy smile that played over her lips as she lay in his bed, his arms wrapped tightly around her waist. They had made love a second time, and while her knees were weak, she couldn't stop the seemingly insatiable hunger that worked through her at his touch.

No matter how it ended up, she knew that this vacation—and the parts of her that Sloane had unearthed—was the start of a new phase of her life.

Nuzzling against his chest, she inhaled the herb-laced scent that was uniquely him. Heat washed through her yet again, and with more bravery than she had had even that morning, she slid her hand down the hard planes of his abs to dance her fingers over the length of his cock.

"Well, then." She could hear the answering smile in

Sloane's voice, and beneath her touch his length hardened much more quickly than it should have, considering how much work it had gotten in the past few hours. He thrust into her hand as she wrapped it tightly around the hot silk of him, and she dampened her lips with her tongue in anticipation.

Sliding up the length of his body, she felt his hard muscles stiffen beneath her softer frame. He grabbed her upper arms in strong hands when she moved against him, holding her still.

"Shh." He cocked his head to the side, and Isla blew her bangs out of her face with an exasperated sigh. She hadn't heard anything.

"I wasn't talking." Sloane quieted her again, sitting up in the bed, the sheets and Isla herself rumpled and in his lap.

The serious expression on his face was enough to have nerves skittering through her blood.

What was with this resort and this island? There had been enough odd occurrences in the past two days to make Isla thoroughly discomfited.

She even felt different, and she had since she'd set foot on the dock. She'd initially chalked it up to relaxation—she was on vacation, after all—but when she thought about it, she'd had more than her share of stressful encounters since arriving.

She didn't believe in vampires, but she was starting to wonder if she might be wrong and if there were some on the island—like that woman Luana she'd met earlier that morning.

"Isla, stay here." Isla's spine stiffened as Sloane lifted her as though she weighed nothing and moved her from his lap to the edge of the bed. Though his actions had

her feeling a bit uneasy, she was still able to appreciate
his nude body as he got off the bed and quickly dressed
in his discarded shorts and T-shirt.

"What is it? What did you hear?" Sloane's entire
manner had changed from the lazy lover he'd been only
moments earlier. In that lover's place was a man who
looked lethal and not a little bit scary.

"I didn't hear something—I smelled it. I'm not entirely sure what, but it's not for lack of trying." He
scowled, his eyes darkening.

He had smelled it? Taken aback, Isla clutched the
sheet to her naked breasts and scooted to the edge of
the bed.

"What are you going to do?" She wanted to think that
he was crazy—it's what her mother would have done
and her sisters, too. Normal people just didn't *smell*
danger, much less take it seriously if they did.

But Isla wasn't her mother or her sisters. She was
going to go with her gut, and it said that she could trust
this man with her life.

Following him to the front door with the sheet
wrapped around her, she found a hand placed flat
against her chest when she tried to follow him out.

"You stay here. I mean it." Isla narrowed her eyes—
she didn't appreciate being spoken to in that manner.
Sloane saw the look and heaved a sigh that she inter-
preted as exasperation.

"Isla, remember yesterday in the jungle? When I
told you that this island can be dangerous?" Hesitantly,
she nodded.

His face softened as he bent down to kiss her on the
lips quickly. Then the lethal expression returned, and
a shiver ran through her frame.

"I meant it. Don't go anywhere." And then he was gone, running across the beach and into the trees.

He was fast, so fast that one minute Isla had him in her sights, and then he was gone.

She looked down the beach. It was deserted, not a soul to be seen, but she still felt exposed. Prickles ran over her skin, and with a shake of her head she tried to rid herself of the notion that she was being watched.

Trusting her gut was one thing, and relying on her overactive imagination was quite another.

She could do something about feeling exposed, though. Moving back through the cabin of the boat, she picked up her discarded yoga shorts and slid them back up her hips. Craving more coverage than her camisole provided, she instead reached for one of the T-shirts that Sloane had in a laundry basket beside the bed.

She had a qualm about doing so, though she didn't truly think he'd mind. Even if he did, it would be worth it, having the scent of him right against her skin.

The knock at the door through which Sloane had just exited made her jump damn near out of her skin. Clutching her hand to her heart, which was now thundering against her rib cage, she inhaled and exhaled deeply, trying to calm herself.

"Um...hello?" From the safety of the bedroom, she called out to the door. Sloane hadn't said anything about that, but she wasn't an idiot. She wasn't going to place herself in danger if there was anything to be concerned about.

"Miss Miller?" The voice was crisp, accented and vaguely familiar. "It is Gaspar. Your concierge. Your buzzer summoned me."

Isla relaxed slightly as the visitor identified himself.

She made her way to the door, her arms crossed in front of her self-consciously.

"I'm so sorry that you came all the way over here, but I didn't use my buzzer." She opened the door with a small smile, feeling guilty.

Gaspar smiled vacantly. Up close, she saw that he didn't look very well—his eyes were glassy and the pupils were dilated.

"May I look at it? Perhaps it is malfunctioning." Pursing her lips, Isla went to slide her hands into her pockets before remembering that she didn't have any in the skimpy yoga shorts. That's right—she hadn't been back to the bungalow since that morning, and she hadn't taken the device with her to the aborted yoga session.

"I don't think I even have it on me." She looked up into Gaspar's face to smile apologetically. Instead she found herself yanked against the man, turned so that her back was to his chest. He tied a cloth gag over her lips, and then flipped her over his shoulder with a strength she hadn't guessed at in his wiry frame.

"You will come with me."

Isla couldn't do anything but try to scream.

Sloane had recognized the vinegar scent the moment it had wafted into his boat. It was the signature of only one of the vampires that he was trying to track, and because of that he was loathe to leave Isla alone.

Where was the second vamp?

Seeing her nerves, though, he determined to end it then and there.

No matter that he had lived for centuries, that he had the experience of active duty in more wars than anyone should ever have to live through—catching a vampire who didn't want to be caught was not an easy prospect, gifted as they all were with strength, speed and highly tuned senses. Because of this he was startled to find the figure that the vinegar scent belonged to hadn't appeared to sense him coming.

"What are you doing?" Building up his vampire speed, Sloane leaped, his movements as full of raw power as a predatory cat. He slammed into the other vampire a moment before the other turned to look at him, eyes wide.

The other vampire slammed into the fat base of a tree, pinned by Sloane's body. He didn't struggle much, not even when Sloane cupped his throat in tight fingers and squeezed.

Sloane recognized the other vampire. He was one of those in Lucian St. Baptiste's inner circle. Why was he in the woods by Sloane's boat? There was nothing else down here.

"Start talking, Marcus." Rage was hot in Sloane's still blood. His fangs sliced down through his gums painfully, as it always was when the flesh parted only to knit back together within instants.

Marcus opened his mouth to speak, but there was no sound. Vampires didn't need to breathe, but air was still necessary to carry sound.

"Why are you following Isla?" Sloane loosened his grip very slightly. His instincts had been honed to a sharp edge over the years, and though he was certain that Marcus's scent was one that had been following Isla, the man wasn't letting off the air that he was a threat to Sloane's woman.

"You don't understand. I'm protecting Isla." Marcus was a strong vampire in his own right—he had to be

as the face of Lucian while the sick vampire couldn't
be seen. But he grabbed at Sloane's hands around his
throat, his fingers scrambling.

The beast inside Sloane wanted to snap the man's
neck.

"Am I supposed to believe that the other one I've
scented with you is protecting Isla, too?" Sloane's voice
was a snarl. He glanced uneasily in the direction of his
boat. He hadn't planned on a lengthy discussion—he
wanted to get back to Isla.

Marcus's face flickered with surprise. Sloane didn't
want to discuss his tracking skills. He wanted information.

"No. Luana—she is the one you have scented. I try
to follow her to make sure that she does not cause too
much trouble." Sloane heard truth in the man's voice
and eased the grip on his neck, though he still stood
positioned to attack if necessary.

Marcus continued. "Usually when Luana escapes,
she runs to the jungle. Given her behavior around Miss
Miller, however, I thought that she might have come
here."

Sloane couldn't have said why, but he believed the
man. But he had a question before Marcus was off the
hook.

"Who the hell is Luana?" Adrenaline pumped
through him as an aborted scream sliced through the
heavy air. The scent of a vampire entered his senses before disappearing, and dread washed over him.

The vampire scent wasn't the one that he had been
tracking, and it would have been bad enough if it was.
He looked to Marcus to confirm his suspicions.

"That isn't Luana. I don't know where she is."

Sloane cursed and, shoving Marcus away from him, broke into a run, sniffing as he went. The way that the smell was dissipating told him that the strange new vampire was on the move.

Mixed with it was the smell of mangoes and vanilla.

Isla was in trouble, and it was his fault for leaving her alone.

Isla was still gagged, her cheeks numb from the fabric digging into her flesh. She was bound to a massive cross made of wood, her arms and legs splayed and fastened with iron cuffs.

Fear made her tremble. Gaspar had brought her to the massive ballroom of Lucian St. Baptiste, bound her and left her here. Oh, but she wasn't alone.

The view in front of her was one that could only be described as an orgy. Scores of figures writhed in scenes that she could not even comprehend. Men cupped the cocks of other men. Women suckled one another. Groups of three and four, the sexes varied, contorted their bodies in ways obviously meant to heighten pleasure. Whips, paddles and other items that Isla had never seen before and couldn't name were used with heavy hands.

Why was she here? What was about to happen to her?

The vampire legends of the island swarmed through her mind. She couldn't wrap her mind around the reality of such a thing, not even after witnessing the freakish speed at which Gaspar had run to deliver her here.

But she wasn't stupid. Of the figures writhing about in front of her, approximately half were the color of snow. The other half had punctures and bruising on their necks, caused by the bites that were delivered often and apparently with much pleasure.

Isla could see the bites, could see the blood that trickled from the wounds. Her mind wanted to think that this was all some sort of very intense role-playing, but a whisper inside of her urged her to open herself to what her eyes told her was real.

What the hell had she gotten herself into?

"Do you like what you see?" The voice was whispered intimately into her ear, the speaker at her back. Isla shivered as a frigid breeze misted her neck.

She felt the pressure of fingers and shouted as the fabric of her gag was ripped from her skin. She wanted to scream for help, but who would she be calling for?

Sloane, of course, was who she wanted. But was he one of them?

"I asked you a question." As she shivered, Lucian strolled easily out in front of her, a long coil of leather in his hand. When she could do nothing more than stare at him with wide eyes and her mouth agape, he flicked the whip between her legs.

She startled but couldn't move away. The burn of the lash striped the skin of her inner thigh, and fury lanced through her.

"Who the fuck do you think you are?" The Isla who would have cowered in fear was not anywhere in sight. She was terrified, but more than that, she was furious. She also had nothing to lose and was feeling an almost animalistic anger rolling over her. She hissed and bit at the air, jerking at her restraints. "Let me go."

Her words were futile, as she knew they would be. But rage was building inside of her, combining with her fear, hazing her vision with red. She didn't know what her face displayed, but it must have been ferocious enough to make an impression because Lucian blinked and took a step backward.

As Isla's stare again flickered to the cavorting couples, however, his confidence was again revealed in the curve of his lips.

"I am pleased at how being on the island, around your own kind, has changed you. Therefore I will allow you to ask a question." Lucian smiled at her as if he was imparting a great gift.

"What are you...what are you going to do with me?" Isla looked into the icy pale eyes of the man who had ordered her kidnapped and chained. What she saw there was...nothing. The man's eyes were devoid of any emotion.

Lucian licked his lips, slowly and deliberately, the movement somehow sensual.

Isla shuddered.

"Let me first tell you a story." Lucian walked toward Isla. When he reached her, he leaned in and sniffed the curve of her neck. Isla tried to jerk away, but her restraints allowed her only limited movement. Slowly he licked her cheek. His tongue was cold on her skin, and she heaved, filled with revulsion.

"I have lived for more years than you can possibly fathom, my dear. For millennia." Lucian pressed his lips to the hollow of her throat, and as his body moved against hers, Isla felt the evidence of his arousal. "Did you know that vampires can bear young, my dearest? We are not dead, as many think, but simply...more... than we were as humans. Our children, though, are human, as we once were, but still with that touch of... more."

Isla stared at the man as if he was mad…and actually, she was pretty sure that he was.

"If you're wondering what any of this has to do with you, Isla dearest, then wonder no more. You are my descendant—my blood runs in your veins. The blood that I had once, before I became so sick. The blood that I have been waiting for, with the latent vampire gene contained within it. Your mother, her mother, and generations before… None has had it until you."

With a sinking sensation in her gut, Isla saw with complete clarity where this was going. Before she could wrap her mind around it Lucian flicked the whip again, and she flinched. This time it struck her midriff, slicing through the cloth of her T-shirt—Sloane's T-shirt.

She hissed as her flesh parted. The copper scent of her blood, welling from the shallow cut, turned her stomach.

Lucian sniffed the air delicately, the movement overly emphasized—for her benefit, Isla knew. Then he turned to face her, his mouth curved into a wide grin.

Protruding from bloodred lips were ivory-white fangs, long and lethally sharp.

Fangs that hadn't been there moments before.

In that moment, Isla knew. The legends she'd heard were not stories at all.

She thought of Sloane, impossibly attractive Sloane, who was so pale even after hours in the tropical sun. Who insisted that they couldn't be together.

Whose lips were cool against her own.

Vampires were real.

And she was helpless in a room full of them.

"What—what are you going to do to me?" This… vampire…intended to drink her blood. She now believed this to be true, but she still had trouble accepting it as reality. But what then? And why her?

A tinkling laugh cut through her thoughts. "It's so very rude to not show more excitement when you're the guest of honor, Isla."

Isla had thought that she couldn't be shocked further that day.

She was wrong.

From one of the groups of copulating creatures, entirely naked and with blood running down the side of her neck, rose a woman with long golden hair, neat features and guileless blue eyes.

"Jessie?" The creature who looked like her friend smiled, but it wasn't the smile that Isla was familiar with. Feeling as though she had been punched in the gut, Isla watched as Jessie walked up to Lucian and draped her naked frame over the ancient vampire.

"Lucian, you promised you wouldn't start without me." Lucian smiled at the woman in the way that someone would look at a favored pet. Stroking a hand down her throat, he cooed softly.

"I told you that you would be rewarded for delivering Isla to me, and you will be." The affection he displayed for Isla's supposed friend disappeared when he turned his gaze on the woman who he claimed was of his blood. "Now, Isla, I hate to rush things along, but I need your blood to return me to health. This celebration of my return to greatness cannot be completed until I do."

Isla looked to the only person she could think of for help—Jessie, the woman who had been her friend for so many years. Utterly betrayed, she wondered if Jessie and Sloane knew one another.

"How did you get here so fast?" It was not the most

pressing question that Isla had, but it was all that she could phrase at the moment.

"Having friends in high places—friends with private jets—is a handy thing." Jessie smirked, then watched with apparent satisfaction as Lucian began to advance on Isla. She did nothing to stop him.

Chapter 8

They knew he was coming. There was no way to avoid that when he was using his body as a battering ram against the heavily barred, ancient wooden door inside the house.

When he had come to Vampire Island, he had wanted peace—he had seen enough death for any one creature's lifetime. Still without a qualm he had broken the necks of the two guards who were stationed throughout St. Baptiste's house. These creatures were protecting a fiend.

And worse—they were keeping him from Isla.

He had managed to extract the location of this room from a guard before breaking his neck as well—to kill a vampire the head had to be severed from the body. Not at all pleasant, so he preferred to injure them in ways that would take them months to heal from. His shoulder ached, but he kept at it until the door finally gave way, splintering inward in a violent explosion.

He burst through, searching the room for his woman. The massive ballroom was a grotesque sight, an orgy the likes of which he hadn't seen since his days in ancient Rome. His stare cut through the swathes of flesh. Many there stared at him with alarm, and some merely flicked their gazes at him before continuing on.

At the far end of the room was Isla. Fury pounded through him when he saw the way in which she was displayed, bound to the wooden frame like an offering.

She was wearing one of his shirts. The realization snapped the final, primal puzzle piece together inside of him. Vampires didn't always mate in this way, this chemical sort of bond, but those who did were bonded for life.

That was his woman. The frail vampire dressed like Dracula was surely Lucian, and he was advancing on her slowly, an animal toying with its prey.

It had been years since Sloane had had to race across a battlefield, but muscle memory took control. He vaulted over the writhing bodies. He had no plan other than to get the ancient vampire away from Isla, and he halted in a crouch, hissing, his fangs bared when Lucian turned on him.

"This is none of your concern." His first impression of Lucian St. Baptiste was one of shock. He had known that the vampire was in failing health, but the white skin of the man was tinted with a sickly green hue that Sloane had never before seen on another vampire.

More than that, though, the shock came from recognition.

"Luca?" Sloane had lived too long to be stopped dead in his tracks, but when he saw the man who had once been his closest human friend standing so frail yet deadly in front of Sloane's woman, Sloane's quick mind had trouble keeping up.

"Goldhawk. It's been a long time." His voice was soft, but Sloane heard the hatred that lay beneath it. Grief washed over Sloane in a great wave.

He had earned that hatred when he had tried to turn Luca's sister. Luca—Lucian—had ended their friendship and sworn vengeance on the hellish creature who had broken his beloved sister's mind.

Now Luca was a vampire himself, a very sick one. And he had a look in his eyes that told Sloane that Luca was close to death and had nothing to lose.

It wasn't a good sign.

"She is mine." The voice issuing from his own throat was raspy and harsh, his beast taking over control. He knew that he would have to push through his shock and his guilt if he wanted to save Isla, though he still didn't know why Lucian wanted her. "Let her go and I'll let you live."

Lucian cackled out a laugh in response, and Sloane realized that he had done perhaps too good a job at hiding his tracks before coming to the island. The old vampire had no idea that he had once been a ruthless killing machine.

It would have been easier if the vampire had feared him. Then he could have saved Isla from what was about to come.

If he had any hope of her accepting his claim on her, it would be best for her not to see what happened when two vampires fought.

"She was mine before she was ever yours, Goldhawk. As was Ana." With a flick of his wrists, a long, lethal blade slid out of Lucian's coat sleeves and into each hand. Sloane eyed the swords warily. They didn't make his task—freeing Isla—impossible, but they certainly complicated it. He had no weapon besides his bare hands.

And his fangs, which he bared at the older vampire. From the corner of his eye he saw Isla flinch at the display, and sickness rolled through him.

He shook it off. He could try to change her mind about him after. Right now, he had to save her.

"You let your thirst for vengeance cloud your judgment, St. Baptiste." Slowly standing from his crouch, Sloane circled the vampire. He was aware of the vampires and fangers throughout the room slowly halting the feeding and the fucking, curious about the scene being played out before them.

If they decided to protect their master, then he was screwed.

The light of insanity flashed through Lucian's eyes as the insult hit him. Sloane was frozen for a moment longer than he would have been normally because the madness he saw in Lucian's eyes was a mirror of what he'd once seen in Ana's.

Lucian cackled again and lunged for Sloane with the blades, showing surprising strength and skill for someone who appeared so frail.

Sloane managed to wrest one of the blades from the other vampire's grasp. It sliced his palm open in the process, and his blood, darker and thicker than that of a human's, oozed to the floor.

If he survived this, he would have to drink—drink live blood, human blood.

It only made him more determined not to lose any more.

"I should never have invited you to the island, but it was too tempting to have my enemy so close at hand. Keep your friends close and your enemies closer...is that not the saying?" Lucian sneered, clearly furious at being divested of one of his blades and thereby humiliated. "And now you have complicated things immeasurably between me and my great—well, we won't count the generations, will we, dear? My great-granddaughter many generations removed." Lucian cast a look of pure lust over his shoulder, directed at Isla, and even as a puzzle piece fell into place the fury and need to protect her overcame him.

Sloane lunged at Lucian with his blade, and the frail vampire parried back. The naked female who was inexplicably hovering around the group squealed and moved closer to Isla, who was yanking on her bonds with desperation and increasing determination, snarling like a caged animal.

The rest of the room was silent and still, clearly waiting to see which way the chips fell. Fangers cared for nothing but their next fix, and vampires were opportunistic and sought self-preservation above all.

Sloane's world narrowed as he fell into the rhythm of a skill that he hadn't practiced for several hundreds of years. He stared down the length of the silver blade, his attention focused on defeating the enemy.

Lucian feinted left. Sloane would have been able to recover, but Isla's sharp cry of concern was so potent, ringing through his being, that he was distracted. The split-second look that he cast her way found Lucian's blade sliding through the flesh of his gut, and the searing pain radiated all the way out to his fingertips.

As the floor sped up to meet him he twisted and, determined to ensure Isla's safety and with every remaining particle of strength left inside of him, he slashed his blade down with brutal force.

His aim was true, severing Lucian's head from his body. Relief flooded through him even as his world went black and still.

Marcus would send Isla away from the island, away from this Luana he had spoken of. She would return to the calm life that she had had before they had ever met.

She would be safe.

Isla's world fell out from beneath her.

Sagging in her chains, she let numbness wash over her entire body.

Sloane was dead.

Sloane was a vampire.

Sloane had died protecting her.

She wanted to weep but felt frozen inside. Only the faint sound of Jessie's rasping breath saved her from an abyss of ice.

Her eyes dry, she turned to the woman she had thought was her best friend in the world. For a woman who didn't make friends easily, the betrayal was all the worse.

"Why would you do this, Jessie?" The other woman turned to her, and Isla saw that the Jessie who had once been her friend was not readily apparent in the pale, emaciated creature who stood before her. Though Jessie was the one who had led her into all of this in the first place, Isla couldn't help but feel a stirring of pity for the person who looked at her with wild eyes.

The pupils were hugely dilated, nearly swallowing the pale blue of her eyes. If Isla had still lived in the reality that she had known back home, she would have thought that Jessie was high on some kind of drug.

Gooseflesh prickled over the lawyer's naked frame. Her neck was streaked with blood that was still sticky. Someone had fed on her, not that long ago. "Don't feel pity for me," said Jessie. Isla had always displayed her emotions clearly on her face. "I made this choice. When Lucian contacted me, told me about this island, I was loyal to you. But then he showed me the pleasure of being bitten. It's the ultimate high. He offered me a lifetime here, where I would be regarded as a goddess for providing blood."

Isla's eyes flickered over to the prone figure of Sloane, lying on the ground. Though she knew that it was just wishful thinking, she thought that she had seen his fingers twitch.

Now she tore her stare away from her lover and returned it to Jessie, incredulous.

"That's why you set me up?" If Jessie had given her up so easily, she'd never truly been Isla's friend, but even that realization didn't help to assuage the burning pain. "For a high and the potential to be seen as an expensive wine?"

Jessie snarled, looking more like one of the vampires who had fed off her than human, at least to Isla's eyes. Pain threatened to break her heart in two.

Jessie had been her friend since university. Her only close friend. She had helped Isla through her trials with her mother, had listened to her crushes, had pushed her out of her comfort zone.

The woman staring back at her was not the Jessie she had known. With a grief that threatened to tear her in two, Isla understood that, whatever Lucian had done to Jessie, her sweet friend was not in that body anymore.

"You would never understand. You're never happy with what you have. You're beautiful and you have a solid job, even if you don't meet your mother's fancy-ass standards. You have me as a sidekick so that you can feel better about yourself."

"What are you talking about?" Her disbelief was genuine and gut deep. Just as she had always played the ugly, unsuccessful duckling to her sisters, she had felt the lesser of the pairing in her friendship with Jessie, though she knew that the other woman also had self-esteem issues—it was how they had originally bonded.

She had never perceived any inequality in their friendship. From the slightly crazed look on Jessie's face, and the lengths to which she had gone to differentiate herself, apparently Isla had been wrong.

"It was delicious to be told why your mother hates you so much." Jessie bent and took the silver blade that had sliced through Lucian's flesh into her hand. Lifting it to her lips, she licked at the vampire's blood, which coated the metal. Closing her eyes as if in reverence, she shuddered with apparent pleasure as she swallowed.

"What?" Isla pulled at her bonds, ignoring the pain, though her skin was rubbed raw beneath them. "You... what?"

"You'll love this." Jessie stalked close, as if she was about to share a secret with her best friend.

They would never be friends again.

"Lucian told me all about it, last night when he... welcomed...me to the island." The satisfaction in Jessie's voice told Isla exactly how Lucian had welcomed the other woman to the island, and she shuddered with revulsion. "Your mother…she knows all about your vampire heritage. So do your sisters. When it became apparent that you were the first to finally be born vampire, rather than just a carrier, she decided to keep it a secret from you. She didn't want the shame of having a bloodthirsty beast for a daughter."

Isla's mind reeled. Deep in pain, she was having a hard time keeping up.

"I'm not a vampire." With a shudder, she looked out over the room, over the creatures who were sucking the life force from humans. "I'm human."

Jessie laughed mirthlessly, moving closer still. Isla felt the heat of the other woman's breath on her neck.

"The change doesn't happen unless you're around your own kind." Realization slammed into Isla as her mind ran down the list of all the strange changes that she'd noticed in the past few days. "And now that you've changed, Lucian needs your blood to get well again."

"He was using you, Jessie." Isla could see that more clearly than anything else. "You were a means to an end for him, nothing more."

The other woman shrieked, slapping her palm across Isla's cheek. It stung, but Isla felt none of the heat, the rush of blood, that should have accompanied such a blow. "Lucian told me that he was going to turn me as a reward for bringing you to him. You would feed him and die, and then I would be the special one." Jessie moved until she was mere inches from Isla, and Isla trembled as Jessie traced the blade up her calf and inner thigh.

She wanted to look past Jessie, wanted to stare at Sloane as she died, but she couldn't see past the taller woman.

"You've ruined it all for me now. I don't know if I'll even be allowed to stay here, without Lucian." Isla wondered if vampire blood acted as some kind of upper to humans because Jessie was starting to tremble with nervous energy. Still, even with her shaking hand, she traced the blade farther, up to Isla's throat.

Isla held her breath and closed her eyes.

Jessie's scream was loud, shrill and all too human, echoing right in Isla's ear. Isla's eyes flew open and her body tensed in time to see a large hand wrap around the other woman's throat.

"Jessie!" She couldn't help her concern—the revelations of the past few minutes couldn't wipe away years of friendship, in her mind anyway.

What she saw then made her throat go dry.

Sloane stood a foot away from her, holding Jessie effortlessly by the throat. Her feet dangled off the floor, and she clawed at Sloane's fingers with her own.

Sloane looked at Isla full-on, and her heart leaped with joy and disbelief. How was he standing there? Lucian had thrust the sword right into Sloane's gut.

The gash was visible in his T-shirt, the cotton shredded and caked with blood. The skin beneath was red and angry looking but smooth and whole.

Isla's mouth fell open and her heart stuttered.

Sloane was alive. He was pale and feral-looking— but alive. He had just healed from a fatal wound in mere minutes.

Her mind couldn't process it any more than she could process the fangs protruding from his upper jaw. His face was drawn and pale, and though she knew next to nothing about vampires, if she had to hazard a guess, she would think that he needed to drink blood to replace what he had lost, which was spread out in a viscous pool on the floor behind him.

"I will kill her for what she's done to you." His eyes on Isla, Sloane set Jessie down on the floor again, keeping his hand clasped around her neck. He paused, and Isla understood that he was waiting for her to give her consent.

Isla shook her head violently and struggled against her bonds. She was done. She wanted to go home.

"No. Please, don't." Finally, she felt her throat thicken and tears prickle at the backs of her eyes. "I won't have that on my conscience. Just—just leave her here." She was going to suggest that Sloane drink from the woman because he clearly needed to, but she couldn't bear the thought. Jessie had said that being bitten by a vampire was a source of extreme pleasure.

She didn't deserve that. More, Isla didn't like the idea of Jessie being in such an intimate situation with Sloane.

Terrifying as his fangs were, he was hers.

As if sensing her struggle, he took his hand off Jessie's neck and deliberately stepped away, moving smoothly toward Isla.

"I don't drink from fangers." He seemed on the verge of saying something else, but then he knelt in front of Isla and placed his fingers on her ankle to remove her bond, and she couldn't help it.

She shrank away from him.

As if she had physically struck him, he seemed to retreat, just for a moment. Inserting a finger between the metal and her ankle, he snapped the bond in half, then repeated the movement with her other foot.

When he stood up to release her wrists, his face was

carefully blank of emotion. He had also retracted his fangs. He still looked wan and weak.

"Sloane. I—" Isla wanted to say that she was sorry, but the words stuck in her throat.

She massaged her wrists, wincing as the blood flowed back into her hands. She was so ashamed and so nervous that her heart beat triple time, her every muscle tensed to flee.

This was Sloane. He had never shown any drive to hurt her, and he had had ample opportunity.

Still, she couldn't erase from her mind the terrifying image of him with his fangs fully extended.

"Do you trust me?" Isla looked up sharply. Sloane's words were brusque, his voice harsh. She turned half-way to look at Jessie, who was crouching on the floor now, at the edge of the vampires who watched the scene play out before them.

She had trusted Jessie implicitly, and the woman had betrayed her in the worst possible way.

Her entire life, Isla had used logic and fact as the basis for her actions.

She hadn't gotten very far.

Something in her gut told her that she could trust Sloane, fangs and all.

Maybe it was time to squelch the need for empricial evidence and trust her instincts.

"I do."

Chapter 9

Sloane set Isla down in the same copse of trees in which he had found Marcus not even an hour earlier. From what Marcus had told him about Luana before they had gone their separate ways—Sloane to save Isla, Marcus to capture Luana—Isla was not yet safe.

It had been centuries, but Sloane would never forget how he and Luca had once been human together. Luca had introduced him to Ana, the only woman Sloane had ever loved.

Sloane had carried the guilt over his first action as a newborn vampire ever since. He would never forgive himself for trying to turn Ana, and for the madness that had stolen the rest of her human life, and her vampiric one, as well.

As soon as Sloane had seen Lucian, had realized that he was his old friend Luca, he had understood that Luana was Ana, the woman he had loved and ruined.

Luca...Lucian...clearly felt that Sloane had not yet suffered enough.

Ana would have as much grievance against him as Lucian had, and hers was tainted with insanity.

They needed to get to a boat and get off the island. Isla would want to explore her heritage, he knew this, but they would do it another time in another place.

His Ana had been sweet but jealous. Luana had centuries of insane rage under her belt, and she would not have taken kindly to Sloane's interest in another woman.

Shaking, Sloane realized that he couldn't go another step without drinking blood—fresh, human blood.

To her credit, Isla didn't shrink away from him when he set her down, the way she had in Lucian's chambers. The fear that he had seen reflected in her eyes had cut him down to the marrow, and he knew that he would remember it for a very long time.

He had never before cared so much about being seen as a beast.

"Isla." At the moment her scent was both the most appealing and most repellant thing he had ever experienced. If he wanted to get her off this island, he needed to drink from her, and she was as intoxicating to him as she had been from the first moment he had set eyes on her.

The idea of drinking from her when she may not be fully willing made him nauseous. Plus, he had overheard what Jessie had told Isla. Unless the woman was lying, Isla was a natural-born vampire. Though he had thought that such a thing was mere legend, he couldn't discount it.

He had no idea what his bite would do to her.

She looked up at him with wide eyes. What he saw in them brought him to his knees.

"I trust you." Her voice trembled with fear, but it wasn't the same as it had been.

Isla tugged at the loose neck of her shirt—his shirt, hanging on her small frame—and exposed the curve of her delicate neck. Without bidding, his fangs came out, and at the same time his cock went impossibly hard.

"I want you to drink. You need to. I trust you." Her voice only trembled a little. Her stare strayed down to his erection, and her eyes widened as she hissed in a breath.

"Sex and feeding are linked. Be sure." He wasn't sure how much longer he could hold himself back. He needed her strength and wondered if he could keep himself from becoming so lost in her that he could still protect them both.

"Do it."

"It has to be fast." He was already striding toward her, and he could feel the surrender in her frame as his arms wrapped around her.

Turning her gently so that she faced the trunk of a large tree, he pressed against her from behind. This way she was covered from any attacks, and he was the vulnerable one.

Trying to keep enough wits about him to look out for the now familiar vinegar smell with the tender curve of Isla's neck offered to him was next to impossible.

"Yes." Sliding his hand over her buttocks and around the curve of her leg, he moved beneath fabric to find flesh and heat. She shuddered when his hand moved unerringly to the pulse of her clit.

She was wet and ready, her response to him as primal as his was to her.

Working her with unsteady yet firm fingers, he traced his lips over the column of her neck. He heard the hitch of her pulse from fear and smelled the syrupy heat of her blood as her heartbeat quickened.

He bit into her flesh slow and firm. She cried out softly at the first stabs of pain before his saliva anesthetized the wound.

Her blood began to flow, hot and rich, into his mouth, giving him life. He could tell the exact moment that the pleasure hit her. Having undone his shorts with his free hand, he fisted his erection while tugging the flimsy fabric of her spandex shorts to the side with his other hand.

He was inside of her in one long thrust. He felt the trembles of her orgasm as the sensation of his cock and his suckling combined sent her over the edge.

He felt her blood flowing through him, filling his veins, restoring his strength. It was more potent than that of an average human, rather as if he was drinking fifty proof instead of a beer. A great roar pushed through his lungs, and he buried his face in Isla's hair to stifle the noise, still aware in some dim portion of his brain that they were in danger.

With a low moan, Isla pushed back against him. He came hot and hard, thrusting deep, and felt another surge of strength in his body.

He wanted to stay inside of her slick heat—wanted to hold her close, wanted to start it all over again. But before he could even withdraw from her tightness, that vinegar smell slammed across all of his senses like an assault.

He growled, trying to shake off the drunken sensation that Isla's ambrosial blood had caused in him. Then he was flying, caught before he was ready by a hundred-some pounds of snarling, enraged vampire.

He had taken too long—he had lingered. He hadn't wanted to make it worse for Isla. And now she was in even more danger because of him.

Snarling, he rolled with the female vampire whose scent was now familiar. He could smell Marcus in the distance, getting closer.

He now understood what had tickled at his memory about the second vampire's scent. She had changed so much that her smell was nearly unrecognizable, but that very faint note was still the same.

Now, though, she was no longer a fragile human girl in love with a vampire. She had had centuries to gain strength. She was also insane.

He rolled with her, trying to gain the upper hand.

He couldn't let her get to Isla.

Shit, but she was strong.

Her caramel eyes, shining from olive skin, were bright with madness. Her hair was a mess of long, matted curls, and when she moved, he caught the overwhelming stench of the mansion's ballroom.

She must have followed them there and just missed them.

He struggled underneath her.

She held him down, threw her head back and laughed.

"No fun being on the other side, is it, Simeon?" Her use of the name he had once called his own dragged him back through the centuries, back to the time before he had been turned, when he had been confidants with a human and loved the human's twin sister.

"Sloane!" Isla was pressed back against the tree where he had just taken her. His loving had made her cheeks flush with blood, and she looked irresistible—would to any vampire.

His mind whirled, trying to figure a way out of it.

"You killed my brother, you little whore." Luana—Ana—stared over her shoulder at Isla, who seemed angry and frightened. "Was it not enough for you to tempt him with your body and your blood? I will kill what you love!" Slamming Sloane's head into the ground hard enough for him to see stars, Luana flew through the air toward Isla.

Isla didn't flinch. Instead she stood her ground, her hands curled into tight fists.

Sloane sprang after Luana, slamming her into the ground so hard that it shook.

"Don't touch her!" Luana struggled beneath him, cackling at the same time with mad glee.

"She didn't kill Luca. I did." Sloane bared his fangs, fully extended, at the woman he had once loved so much that he'd tried to keep her for eternity. Though he was still racked with guilt, seeing her go after the woman who had stolen his heart fully removed the last scourges of tenderness that he had held on to for this creature.

"She might as well have!" Thrusting at his chest with both hands, Luana freed herself and flew toward Isla again.

Then Luana was flying back in his direction, landing on her ass just a few feet away from him.

Sloane leaped to his feet. Isla was looking at her hands with astonishment.

"I— What?" She looked helplessly at Sloane.

Luana rose to her feet again, circling the tree to which Isla was pressed. Sloane jumped to Isla, wrapping his body around her protectively.

He had no idea what had just happened.

"Interesting." Luana appraised Isla as she circled, a shark with its prey in sight. "My great-granddaughter so many times removed, this new power in your blood—it is from the bite of a vampire. It was supposed to heal my twin."

Her great granddaughter? Lucian had said the same. That meant...

In a sickening rush, Sloane saw why Luana had lost her mind when he had turned her. She had already been twisted—a family trait. She in turn must have done the same to Lucian, which meant that it hadn't been his specific bite at all.

Luca and Ana. Together.

She had never been his, after all.

That meant that Isla... Isla was the generations removed product of the madness of *both* Luca and Ana, of the relationship that they surely hadn't confided in him about.

Never had Sloane been so thankful for the distance that time created. Though Isla's ancestors had been twisted and mad, the traits hadn't been passed down to her.

But Luca...Ana...the vampire before him, the woman he had once loved and who had played him for a fool, seemed an entirely new creature, his knowledge giving him perfect vision. He listened intently as she spoke, afraid that if he missed something, it would cost Isla her life.

"Now the power of this natural-born vampire will be mine—your gift to me for stealing what I love."

Isla's hands were trembling, but it wasn't with fear. She could feel something surging through her veins, something hot and potent that was overwhelming her.

It burned.

It made her feel alive.

When Luana had come flying at her with murderous intent written on her face, Isla had reacted out of sheer instinct. She had felt the force of her own strength shoving against the vampire.

She had no idea how it had happened or what was happening to her.

Now Luana was circling her again—Isla knew that she wasn't out of the woods yet.

"But…I don't understand. Lucian is my great something grandfather. How are you…" Her voice trailed off as understanding hit her.

Lucian and Luana were twins…brother and sister who clearly had an affection for each other that ran far deeper than it should have. She was descended from these two insane creatures.

And Lucian had been killed to save her.

"Now you understand." Luana came closer again, though she kept a bit of distance, clearly appraising the situation—and Isla's strange new strength—before acting.

From the corner of her eye Isla saw Sloane lift his head, sniffing the breeze. Luana did the same, and a flicker of an emotion that Isla couldn't identify skittered through the vampire's eyes.

"You don't need to keep watch on me anymore, Marcus." Luana called out the words into the sticky air, her stare still focused on Isla, who was wondering if she could truly hold off the vampire when she went for her throat.

"Luana. Don't do this." The man Isla had seen with Luana in the yoga tent appeared through the trees. He looked agitated and weary. "Lucian is dead. He doesn't need the girl's blood. You don't need her blood. Let them go. You cannot defeat us both to get to her."

Luana hissed, baring her teeth at the man who demonstrated affection underneath his obvious fatigue. "She killed Lucian. She will pay. And I can do whatever I want, overpower anyone I want, after I have her blood flowing through my veins! No one will ever hurt me again!" Luana looked at Sloane, and Isla saw an undercurrent run between the two.

They had a history, and the realization was like a punch in the gut. But before she could begin to withdraw, to cry in a corner as was typical of her, she felt a surge of emotion stronger than anything she'd ever experienced.

Rage, jealousy and possession filled her veins. Sloane was *hers*. He had marked her with his body. Luana couldn't have him.

Isla howled. Sloane's eyes met her own as she did, and she saw her fierce need to possess reflected there.

She was not entirely human anymore. She was vampire, and although she didn't know what that entailed in the relationship department exactly, she knew that she and Sloane belonged to one another.

Isla was expecting Luana's lunge this time, but the vampire still managed to take her to the ground. She struggled and fought to keep away from the deadly length of those fangs, which came ever closer to her neck.

"Isla!" Sloane was trying to pull Luana off Isla, and Isla was fighting for all that she was worth—for her life and for Sloane. Then Marcus was shouting not to hurt Luana, and jaws were snapping as the two women rolled in a tangle of sleek limbs.

"I want my brother back! Luca, my love!" Forgoing her fangs, Luana wrapped her hands around Isla's throat. Isla gagged as oxygen was cut off.

From over Luana's shoulder she saw Sloane. His fangs were fully extended, and her blood still stained his lips. He looked closer to a beast than a human, but what she saw was simply Sloane, the man she had connected with on a level she had never thought possible. The man who had killed for her.

The man who would do so again, just to save her life.

He gave her the strength she needed. As her vision grayed from lack of oxygen, Isla drew everything that she had and shoved at Luana, freeing herself.

Sloane caught the female vampire by the tips of her hair and held her tightly in a stranglehold. Isla rolled to her feet, amazed that she was able to do so after such a blow. She didn't know what, exactly, she could do to help keep Luana subdued, but whatever was necessary, she would do it.

"Luana." As he crossed the clearing, something seemed to break inside Luana as she heard Marcus's voice. She began to sob, falling limply in Sloane's arms. Isla didn't trust that the vampire wasn't trying to trick them. Neither did Sloane, it seemed, who kept his hold tight.

"I have nothing left." When Luana lifted her head,

Isla gasped with alarm—blood tracked down the vampire's cheeks, striping her golden skin with crimson. Sloane saw her alarm.

"Vampires cry blood." He tensed, seeming ready for her rejection. After everything that had just happened, tears of blood were not as shocking as they could have been.

Marcus didn't appear to even notice the exchange between the pair. His pale eyes were focused entirely on Luana, and his face reflected incredible patience and love.

"You have me." As he spoke, Isla saw why he had been following the vampire so diligently—to protect her, yes, but also to save Luana from her own destructive insanity.

Lifting his wrist to his mouth, Marcus tore the skin open with his fangs. His blood, dark and thick, welled to the surface.

"Can you please hold her mouth open for me?" Marcus's voice was soft, his eyes focused on Luana.

"What are you doing?" Isla was still ready to be attacked. Her stare was riveted to the viscous vampire blood.

"Vampire blood acts as a sedative to another vampire." Sloane loosened his hold on Luana with one arm, reaching over her jaw to open her mouth for Marcus. She shook her head before he could hold her lips apart.

"I'll do it myself. I won't hurt Marcus. I'll do what he wants." Parting her lips, she lapped at the blood in Marcus's wound, cleaning the cut with her tongue.

His skin healed within moments, the incision from his fangs shiny and pink. "I'll take care of her now. You two go now."

Isla still couldn't quite believe that it was over, not even when Luana sagged in Sloane's arms and was passed off to Marcus, who cradled her gently.

This woman—this vampire—had given birth to someone long ago in Isla's family tree. No matter what she had done to Isla, she was glad that the vampire hadn't been killed.

"Why would you do this?" Sloane only relaxed once the drugging effects of the vampire blood had taken hold on Luana. Striding across the small space that separated them, he caught Isla in his arms, not unlike the way that Marcus held Luana. Strange new strength or not, she was only too happy to be lifted off her feet and pressed against his firm chest.

Marcus looked down at the now unconscious vampire in his arms. His smile was bittersweet.

"I have loved Luana for a long time. Her relationship with Lucian has never bothered me. And you don't stop loving someone when they become unwell." He lifted his head and cast a level look at the other couple.

"I have cleaned up after her and Lucian for centuries. It is what I will do again now. But you need to go—it is not safe for you here anymore." As if coming down from an extreme high, Isla felt fatigue washing throughout her entire body. She sagged against Sloane, aware that the two men were conversing but not able to follow the conversation.

Still, she had one lingering question.

"You said that vampire blood acts as a sedative to other vampires. I—everyone seems to think that I'm a natural vampire. So why didn't my blood drug Sloane?"

With the unconscious vampire cradled in his arms, Marcus looked back at Isla and shook his head. "There aren't enough natural-born vampires to know. The last one I heard about was born centuries ago. I do not know why you still breathe, where your strength came from or how long you will live. I am sorry."

Isla murmured when Marcus left with Luana and Sloane lifted her completely off her feet and ran jaggedly to his boat. It was so strange to think that it had been so close all this time.

Setting her down on the lower deck, Sloane moved swiftly to the control panel, his movements no longer restricted to what she now saw must have been an attempt at appearing human. Soon they were chugging away from the beach, picking up speed as they went.

"I should take you home." Isla shuddered at the thought. She would have to confront her mother at some point—the mother who had kept her vampire ancestry from her deliberately, who had made her feel unloved her entire life because of it—but she needed some time first.

"No." Her voice was panicked. She had known of the existence of vampires for mere hours. She couldn't imagine having a discussion about them with her mother.

Not yet.

"Where should I take you then?" Isla hadn't even heard Sloane approach—she was asleep on her feet. She eyed him warily, not sure what answer he wanted her to give.

"Well, logistics first. That's what I'm good at, after all." And she now saw that who she was wasn't that bad, after all. "My passport is still in my cabin at the resort."

Sloane smirked. "A perk of being a vampire, of living so long, is connections with shady individuals who can obtain legal documentation. We'll buy you a new passport. It's not a problem."

"Well, then." Inhaling deeply, Isla told Sloane the truth.

"I want my damn vacation." Sloane barked out a laugh, and she couldn't help but join in.

"Any requests?" The smile that played over the vampire's lips was one that she wanted to see for as long as possible.

Isla bent forward and pressed a kiss against his chest, then splayed her fingers over the place her lips had just touched. She hadn't noticed before, but there was no discernible heartbeat there.

"Yes, someplace as different from here as possible. Like Iceland." She shuddered lightly before her laugh dissolved into Sloane's.

No matter how crazy her life had gotten in the past few days, she wouldn't have gone back for anything.

She had Sloane.

For the first time in her life, she was truly happy.

Epilogue

It was an entire week before either of them discussed what had happened on the island. In that week they talked, ate, made intense love and put as much space between themselves and Vampire Island as possible.

They would go back someday, she knew. Isla wanted to talk to Marcus and wanted to ask questions about her heritage.

As long as Luana was far away while she did.

They had just docked in a harbor in Maryland—they hadn't quite made it to Iceland yet. Sloane had left the boat just long enough to procure crab cakes and locally made root beer for them both.

Like a couple who had been together for years, they wanted nothing more than a quiet night.

"I want you to turn me into a vampire." Sloane had just bitten into his crab—Isla had been fascinated to learn that vampires enjoyed food as much as humans— when she finally said what was on her mind.

Sloane eyed her narrowly, chewing and swallowing before he replied.

"You *are* a vampire, Isla." Isla inhaled deeply—she had her speech all planned. But what came out of her mouth was not rehearsed.

"I want to be with you. Forever. We don't know anything about me, about my condition. I still breathe. I still have a pulse. So I might still die, and I can't handle the idea."

Sloane sipped at his root beer, then reached over and pulled Isla into his lap. She buried her face in his chest.

She had already decided that she wasn't going back home. She would rebuild her relationships with her family once she'd had some space and was strong enough not to buckle beneath their pressure.

She didn't know what she would do for work, but she had enough savings for another week or two. So far Sloane hadn't let her pay for a thing, muttering something about being the head of a major company and wanting to share everything that he had with her.

"I can't do it, Isla." Sloane stroked his hand over her thigh, teasing with the hem of her sundress. She shook her head vehemently at his words, even as she arched into his touch.

"Please." She was haunted by nightmares in which she was bound and helpless and Lucian drank her dry. She wanted to be fully vampire so that she was never that helpless again.

"I understand now that it wasn't my specific bite that made Luana insane. It's been an enormous relief not to carry that guilt around anymore." Sloane stroked the same patch of her skin over and over again.

"But I have no idea what would happen if I tried to

do what you're asking to someone who is, for all intents and purposes, a vampire already. I won't risk it. Once I thought that I loved the girl Ana was. But what I felt for her is pale, pale pink compared to the crimson that I feel for you."

Isla shivered at the words. The bond that was between them was, so Sloane had told her, a vampire mating bond. Still new, still forming but very much there.

It connected them on a level so deep that if one of them were to die, she wasn't sure what would happen to the other.

"That strength that you found in the woods…I noticed you haven't tested it this week. You're afraid of it, and that's okay for now. But you need to accept that, despite the difference, you are as much a vampire as I am." Furrowing her brow, Isla turned to look into his face.

Those golden eyes were set and serious.

"You might die in sixty years. Given how quickly you heal, I am inclined to think not, but you might." Isla gaped at Sloane's brutal honestly, not liking where he was going with it.

"I don't want to leave you." Sloane nuzzled his lips into her neck, and she felt frustration and sadness move through her.

"You won't, Isla. We are mated now." He didn't sound nearly as upset as she thought he should, and she glared at him.

He sighed with exasperation.

"One vampire cannot outlive their true mate. Luana and Lucian—their relationship was not that of mates. It was twisted. Ours, though, is the rare and real thing. When one of us dies, the other will, too. We will pass on to the next world together. And though I still think you're going to live a very, very long time, if you don't, I will have been happy to have lived as many years as possible with you."

Sloane kissed her fingers, and a surge of emotion washed over Isla. The unknown was terrifying, but she had lived her life without the promise of immortality. She would wrap her head around this. And they would know within a few years, after all, whether she was immortal or not.

She would age, or she wouldn't. They would deal with it then.

Swamped with love, she threw her arms around Sloane's neck and smothered him with kisses. The small kisses turned into one long, heated press of the lips, and his fingers surged higher under her skirt, to the heat of her.

"I take that to mean that you still want me." Sloane's laugh was breathless as she straddled his hips, rocking her pelvis against him.

He sucked in a breath when he found that she wasn't wearing underwear.

"Oh, I want you, all right." Isla pressed herself into his touch, smiling and breathless.

"I want you forever."

* * * * *

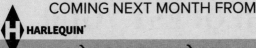
#163 KEEPER OF THE DAWN
The Keepers: L.A.
by Heather Graham

In this last book of The Keepers: L.A. series, Allesande Salisbrooke returns to Los Angeles when she receives a cryptic message from a friend who had been researching illusionists. But once she arrives, she is shocked to find that her friend has been gruesomely murdered, and by the looks of it, at the hand of a vampire. Now there's only one person who can help—Mark Valiente. The sexy vampire cop will help Allesande investigate the murder...and the chemistry growing between them.

#164 BEAUTIFUL DANGER
by Michele Hauf

The Order of the Stake, an ancient order of slayers, gave Lark a reason to live after her husband's death—and a reason for revenge. Her mission: to track down vampire Domingos LaRoque and kill him. Determined to achieve her goal, Lark is blindsided by the deep attraction Domingos elicits from her at first sight. Now Lark is faced with a tortured choice: let her guard down and surrender to their building desire or obey her one order as slayer.

REQUEST YOUR FREE BOOKS!

2 FREE NOVELS FROM THE PARANORMAL ROMANCE COLLECTION PLUS 2 FREE GIFTS!

YES! Please send me 2 FREE novels from the Paranormal Romance Collection and my 2 FREE gifts (gifts are worth about $10). After receiving them, if I don't wish to receive any more books, I can return the shipping statement marked "cancel." If I don't cancel, I will receive 4 brand-new novels every month and be billed just $22.76 in the U.S. or $23.96 in Canada. That's a savings of at least 17% off the cover price of all 4 books. It's quite a bargain! Shipping and handling is just 50¢ per book in the U.S. and 75¢ per book in Canada.* I understand that accepting the 2 free books and gifts places me under no obligation to buy anything. I can always return a shipment and cancel at any time. Even if I never buy another book, the two free books and gifts are mine to keep forever.

237/337 HDN F4YC

Name	(PLEASE PRINT)

Address		Apt. #

City	State/Prov.	Zip/Postal Code

Signature (if under 18, a parent or guardian must sign)

Mail to the Harlequin® Reader Service:
IN U.S.A.: P.O. Box 1867, Buffalo, NY 14240-1867
IN CANADA: P.O. Box 609, Fort Erie, Ontario L2A 5X3

Want to try two free books from another line?
Call 1-800-873-8635 or visit www.ReaderService.com.

* Terms and prices subject to change without notice. Prices do not include applicable taxes. Sales tax applicable in N.Y. Canadian residents will be charged applicable taxes. Offer not valid in Quebec. This offer is limited to one order per household. Not valid for current subscribers to Paranormal Romance Collection or Harlequin® Nocturne™ books. All orders subject to credit approval. Credit or debit balances in a customer's account(s) may be offset by any other outstanding balance owed by or to the customer. Please allow 4 to 6 weeks for delivery. Offer available while quantities last.

Your Privacy—The Harlequin® Reader Service is committed to protecting your privacy. Our Privacy Policy is available online at www.ReaderService.com or upon request from the Harlequin Reader Service.

We make a portion of our mailing list available to reputable third parties that offer products we believe may interest you. If you prefer that we not exchange your name with third parties, or if you wish to clarify or modify your communication preferences, please visit us at www.ReaderService.com/consumerschoice or write to us at Harlequin Reader Service Preference Service, P.O. Box 9062, Buffalo, NY 14269. Include your complete name and address.

SPECIAL EXCERPT FROM

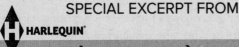

HARLEQUIN®

NOCTURNE™

Alessande Salisbrooke has been warned
about the legend of the old Hildegard Tomb.
But when she narrowly escapes becoming a
sacrifice herself and the bodies continue piling
up, working with vampire cop Mark Valiente
may be her only hope for finding answers. But
can she trust her feelings for her new partner?

Enjoy a sneak peek of

KEEPER OF THE DAWN

by *New York Times* bestselling author
Heather Graham, book #4 in
THE KEEPERS: L.A. miniseries.

As Mark approached the iron-gated entry to the grand mausoleum, he could hear chanting. Night had fallen, but peering inside, he saw that the people who stood around the tomb of Sebastian Hildegard carried firelit torches. A caped figure stepped forward carrying a burden—a woman who was dressed like Fay Wray in the old *King Kong* movie; she wore a white halter dress with her long flowing hair falling around her. She was either dead or unconscious.

And then he saw her fingers twitch. She wasn't dead, Mark thought. At least not yet.

There was still no sign of his partner, Brodie, but the chanting in the tomb was growing louder. Friends in the L.A. Underworld had warned them that they'd been hearing tales about a growing belief that blood sacrifices on the tomb would bring the old magician back to life, and bring stardom, power and glory to those who worshipped at his feet.

Fearing they were almost out of time to save the "sacrifice," he forced his way past the locked gate and shouted, "LAPD! Stop where you are!"

The tomb erupted in chaos as mist filled the room. Mark could hear Brodie catching up with those who tried to escape.

When the mist finally began to clear, he could see that five people lay cuffed on the ground. The others had seemingly vanished into thin air. Whoever was at the head of this wasn't one of these humans. The head of this particular operation was a shape-shifter. And they had missed him.

Or her.

"The woman… She can't be dead…they needed her alive," he said. But when he reached the woman and saw her face, he nearly froze.

Even though he'd never seen her before tonight, she had been the bride in the daydream he'd had just prior to entering the tomb—a wedding that had ended in bloodshed.

Discover the dramatic conclusion to THE KEEPERS: L.A. miniseries, *KEEPER OF THE DAWN* by Heather Graham. Available July 1, 2013, wherever books are sold.

Could Her Sworn Enemy Lead Her Out of Darkness?

As a member of an ancient order of slayers, Lark has found that eliminating dangerous vampires is about more than duty. It's personal—a kill for every day her husband was held captive before his death. Staking her prey isn't a challenge until she confronts Domingos LaRoque. Mad with vengeance and the blood of a powerful phoenix, Domingos tests her skills…and seduces her soul.

Yet as he and Lark become allies to defeat a mutual threat, loving the enemy may be the ultimate sacrifice.

BEAUTIFUL DANGER

by

MICHELLE HAUF

**Be seduced by danger this July.
Only from Harlequin® Nocturne™.**

HN88574